RED RAIN

PARADISE CRIME MYSTERIES BOOK 11

TOBY NEAL

Red rain, in Hawaiian culture, is an omen associated with royalty. An incident of "blood" or red rain, such as a primarily red rainbow, a shower at sea colored red by sunset, or an unusual red mist of cloud—all of these things—heralded the birth, death, or transition of a chief.

–Summarized from The Fornander Collection of Hawaiian Antiquities and Folklore

This book is dedicated to Nalu, the biggest little dog I've ever known, and the inspiration for Keiki. Thank you for joining our family for sixteen years of wonderful, heroic dog love. You will never be forgotten.

June 1999 - to November 28, 2015
RIP

CHAPTER ONE

THE CHILD'S SKULL, stained red by iron-rich Hawaiian soil, rested on Captain Omura's desk, its empty eye sockets gazing at Lei through the Ziploc bag it was encased in.

"Shut the door, Sergeant Texeira." Captain Omura looked away from her monitor, the bell of her immaculate bob swinging. "You said you wanted a private meeting."

"Yes, sir." Lei clicked the office door shut and sat down in one of the hard plastic supplicant chairs in front of the captain's desk, trying not to look at the skull. "While I was on Oahu this weekend, I had a visit from an army liaison with the company Stevens went to work for overseas, Security Solutions." Lei pushed her hair behind her ears, groping for words, forcing them past the lump in her throat. "He informed me that Michael was captured."

"Captured? What does that mean?" Omura's carefully groomed brows snapped together, and she leaned forward. "What kind of operation was this?"

"A training camp for military police somewhere in Central America. They wouldn't tell me where. His role was to work with armed forces personnel on investigation techniques, and he and several others were kidnapped. The army officer who informed me

1

said that they expected a ransom demand anytime now, and that they'd handle it. The men were insured."

"So they expect that kind of thing?" Omura's dark eyes widened. "That's our tax dollars at work?"

"I don't know about that. I don't know much of anything." Lei threw up her hands, stood, and paced back and forth in front of the captain's desk. "I'd like permission to take some personal leave."

"Denied," Omura said immediately. "I can't spare you."

"Come on, Captain! He's your man, too!" Lei's husband, Lieutenant Michael Stevens, was one of Omura's steadiest officers, in charge of training new detectives, always working a full roster of lieutenant duties. "Don't you want to know what happened to him?"

"So this leave is for you to hop on a plane to God-knows-where, trying to find your husband 'somewhere in Central America'?" Omura made air quotes. "First of all, I don't like hearing this news any more than you do. But seriously, Lei—I can't spare you! I'm shorthanded, as you know, and Stevens taking that military leave really put me in a jam, as I wasn't shy to tell him. So any personal feelings aside, I couldn't let you go even if I wanted to— which I don't. You're a mother. Or have you forgotten you have a son who needs you, more than ever now that his father's missing?"

Lei's stepson, Kiet, aged five, wasn't handling his dad's absence well. Lei rubbed her hands up and down on her black jeans, wicking away nervous sweat. "I haven't forgotten. But I have family who've been helping with Kiet already..."

"No. Just no. And if this officer told you to wait, you need to do that." Omura stood, came around her desk, and did an unprecedented thing—held open her arms. "Hug."

"Captain?" Lei cocked her head in surprise, but she smiled as she leaned carefully into the other woman's space and shut her eyes for just a moment. The Steel Butterfly was hugging her. It was an awkward and stilted embrace, like two triangles leaning against each other—but the emotion clouding the captain's eyes was genuine as she pulled away.

"I'll do all I can to support you during this time. Flex time for your pickups with the kid, short days, swapping shifts, whatever. But I can't grant any leave, especially if I think it might end up like that other trip."

That other trip.

Lei's belly tightened at the memory. She'd taken off for the Big Island to deal with an enemy in her own way, a move that had worked in some ways and cost too much in others.

"Shit." Lei's shoulders sagged. "Okay."

"Good." Omura tip-tapped on pointy-toed sling backs around her desk and sat down. "I have a new case for you. Something a little different, in addition to your regular cases with Pono. I'd like you to handle it as a side project."

She held up the Ziploc bag containing the skull. A fracture mark on the bone where the forehead would have been testified to possible cause of death.

"Where'd this come from?" Lei accepted the bag and turned the skull in her hands.

"I logged it into evidence already. It was brought in this morning. Apparently it washed up on the beach near one of the Hana streams. A woman named Iris Yamaguchi found it in some driftwood. She bagged it and brought it in. Didn't realize she should have left it there and called us."

"Have you had anyone look at it? To date it, or anything?"

"No. That's for you to figure out, and if there's anything more that can be found out about this poor kid—who it was, when it happened, if there was foul play involved." Omura pinned Lei with her dark gaze. "I plan to keep you so busy you don't have time to worry about getting that man back. Now go find me a cold-case child killer."

I woke with that jerk that happens in a falling dream, my whole body a-jangle with alarm and a sense of impending disaster.

But the disaster had already happened, when we were captured.

I blinked my eyes in a darkness as thick as if a velvet bag had been dropped over my head. The plane had crashed in my latest dream, and I'd been on fire at the end. Crawling. Dragging my dog, burning and desperate.

Like the most recent time the house was on fire.

But the plane hadn't crashed, really. Must have been another dream. Or a memory. Maybe it had crashed. Who the hell knew?

I wasn't sure about anything right now. Dreams and memories ebbed and swirled through my mind, and I couldn't tell which was which half the time. I shut my eyes, since I couldn't see anything anyway, and tried to remember the real plane ride here to Honduras —because that's the particular ring of hell where we'd landed. I was sure of that much.

The military transport C-130, open and echoing, had roared along on its journey to whatever the godforsaken mission destination was—I hadn't known at the time. I was strapped into the over-hard upright seat against one wall, alongside a couple of other civilian contractors. Military police troops I'd be training when we arrived occupied the rest of the seats.

At least I'd finally slept on the flight. I rolled my sore neck, using the occasion to gaze around the interior of the aircraft. Several heavy-duty Jeeps were strapped down the length of the plane, along with a huge pile of supplies held down with a webbed net. I unstrapped from the five-point harness and stood, stretching my muscles. I took a walk up and down the length of the plane, getting circulation back into my legs.

I felt shitty. Throbbing headache, dry mouth, a twitchy sense of frayed nerves. Perhaps left over from the dream I'd been having, but more likely that other thing. I dug in my olive-drab backpack, stuffed with all the personal possessions I'd have for the next six months. I took out my shave kit and went to the head.

4

It was a bare-bones closet with a metal toilet and sink with a steel mirror above it. I did my business and opened the shave kit.

I had a flask inside filled with booze, disguised as a shaving cream can. It had been a simple enough thing to buy online. This ration was all I going to get, and it was strictly for medicinal purposes, so I could stave off the DTs as I dried out.

Because that's what this stint overseas was all about. Kicking the booze, and the other mental shit, too. I swigged a gulp of the cheap scotch, gazing at my hollow-eyed reflection in the steel mirror with contempt.

The foul stuff seared my throat and made my eyes water, burned my esophagus, and went off like a bomb in my empty belly. It tasted horrible. I wanted to retch. Instead I felt immediately better as flu-like symptoms of withdrawal receded.

Just one more hit.

The scotch still tasted horrible, but it felt good, and that second drink activated a fierce longing to finish the rest. But I was in trouble if I did. This had to last, and then I was done. I screwed the top back on. Feeling steadier, I shaved with a sliver of soap.

Working the razor around that stubborn square edge of my jaw, I caught sight of the hook pendant Lei had given me. The white bone seemed to glow in the dim silver of the mirror, filling the shadow at the base of my throat, almost hidden in the olive of my uniform shirt.

I still remembered her small hands pressed together over the pendant, her curly brown head bent before me as she murmured a prayer of blessing over it. She'd risen up on her knees in the bed before me and fastened the slightly scratchy coconut-husk closure behind my neck.

My face had been close to her breasts: small, round, and perfect. I'd looked my fill at them and breathed in the smell of her. I'd shut my eyes and felt the love in the gift wash over me. I'd soaked it in, reveled in it—as I had in her body.

I didn't deserve any of it. I'd almost destroyed us. But I'd make up for it now, by dealing with my shit and making some money. The company I was working for, Security Solutions, paid very well. This six-month stint would be a good start for our son Kiet's college fund, if nothing else.

I finished shaving. Splashed my face. Buttoned up that last button so that the bone hook I told her I'd wear until I returned was hidden. Zipped up my kit. Returned to my seat.

When I shut my eyes, for a moment I could still smell her.

I slept again. I didn't want to. Bad things came when I slept.

CHAPTER TWO

"Dad! I see a wave coming!" The ocean off of Maui was always warm, but the currents and waves were strong. I was on my long-board with Kiet in front of me, out at the cove at Ho'okipa, our favorite break. Kiet wore a flotation device just in case he got into trouble. Sunlight sparkled on the water. The clouds, piled against the West Maui Mountains off to our left, looked like mounds of shaving cream. Out to sea, I saw the rise in the horizon that meant a wave was coming. I spun the board, Kiet sliding down against me.

"Paddle hard!" I yelled. My boy's little brown arms churned as hard as they could as we headed toward the yellow-gold of shore. I arched my back, lifting my chest above his little body as he thrashed and splashed in front of me. For five, Kiet had good focus and physical effort. I stroked hard, too, and in a moment we both felt the lift and surge beneath the board that meant we'd caught the wave.

Kiet popped up to his feet. He looked good, braced strong, black hair gleaming with water and sun. As soon as I was sure he was up and stable, his arms outstretched, I jumped up behind him, angling the board to catch the wave's peeling break off to the right.

"Hang five, buddy!" I yelled. Kiet sidled up toward the front, and I whooped as he inched to the nose of the board, extending one foot to hang his toes over the end.

He looked back to smile at me, so like his murdered mother, Anchara, that I lost my balance. We wiped out, the board flipping into the churning curl of the wave and sucking us under.

All was churning dark water, roiling and deep. I fought for the surface, certain that my son was drowning. My eyes were open and burning under the water, filled with nothing but black. I was unable to find him, reach him, help him.

I woke abruptly.

I was shaking with the bone-jarring, full-body shudders of hypothermia. My jaw ached with tension from trying to keep my teeth from clattering together. I shivered so hard the water around me made tiny waves.

Tiny waves that splashed against the mud walls of the deep pit I was in.

Oh, yeah. The pit. I must be remembering this. I wasn't in the pit anymore. I was lying flat on my back somewhere dry, musty-smelling, and darker than a coal mine. Probably a storage shed. I remembered what happened next, in the pit, but not how I got where I was now.

"Lieutenant. Move back here." A man hauled me under the armpits out of the puddle I'd fallen over into, propping me against the slimy mud wall. Rain continued to pelt down on us through a bamboo frame covered with palm fronds. I couldn't stop shivering; my teeth chattered and my body quaked. I couldn't even form words I was so racked with shudders.

"I think he's sick," the man who'd helped me said to someone else. I tried to remember his name. I knew this man, this fellow prisoner, filthy in his mud-crusted clothing. His eyes were dark and shiny as he looked into my face, briefly touching my head. "He's got a fever."

He was talking to someone on the other side of me.

"You think they give a shit?" The other guy's voice was scratchy and hard.

"But we should tell them. He's no good to them if he dies," my helper said. He sat down in the mud beside me and threw an arm over me. "Relax, LT. We got you. Carrigan, get over here. Lean against him on that side. Let's warm him up."

I felt the reluctance in Carrigan, but he shuffled over and pressed against me. Sandwiched between the two men, I eventually began to thaw a little as our shared warmth loosened my locked muscles. "Thanks," I whispered through cracked lips.

I rested my forehead on my knees.

A dim memory came to me. Carrigan was another of the civilian contractors. We'd all gotten to camp together—and the plane hadn't crashed. Definitely hadn't. I remembered his cold blue eyes. We hadn't hit it off—I thought he was an entitled asshole. He wouldn't change out of his polo shirt and Bermudas into the uniforms they'd issued us.

"I'm in charge of tech. I don't need to wear this hot, shitty uniform," he'd said. Yeah, Carrigan was a jerk.

"Hey, man, relax." It was my friend whose name began with a "K." He was pounding my back, because I was choking. Somehow I'd sucked water, and though I coughed and coughed, my lungs didn't clear.

"Hey!" K-Man stood, bracing his legs to pull me up. I felt hot but cold, too, and the shivering wouldn't stop. "Hey! This man is sick!" He yelled up at the entrance of the pit, and this time Carrigan yelled, too, and then two more voices joined in, shouting up into the mouth of the pit. "Help! Ayuda aquí!"

Things looked very close to me: the grains of soil in the walls were big as boulders, the puddle I knelt in, deep as a lake rising to swallow me. But then everything was far away, as if I were seeing through the wrong end of a telescope. The slurry of the mud walls formed distant, fascinating patterns.

Patterns like the path of blood, sliding down a wall. So much blood could come from one body. They said it was only five to eight pints for most people, but when it all emptied out of dying veins, it looked like a lake. I'd wondered sometimes if it only seemed that way because of the color—so intense. So permanent.

And blood had so many textures.

Pooling blood, with a skin of coagulation, like Jell-O beginning to set.

Spattered blood in abstract patterns, bizarrely beautiful at times.

Blood with flies stuck in it and scabbed blood in dried puddles. Blood hardened into black strings, blood speckled like freckles on skin.

Bloody hands reaching for me.

I cried out, adding my hoarse voice to the yelling of the rest of the men.

The palm fronds lifted, and a round brown face looked down.

"Ayuda esta, por favor!" cried K-Man. His hands dug into my armpits as he tried to haul me upright, but I collapsed face down in the water. "This man is sick!"

The black of the wipeout at Ho'okipa rolled over my head, and I was gone.

LEI SET the child's skull down on her desk. Pono Kaihale, her longtime partner, barely back at work from a minor gunshot injury, recoiled at the sight.

"It's a kid." No one liked kid cases, but Pono's aversion was almost at the phobia level.

"Don't worry. The captain gave me this one to work on my own," Lei said. "She thinks this is an old skull. Someone found it washed down a stream in Hana." She leaned over, inspecting him. "Show me your arm."

He held out that thick, brawny appendage. A triangle tattoo pattern encircled the biceps that had been gouged by a drug dealer's bullet in their last case. Lei winced inwardly, remembering how terrified she'd been when Pono was shot. She traced the white edge of the bandage with a finger, wishing again that she'd remembered to call out that the suspect was armed.

"Told you, just a flesh wound." Pono's cheeks creased in a wide grin. "Did I tell you Tiare thinks it's hot?"

"You did. And you told me you'd always wanted to get 'just a flesh wound' for bragging rights." Lei sat, booted up her computer. "Captain wouldn't grant my request for leave."

Lei had called Pono from Oahu to tell him the news about Stevens. She had no secrets from her partner, who'd become like the brother she'd never had.

"Nothing you can do for Mike with him way over there in some classified hot zone." Pono squeezed Lei's shoulder with a meaty hand. "I know that doesn't make it any easier. But Kiet needs you. He still having sleep problems?"

"Yeah." Lei sighed, looking down at the pathetic little skull. She picked it up, hefted it. "This skull doesn't look much bigger than Kiet's head."

Pono looked away with an exaggerated shudder. "Get that thing out of here. It's bad juju."

"So superstitious, you." But Lei stowed the skull out of sight in her desk drawer. She deliberately pushed Stevens out of her mind as she opened her departmental e-mail. She'd tried. She really had. And she wasn't going to risk leaving her job without permission after that last time. Her hand rested in a brief habitual gesture on her belly.

Lei was flipping her notebook to the number for Maui Memorial's morgue when she heard a delicate throat-clearing at the door of the cubicle.

Both Lei and Pono turned their office chairs. An attractive

woman stood in the doorway, and there were spots of color on her high cheekbones. "Hi, Sergeant Texeira. Detective Kaihale. I wonder if I could have a moment of your time."

"Sergeant Fraser." Lei took in her husband's partner's appearance. As one of the MPD's training officers, Fraser wore a uniform. She'd opted for a pencil skirt and low heels instead of trousers, and Lei could see why—her legs were stunning. The crisp navy fabric of the uniform brought out the woman's deep blue eyes. Creamy skin, smooth dark hair in a French braid, and shiny winking brass finished a look worthy of any recruiting poster.

Lei suppressed the instinct to smooth her own springing curls and straighten her wrinkled tank top. "How can we help you?" She was proud of how calm she sounded, when every cell in her body wanted to leap up and tear the woman's hair out by the roots.

Stevens had never told Lei he had a partner. She'd found out by accident, going up to his office after his deployment for a missing set of keys and finding Kathy Fraser sitting at his desk. That was also when she'd found out that Fraser had known his deployment date for months, though he'd told Lei only the day before he left.

What was this woman to him?

"Could I speak to you privately, Sergeant Texeira?" Fraser was obviously uncomfortable, and Lei's stomach tightened. There was nothing this woman could say that Lei was going to like.

"I need another cup of coffee, anyway," Pono said. "Nice to see you again, Sergeant Fraser."

"You too," Fraser said.

Lei shot her partner a look of shock as the big Hawaiian stood and sidled out past Fraser, not meeting Lei's eyes. Was she the only person in the whole department who had never met Kathy Fraser or known that she was Stevens's partner?

Fraser entered and closed the retractable privacy slider. The roof of the cubicle was open, but soundproofing inside helped cut down on ambient noise as the detectives worked their cases. The woman took a seat in Pono's chair.

"You've got a hell of a nerve coming and talking to me." Lei could feel herself arching and stiffening, like a cat reacting to a threat.

"I came because…" Fraser licked her lips, and a tiny bit of lipstick got on her teeth, a small comfort to Lei. "I wanted you to know there was nothing between Michael and me. I could tell you —jumped to some conclusions when you found me at his desk. But there was nothing you need to worry about."

Lei stared at Fraser, unblinking. Her eyes felt hot as lasers, like she could burn holes in the other woman's uniform. "Maybe not. But he didn't tell me about you. And you knew his deployment date, and I didn't. Both those things are a problem, but nothing to do with you."

"Okay. I can see how that's upsetting. But I swear, he never did anything…" A deep flush rose up the woman's fair chest and neck like the red in a thermometer, and Lei, no stranger herself to unwelcome blushes, knew that there had been something between them. At least, on Fraser's part.

"You need to get out. Now." Lei spoke through gritted teeth. "Before I do something I'll regret."

"I understand. But I'm covering his duties, and I heard that something happened to him. That he was captured. I'm really worried. I wonder if there's anything you could tell me?" The blush happened again. Fraser looked way prettier blushing than Lei did.

Lei could stab the ballpoint Bic she was holding into Kathy Fraser's neck. Oh, it would feel so good. Blood would spurt in an arc as she ripped it back out. On the second stab, she'd go for the woman's eye and pierce her brain. "He has been captured, but I don't know anything more than that. Please leave."

Fraser stood. "I wish you would believe me. And be mature about this." She sounded sad, and a little huffy. She spun on a heel, opened the privacy door, and left.

Lei waited until the tap-tap of Fraser's heels had disappeared before she surged to her feet.

"Mature!" she snarled. Too furious to do anything but swear, and not wanting to draw unwelcome attention, she headed for the MPD gym, where she could hop on the treadmill and run it off. She paused in the locker room to throw on her gym clothes and shoes.

She was running all out on the treadmill when Pono eventually found her. "Thought you went to see Dr. Gregory."

"I wanted to work out first." She didn't slow down. The thunder of her heart and the pounding of her feet on the treadmill's track were finally dissipating her rage. "You knew about her and you never told me." Her voice was accusing.

Pono glanced around, but they were alone in the soundproofed, air-conditioned gym. "Slow down a minute while I'm talking to you," he growled.

Lei punched the button that lowered the speed of the treadmill to a fast walk and shot Pono a glare.

"I never told you because there was nothing to tell. I heard Fraser'd been assigned about a year ago to work on the third floor in recruiting and training new hires. I met her at something." He flapped a hand. "There's no conspiracy here. Far as I know, she just shared Stevens's office. She's covering his duties. There's nothing there, Lei. You're being paranoid."

"No, I'm not." She brought the treadmill to a full stop. "But I won't get any answers until Stevens is back, safe and sound. Then I can take a strip off him for not telling me his departure date. But he told that woman months before."

"Ah. Well. If the guy weren't already in the doghouse, he definitely deserves to be for that." Pono trailed Lei as she got off the treadmill and headed for the locker room. "But if you think he had something going with Fraser—my vote is no."

"I didn't ask you." Lei flicked him with her gym towel. "But tell me any rumors you hear about this woman. Anything at all. I want dirt."

"Be careful what you wish for." Pono smacked her on the shoulder, making her stagger. "Now get back to work. And take that skull with you. I don't want it in our office."

CHAPTER THREE

SOMETHING WAS BADLY WRONG. Anchara would never have called me if it weren't serious. I reached the ugly Kahului hotel with its terrible whale murals, parked the Bronco, and ran up the metal stairs on the side of the building two at a time to her room.

"Anchara!" I cried, and pounded on the cheap, hollow door. Even as I turned the knob, I knew what I would see, because this was memory as well as nightmare. I didn't want to see, and yet I had to. I opened the door.

She was on the bed, naked.

The blood was everywhere around her, soaking the bedding, splashed on the lamp, dripping onto the cheap carpet. The mountain of my son, the son I didn't know yet and hadn't known about, distended her slender, naked body.

Everywhere, blood. Her reaching hands, her begging eyes, and her voice, a thread: "Take the baby, Michael. Save the baby."

I woke screaming, thrashing, and shivering, as I so often did since this nightmare began. Five years ago, it had begun in that hotel room. With finding her like that. It had fucked me up, big-time. All the rest that followed, all the other that was before…it was like I was a jar full of rocks, and then that final rock landed right on top of me and the jar broke.

I'd been picking up my own pieces ever since.

My throat was raw when I stopped screaming.

I wasn't in the pit anymore. I was in a dark place that smelled of wet and mold. I could hear the rain, the ever-present rain, drumming on the roof. Relief to be out of the pit warred with guilt that the other men were still in it.

I was lying on something. Feeling along, I could detect the harsh weave of a blanket. I sat up slowly and felt the tug of some sort of restraint on one of my wrists.

I was so weak. Periodically, shivers swept over me like wind over a grassy field. I waited for my eyes to adjust to the dark.

Across the room, which had a very low ceiling, I could see the faintest lighter area around what must be the door. On either side of me were dark shapes. Feeling with my hands, I discovered bags of something on one side and boxes on the other. There were no windows.

I was in some sort of storage shed, wedged between stacks of supplies. Tied up like a dog in a kennel. My brain was spongy and glitching, like it had a computer virus. Random memories booted up and cut off.

Throwing a ball for Conan at home, barely registering the beautiful Rottweiler leaping after the ball, the happy prance as he trotted back—I'd been biding my time until I could go to my workshop, where I kept a bottle. Keiki, our old girl, was already sitting by the workshop door. Her brown eyes on me were accusing. But that was probably just my guilty conscience...She was a dog, for God's sake, though no one had the heart to tell her that.

Snuggling Kiet against me on the couch that last morning. "Son, I gotta tell you something."

"What, Dad?" Eyes still on cartoons.

"I'm going away for a while. Six months. But I'll be back before you know it."

Silence. I looked down at the crown of his shiny black hair. My arm was around him, and under it, his body felt fragile but strong and warm. He was still watching the cartoons, his mouth open a little, a sign he was absorbed in something.

"You understand, little man?"

He nodded. "You're going on a trip."

"Yeah. It's a long one. But I'm going to be helping people who need it."

"Okay."

But when I drove him into the turnaround at school, the crying started. No words, just tears and clinging. I had to get help from one of the crossing guards to even get him out of the Bronco's cab. It felt like getting stabbed in the heart, a breathless pain, as he was carried off, sobbing.

Another memory floated up. Watching Lei from the bed as she came into our bedroom one morning, from that back room where she'd slept since I told her I was leaving. Early-morning sun on the tangle of her hair as she bent to get some clothes out of the dresser. The shape of her, familiar and sweet. She could wear a flour sack and I'd know it was her under there. I still wanted her so much, but I hadn't known how to break down all that was between us.

I kept my eyes almost shut, pretending to be asleep, when she looked over at me. But I hadn't slept all night, trying to avoid the dreams.

Another memory.

My partner in the training program at MPD. Kathy's face coming toward me, those dark blue eyes so intent on mine, pretty mouth so soft. She wanted me to kiss her.

I opened my eyes and blinked. Kept blinking. There were shapes in the corners of the shed, dark snakes wriggling along the walls. Probably not real, but who knew in this place?

I coughed. My throat made a sound like ripping wet cloth.

That wasn't good. I felt around a little more. The floor was dirt, and my hand encountered some sort of jar or bottle. I rolled over onto my side, my head swimming at even that small exertion, and explored the jar. It seemed to be of glass, and it had a screw top.

Probably water. The dryness in my mouth told me I was well past the point of thirst.

Slowly I hoisted myself upright onto an elbow. Clumsy with the restraint on my wrist, I got the lid off. I drank, spilling some, and when my stomach protested, I put the lid back on and lay back down. Was it worth it to try to get out? I plucked at the rope on my wrist, but even with the water, still felt too sick to investigate further.

I drifted.

The plane had landed without incident, unlike at least one of my dreams.

I'd jumped up and hurried down the slanted ramp first, eager to get my boots on the ground. I hadn't known where we were going and now I didn't know where we were. That felt shitty, no matter what I was getting paid.

The muggy air of a jungle setting hit me like a wall when I got off the plane. The smell of mud and damp things held a note of rotting fruit. I ran into a cloud of gnats as, carrying my kit, I walked up to two men. They were dressed in jungle camo, and the sergeant held a clipboard. Major's bars on the other man's uniform identified his rank.

"Michael Stevens, reporting for duty, sir." I saluted. I still had the salute from long-ago Marine days. The sergeant ticked a box on the clipboard.

"Welcome to Camp Erehwon. I'm Major Forsythe," the other man said. "Let's greet the rest of our happy group."

I had at least six inches and fifty pounds on Forsythe, and I could tell by his stance that he didn't like it. I moved to the side, flanking him and pitching my voice low and respectful. "Camp Erehwon, sir?" I asked.

"An old joke. 'Nowhere' backward. Our fond nickname for

Operation Trifecta, the jungle shit storm. How much were you briefed?"

"Not at all, sir. I don't even know what country we're in."

"Well, I only like to do this once, so let's wait for the others to get here." We watched the civilian contractors, supplies transport, and military police staff coming our way. "Did you have a civilian rank?" Forsythe asked.

"Yes, sir. I'm ranked lieutenant in Hawaii's police department. Did a stint as a Marine a long time ago." I kept my eyes front.

"Well, then. We'll use your title with the men."

"Thank you, sir."

The other men had gathered in front of us, and the sergeant addressed the enlisted, marked by their uniforms. "Attention!"

They formed up an uneven line, dropped their kits, and saluted. The sergeant began calling out names off a list on a clipboard. The other civilian contractors were easy to spot, walking slowly, staring around in bewilderment. One guy was even looking pissy about the mud getting on his expensive shoes.

I took a chance to look around myself. The airstrip was a packed-dirt track laid down in the jungle. Tall, unfamiliar trees bordered it on all sides. Strange birdsong filled with screeches and trills sounded in the air. The air was thick, and the sun felt like a superheated helmet on my uncovered head. Mosquitoes buzzed, even in the broad daylight. I resisted the urge to smack at them, though the yuppie-looking guy in the expensive shoes had no such restraint, muttering and scratching like a monkey with fleas.

Carrigan. He'd been with me in the pit.

Somehow I'd been moved from the pit to here. And I was alone. Had they just parked me in here to die? It seemed like a good possibility.

I'd have to prove them wrong. I sat up slowly and drank more water.

LEI DROVE the short distance to Maui Memorial Hospital and took the elevator down to the basement where the county morgue was located. As she always did, Lei paused for a second outside the swinging doors to steel herself against the smells.

And the memories.

Then she pushed through doors made for gurneys and walked through the entry where bodies were identified. She buzzed the locked interior door into the main work area, peeking through a wire-threaded interior window.

Dr. Gregory was wearing a bright yellow rubber apron covered with smiley faces, and he was elbow-deep in a chest cavity. His assistant, Dr. Tanaka, was manning the recording equipment on the other side of the body. He looked up, blinking through magnifying glasses. Recognizing her, he gave a head nod and pointed his chin toward Tanaka. Tanaka shut the recorder off and came over, opening the door for Lei. "Sergeant Texeira."

"Dr. Tanaka. Nice to see you."

Tanaka was an attractive young Japanese woman with one of those asymmetrical haircuts that looked like the points of a handkerchief draped all over her head. Lei had heard a rumor that she and Dr. Gregory were living together, but Tanaka, whose first name Lei couldn't remember, wasn't very chatty. Perhaps that was a good balance for the man Lei fondly called "Dr. G," who loved to talk.

"We're in the middle of a post. Can you wait over at my desk?" Dr. Gregory lifted a pair of lungs out of the body and plopped them, with a slurpy sort of noise, onto a big steel scale. They looked like red-streaked, slippery, pale pink water balloons.

"Sure. No problem." Lei went to Dr. Gregory's desk, an island of refuge, tidy and hidden from the rest of the chamber of horrors by a beautifully painted shoji screen. Dr. Tanaka's desk was directly opposite Dr. Gregory's, and her screen was even prettier. Lei kept her mind off the post going on and the doctors' murmuring voices by looking around.

One wall was taken up with a bank of refrigerated steel storage units. There were three bodies on tables in the main room, each equipped with its workstation of flexible steel hose, drill, saw, and other implements on a tray. Right now the only uncovered body was the one Tanaka and Gregory were working on.

Lei set the skull down on Dr. Gregory's desk and leaned back in her chair. This was the first unoccupied moment she'd had in days.

Stevens. Where was he? Was he okay? She pictured his face: those crystal-blue eyes under dark brows, the chiseled cheekbones and angled jaw, his mouth that could be so hard—or so tender. God, she missed him. Her body and bones ached with it, in spite of Kathy Fraser's visit—or maybe because of it.

She felt a buzzing sensation in her pocket and jerked to her feet. The call was on the phone Stevens's company, Security Solutions, had issued her.

"Got a call. I'll be right back," Lei told the medical examiner, and hurried out into the hall.

CHAPTER FOUR

I woke abruptly as the metal door of the shed gave a screech. The light hit my eyeballs like a blow. I wanted to see what was coming, but I shut my eyes involuntarily, my arm coming up to block the searing sunshine. Someone grabbed me by the arm.

"Outside for bathroom," he said in Spanish, pulling me up.

I nodded to show I understood. I still had a little Spanish from growing up in California.

I did need the bathroom, but my legs didn't want to cooperate with this plan. They felt like rubber, and I ended up on my knees as the man, smelling strongly of sweat and tobacco, untied the rope around my wrist. By the time he'd untied me and hauled me up from under the armpit again, I was able to stand.

The man was shorter than me, as many of the native people here seemed to be. I wished I was feeling better, not such a burden, because he staggered with my arm over him, as he led me through squelching mud to a ramshackle outhouse.

Inside, I collapsed on a wooden support made of branches over an open hole and tried to get my bearings. I had some griping pains in my abdomen. A bit of diarrhea. Still, it was good to be outside the storage shed for any reason.

I wished I could remember more about what happened.

We were in a hidden camp in the jungle. I could tell that much from my brief trip from the storage shed to the latrine. Camouflage netting hung from the dripping trees overhead, and tents in mottled greens and browns hunched beneath the trees. Still on the latrine, I applied my eye to a knothole in the crude wall. I spotted a few guards wearing plastic ponchos leaning against trees.

They had machine guns—M16s. American.

No one looked American, but I could swear the tents, camo netting, even the ponchos were American. What was going on here?

"Hurry up!" My guard pounded on the door.

There was nothing to wipe with but damp leaves in an old paint bucket, so I used some of those.

I realized I was feeling slightly better, but still not moving fast enough for my damp and irritated guard as he threw open the outhouse door and hauled me out. I tried to fasten my pants, stumbling and slipping in the mud. He kept me from falling on my face, but that was the extent of his help as he shoved me back into the shed. I collapsed on my pallet and he tied the rope back onto my wrist.

A tied knot could be untied.

He threw something at me, and it landed on my chest. A ball of rice, wrapped in plastic. He stomped out. The door screeched shut, and it was dark again.

Lei tried to keep her voice even as she picked up the call on the sat phone in the hallway outside the morgue.

"This is Sergeant Texeira."

"This is Lieutenant Colonel Westbrook. We spoke on Oahu when I notified you of your husband's capture?"

"Of course. Do you have news?"

"Yes. We've received the ransom demand we were expecting."

A long pause.

"And?" Lei reached up to grasp the bone hook and white metal pendant that hung at her throat. "What's happening?"

"We're sending a crack team over. And we're authorizing the release of funds."

Lei let a breath out in a whoosh. "That's good."

"But paying the ransom is a last resort," Westbrook said. "We have to try other means to get the men back first. Our policy is not to negotiate with terrorists."

"Are these terrorists?"

Westbrook cleared his throat, apparently deciding he'd told her too much. "I'll keep you further informed as I'm able." He hung up abruptly.

Lei wanted to swear and throw the phone. Instead, she pressed Call Back to Westbrook's number. It rang and rang and then went dead. No voice mail.

No way to do anything about any of it.

Lei walked up and down the hall, getting herself under control before she returned to the morgue. Westbrook hadn't had to disclose anything to her, really. If she antagonized him, he'd simply cut her off.

But Lei knew someone who could find out just about anything about anybody, anywhere. She wasn't out of options yet. Lei marched back to the sally port leading into the morgue.

Dr. Gregory had unlocked the door for her, and she joined him at his desk. She was relieved to see he'd taken off the blood-spattered rubber apron and gloves. Today's aloha shirt was emblazoned with cartoon cats wearing leis. He eyed the skull on his desk with an expression of delight.

"You bring me the best presents." He had a lopsided grin. Lei heard Tanaka give a snort from the other side of the shoji screen. "Where'd you dig this up?"

"It wasn't dug up. At least that's not how we got it." Lei

opened the Ziploc bag, and Dr. Gregory, gloved up, removed the skull and set it on the plastic bag. "It washed down one of the streams in Hana and was discovered in a pile of driftwood. Captain Omura thinks it's probably old, so she didn't call out the cavalry on it."

"Yes. It's old, but not that old." Dr. Gregory picked up the skull, turning it gently. "This red-brown color is staining picked up from the soil in the area where it was buried. If it were older than five years or so, the bone would be more porous." Dr. Gregory turned the bone back and forth. The skull looked small in his hands, the eye sockets empty and staring. "I'd say a male, aged ten or so. This fracture—don't think that was cause of death. It looks fresh." He turned on the gooseneck lamp on his desk, aimed the light at the break in the rounded front of the skull. Picked up a loupe and gazed at the cracked area. "See how the interior of the bone is white inside the crack? You can see where the soil staining ends and the break begins. If this were premortem, the coloration would be the same inside the broken area."

"So this may not have even been a homicide," Lei said.

"Right. The captain's a savvy lady. I'm guessing she took a look and knew that right off."

"Okay. Anything else you can tell me?"

He weighed the skull in his hand thoughtfully. "I can send a bone sample to Oahu for dating."

"That would be great. In the meantime, I'll take a trip out to Hana and talk to the woman who brought it in." Lei stood. "Can I leave it with you?"

"Sure thing. I have a special storage drawer for bones." Dr. Gregory pulled out a toe tag. He labeled it, John Doe male skull approx. aged 10, Hana, added the date, and put the tag in the Ziploc with the skull. "I'll keep him for you."

"Thanks. We're in between big cases, so this is a good time for me to try to find out a little more about this artifact. Call me when you get the dating back."

"Will do." Dr. Gregory was already wielding a handheld bone cutter that reminded Lei uncomfortably of pruning shears, snipping off a bit of bone from near the occipital cavity.

What a small, tender neck that would have been, attached to that delicate sphere of bone. The pathos of it shuddered through her. Children were so vulnerable.

"Thanks again." Lei let herself back out of the morgue and took the elevator to the ground floor. The hospital was built on a hill, so it commanded a fine view of the town, the ocean, cruise ships in the harbor, and the imposing blue-purple bulk of Haleakala across the valley. Once outside, she took some deep breaths of the fresh air blowing up from the direction of the ocean.

It felt like wasted effort to run down the woman who'd found the skull of a cold case that might not even be a homicide, when somewhere in Central America, her husband was in danger.

She had time for an important phone call. Lei got into her truck and called Sophie Ang. A friend since Lei's FBI days, the computer tech expert was never short of ways to get at things that seemed impossible.

"Lei! I heard from Marcella what happened to Stevens!"

"Yeah." Lei felt her throat close. Relief swept through her that she wasn't going to have to explain. The three women were close, but her FBI friends Marcella and Sophie lived near each other on Oahu, and so were able to spend more time together. "I have to call her, see how the baby's doing."

"He's doing great. Marcella says Jonas put on weight before they even left the hospital."

"When I met him he appeared to be figuring out breastfeeding just fine." Lei pinched the bridge of her nose. She'd flown over to Oahu and gone to the hospital for the occasion of her friend's delivery. "I'm sorry I didn't get to see you when I was there. I barely saw baby Jonas before I got the news about Stevens and needed to get home."

"I understand. I'd hoped you might call, to see if I could do anything to help."

"You read my mind." Lei took a breath, blew it out. "Security Solutions. What do you know about them?"

"A lot, as a matter of fact. They've got an office here in Honolulu."

"Well, that's the outfit Michael was working for. Westbrook, the army liaison who informed me, called me today to tell me they'd received a ransom demand." Lei filled her friend in on the little she knew. "I tried to get some leave authorized to do my own investigation, maybe go over there and help, but I got shut down. Westbrook won't even tell me what country he was in, and the captain wouldn't authorize my leave. So I was wondering if there was anything you could do to—find him. Where he is. What's going on."

"Definitely. I think it's interesting that the army is liaising with the families and not the company."

"I'm guessing it's to provide an extra layer of 'don't hassle us for information,'" Lei said. "Westbrook seems like an okay guy. He probably told me more than he should have. I did get a satellite phone, supposedly issued by the company. Want the number?"

"Absolutely. I can track the carrier and more with that."

"I won't ask how you're gonna do that." Lei smiled.

"Better not to. But before I start getting into all this—and trust me when I tell you, it's not going to be authorized access—what's your goal with this? You aren't planning to go over there and do something crazy, like that other trip. Are you?"

That other trip. It was always going to haunt her.

"No. I can't lose my job, and the captain isn't giving me the time off. Not to mention, I have a son who needs at least one parent who's willing to stick around." Lei couldn't help the bitterness that had crept into her voice.

"Oh, Lei. I'm so sorry this has happened. Really." Sophie's slightly husky voice was soft. "I know you'll forgive Michael when he's back and safe. You know he loves you and Kiet. He must have had his reasons."

"I don't have to understand them or like them, especially now that this has happened," Lei said. "So what's my goal? I want to know all that I can about his operation. Where he is. What they were doing there. And mainly, if there's anything more that can be done to get him back. If there is, then I want to be in a position to make it happen."

"That I can understand," Sophie said. "I'll check back in with you as soon as I've got something."

"Thanks so much, my friend."

Lei heard the smile in the tech's voice as Sophie said, "Right back atcha, girlfriend," in a tone that told Lei she meant it, even while making fun of the Americanism. Sophie was half Thai and had grown up overseas, immigrating to the United States when she became an agent.

Lei ended the call and got on the long, winding road toward Hana.

CHAPTER FIVE

I SAT up in the dark and ate the ball of rice. Drank more water. Lay back down and rested. Lying there in the dark, afraid to fall asleep, I reviewed the first days in camp.

Sitting in the orientation briefing with the other private contractors under a big canvas tent, I'd positioned myself near Major Forsythe. He took a spot at a battered metal stand that served as a podium and pulled down a large map from a metal roll.

"We're here." He used a laser pointer to highlight a squiggly line on a large topographical map. "We're in Honduras, in this area. This line here is the Río Coco River. On the other side of this river is Nicaragua. We're inland about five miles from the river, and we are a ways off from the capital of Honduras, Tegucigalpa. Our mission here is to train the local police in investigation techniques and support the Drug Enforcement Agency in efforts to prevent drugs from entering the United States."

"I was told I was training U.S. troops on computer security and investigation," Carrigan said. I was glad he was the one to open his mouth. I'd had a whole different idea about the gig, too. I smacked a mosquito that had found an uncovered spot on my arm. The pay that had seemed outrageous back on Maui might not be enough.

"You are training our troops. This is a joint operation. We're working with the local Honduran police, whose cooperation the U.S. government is interested in keeping, as well as our own MPs stationed in nearby countries. Perhaps you could let me get through the briefing before you ask any more questions?"

Carrigan had the nerve to lean back and flap his hand in a "go-on" gesture. Forsythe swung back to his map.

"We're going to be doing operations in and around the jungle here. Michael Stevens is in charge of basic investigation techniques, including evidence collection and processing. Ed Carrigan is in charge of phone surveillance and online investigation. Pat Smithers is in charge of interrogation techniques. Brad Falconer, you're in charge of survival skills, search and seizure, and capture of targets. Each of you will have a tent, much like this one, set up for your daily classes. There will be three rounds of class per day, and you'll each be provided an interpreter for the Honduran investigators in your group. Questions?"

There were many, but I didn't ask any, preferring to extend my legs and rock my chair back a bit as I took it all in, fingers laced over my belly. It didn't matter really. I had six months of this to get through, and asking questions, not to mention arguing, was just an illusion of control.

The upshot was that we had two days to set up our instruction areas before the Honduran police and our U.S. trainees arrived and the program got going.

I was billeted in a tent with Falconer, a large and silent black man. He immediately set up a workout area in the corner of our tent, filling up a portable plastic weight set with water, and a computer area in the other corner, with a space-age laptop powered by a small solar battery source, which he set up on the roof of the tent.

"You can tap in, if you like," was the extent of his conversation. I was glad. I didn't feel like talking either. I took him up on the offer, plugging my laptop into the power strip he ran off the solar battery even though the tent had electricity from the ever-rumbling generator out by the mess tent.

Lei had sent me a text asking me to call. I walked outside for a little privacy to call her back, but when I tried, the satellite phone wouldn't connect.

That first night was long, even under that white veil of sanity, mosquito netting, which our cots were covered with. The sounds of the jungle outside, the relentless humidity, the screeches and cries of unseen animals, darkness that felt thick as paste—all of it, and the last nip off my flask, combined to make the night seem endless.

Just as it did now in my storage-shed prison.

It wasn't even night yet. I picked at the rope tied to my wrist for something to do. Even if I got it off, the door was probably locked. I chewed on the knot, but I still wasn't sure of the best strategy to escape. More than likely we were all being held for ransom and the best thing to do was wait for payoff and rescue. Where would I go in this jungle, when the map I'd seen the first day, with its wiggly lines, was the only idea I had of where I was?

And yet I still picked at the knot. The rope was cheap hemp with a fuzzy natural fiber feel to it. Using my teeth, I had it off before long. I was still racked with periodic shivers from the fever, but I felt stronger having eaten the rice ball.

It couldn't hurt to explore the storage shed, get a good sense of where I was being held. I rolled carefully onto my side and up onto my hands and knees. My clothing had dried, stiff with mud from the pit, but at least it no longer caused a wet chill, aggravating my illness.

I stayed on my hands and knees to explore the shed, swinging my arms slowly as I crawled, feeling my way around the different objects in the shed. I reached one of the walls and felt around the bottom.

As I had suspected, the wall was embedded several inches in the dirt, probably to keep the copious rain, which mercifully seemed to have stopped, from oozing in underneath the wall.

I tested the area where the door was, a faint line of light.

Locked, of course. There were two sides to the door, and rust was definitely impinging the hinges. I pushed, and the doors bowed out slightly but held, even when I put all my weight on them.

No surprise there.

The exploration had wiped me out. I crawled back to my pallet and clumsily replaced the rope, looser this time, and curled up to sleep.

I managed to get some hours of sleep before I woke up screaming. I didn't think it was close to morning, because with my eyes open, I still could hardly see a hand held in front of my face.

I kept seeing things moving at the corners of my vision. I was pretty sure they were hallucinations, but there was a weird fluidity to them, like they were snakes undulating down the walls.

Closing my eyes didn't help. I still saw them. So I opened them again. This time, a tiny light fluttered around my pallet. The light seemed to intensify, coalescing into a glowing object that danced around the darkness like a grave light.

The hairs on the back of my neck rose. I eased myself up into a sitting position, leaning my back against the metal wall on one side, drawing my knees up.

The glowing bug, moth, or whatever it was landed on the edge of my blanket near my feet. It rested there a moment. I blinked, looking at it.

Probably some sort of bioluminescent insect.

It swelled, expanding, its intense greenish yellow light spreading and dimming, and it seemed to be the shape of a woman. I could see through her to the far wall, and her features were blurry —but I recognized her anyway. I knew that petite, slender shape, the outline of hair long enough to brush her hips as she knelt.

My ex-wife, Anchara. Kiet's murdered mother.

At least she wasn't covered with blood in this hallucination. I raised a hand to rub my eyes, refocusing them.

She was still there.

"What are you doing here?" I must be dreaming. She didn't answer. The expression on her translucent face was sad.

"I am releasing you." Anchara's voice was a rustling whisper that sounded like wind in the tops of the trees, but I understood her perfectly. "I was angry. I thought it wasn't fair, what happened, that you got to raise our son. I didn't go when I was supposed to. But now I see that driving you mad has led you here to an unsafe place, and our son needs you."

I blinked repeatedly. It felt unnatural because my eyes were open so wide. My mouth had fallen open, too. "You aren't real. You're a hallucination. You're dead."

The rain started up again on top of the metal roof, just a gentle patter. Anchara was still there, even after I rubbed my eyes. "You've been haunting me? Why?"

"Because you lived, and I didn't," she said. "It wasn't fair."

The hairs rose all over my body, but I controlled the urge to back as far away from her as I could. There was nowhere to go with my back against the wall, and she'd already done her worst in my dreams.

"You won't see me again. I forgive you. Now you must forgive yourself." Anchara looked right at me then, a feeling like a search-light passing over me. She faded, wavering in the air. The luminescence that had spread to assume her shape contracted back down to a moth, and it fluttered around the space.

My eyes couldn't stop tracking it. It was going somewhere, flitting and darting, bright as a flashlight in the total darkness. I tugged at the loose knot on my wrist and got it undone, and followed the glowing insect as it flitted into one of the corners of the shed and disappeared.

It had gotten out somehow.

I was probably still dreaming or hallucinating. I kept waiting to wake up as I made my way to the corner where I'd last seen the flying glow-bug, and felt my way up the wall.

The moth had disappeared through a sort of window or ventilation hatch, a simple square opening with a metal shutter hanging down over it. And when I pushed, that metal shutter wasn't locked.

My mind raced. I could get out. Maybe I could free the men in the pit. Maybe I could find my way…to where?

This was nuts. I was probably dreaming the whole damn thing.

But the patter of rain hadn't stopped, and the metal under my hand felt cool and sharp. I should have woken by now. If it was a dream, it was the most realistic one yet.

I pushed the shutter outward slowly, looking around. The shed butted up against a wall of dark, dripping trees. A sliver of moon barely lit the area enough to see anything, but fluttering and dipping, deep into the shadows, was the glowing moth that might have been Anchara.

MAUDENE YAMAGUCHI PEERED at Lei through a screen door green with mold. Split coconuts in wire hangers, sprouting orchid plants, bracketed the doorway. "What you like?" The old woman's voice sounded like a rocking chair on a wooden porch.

"Hi, Mrs. Yamaguchi." Lei identified herself. "I'm following up with you about something you found on the beach? A skull?"

The old woman pushed the door open slightly. "Come in."

"Thank you." Lei toed out of her athletic shoes and set them on the low shelf filled with rubber slippers. The cottage was one of the old plantation style homes Lei had always loved, single-wall construction with a tin roof and wide, painted-wood floors interspersed with lauhala matting.

"You came all this way to talk with me about that?" Mrs. Yamaguchi gestured to a futon couch. "Go. Sit. I get the tea."

Lei was reminded of visiting with her grandfather Soga Matsumoto on Oahu. There was no rushing a Japanese elder, no matter the mission. The house smelled faintly musty, with notes of ginger and soy sauce. Mrs. Yamaguchi was cooking—probably something with homemade teriyaki sauce.

Lei seated herself on the couch, glancing around. A kneeling desk made of old crates doubled as a coffee table in front of the couch. On the walls, three traditional silk paintings made a triptych. Through the sash-style window, Lei could see a square of neatly mowed, very green lawn, and beyond that, the variegated tops of jungle trees rolling downhill to a wind-whipped ocean.

The drive to Mrs. Yamaguchi's house in Hana had been beautiful, and Lei had been able to flash her lights to get around dawdling tourists blocking the road in front of the many waterfalls in order to get to the remote village in much less than the usual two hours. She'd focused on the challenging act of driving to keep her mind off of Stevens. The road was mostly one-lane, encroached upon by stands of bamboo, lush flowering trees, and extreme hairpin turns.

Sitting here now, her hands resting on her thighs, Lei breathed out a long exhale of held tension. Mrs. Yamaguchi was not going to be interested in her agenda. She would tell her story how she wanted to, at her own speed.

Lei looked at the wall across from the window. On it was a sheathed samurai-style sword with a bamboo practice katana below it, resting on simple wooden pegs. Just above the swords was a line of photos of Japanese men in uniform.

Mrs. Yamaguchi came shuffling back. She was carrying a lacquered tray. It held a small clay teapot, two handleless cups, and a couple of nori-wrapped rice crackers on a plate.

"The water is still getting hot," the elderly woman said.

"Can I help? Please, Aunty. Let me do something."

"Okay, then. In a minute you can fetch the hot water from the stove."

"I will." Lei leaned forward, opening the file she had brought and set it beside the tea tray. "So I have been assigned to investigate the bone you found on the beach. Please tell me about your discovery."

"I was doing my morning walk." Mrs. Yamaguchi pointed to a wooden stand in the corner where several hand-carved canes rested. "I walk every day. How I made eighty-five last week."

"Congratulations. That's a big milestone. My captain said you brought the skull in? I was wondering why you didn't just call us so we could see it where you found it?"

Mrs. Yamaguchi's dark eyes, so deep a brown that Lei couldn't see her pupils, seemed to sharpen in the fans of crepe-like skin surrounding them. "I didn't want someone to take it away while I was calling you. And I don't believe in those cell phones. So I put it in my trash bag and I brought it home. I had to do my shopping in Costco anyway, so I just took 'em out myself. You can go get the water now."

"Of course." Lei got up with a respectful inclination of her head. She walked into the modest kitchen. Sure enough, an old-fashioned white enamel teakettle was just beginning to whistle on the small gas stove. Lei turned it off, glancing around the pristine space with its small round table and two chairs.

She saw no other evidence of anyone else living with the elderly lady, and the thought of Mrs. Yamaguchi driving that hazardous road in the rusting truck she'd glimpsed in the lean-to garage gave her a bit of a shiver. Still, Mrs. Yamaguchi seemed steady enough.

She carried the kettle back out to the tea things. "Is it okay if I pour it in?" She was unsure of the protocol.

"I put the tea in the pot already," Mrs. Yamaguchi said. "You may pour."

Lei carefully filled the heavy earthenware pot with the boiling water and replaced the lid. She took the kettle back to the stove and rejoined the old woman. "Now, you took the skull in. What made you think someone might take it from where you found it?"

"Someone knows who that child is. That someone wouldn't want anyone to see the bone," Mrs. Yamaguchi said.

Lei frowned. "You know who these people are? Who would take the skull and hide it?"

Mrs. Yamaguchi just shrugged. She opened the teapot and stirred the loose tea inside with a bamboo whisk. She placed a china strainer over each cup and carefully poured.

Lei followed the older woman's lead as she lifted the teacup, sniffed, and sipped. The tea tasted like flowers and green things.

"Delicious." Lei's grandfather had a kindred spirit in Mrs. Yamaguchi.

The woman gave a brief nod. "You want I take you to where I find the bone?"

"That would be perfect." Lei opened the file again. "I just wanted to tell you a few things we have found out so far, in case you might know anything about it. The skull belonged to a male child, aged ten or so. The hole in the front?" Lei tapped the photo, drawing the woman's gaze to the disturbing break in the forehead. "This happened after the skull was buried. Perhaps when the flood washed it down the stream. There's no evidence of foul play so far."

"I am glad of that," Mrs. Yamaguchi said. "Finish your tea. Then we go. I have to be back by three."

"Three?"

"General Hospital is on." Mrs. Yamaguchi jerked her head toward the sleek, wall-mounted flat-screen in the corner. "I always watch."

Lei hid her smile by slurping her tea. Finishing it, she stood. "I'm ready if you are."

CHAPTER SIX

I WASN'T sure what I'd just experienced.

I'd just had a hallucination visit from the ghost of my ex-wife, and while I appreciated that Anchara had decided to forgive me and wasn't going to haunt me anymore, her direction that I get back to our son was about as loony tunes a moment as I'd had in my life.

Looking out into the darkness, at the glowing moth fluttering among the dripping trees, I heard the thin, high scream of some small animal, abruptly cut short. Mosquitoes buzzed in my ears. The moth zigzagged out of sight into the depths.

I had no idea where I was being held prisoner, or how to get anywhere that would get me out of this place. If I'd had anything to drink, I'd have downed it. I longed for that anesthetic, that oblivion. But I didn't, and I still hadn't woken up. I pinched my own arm, hard.

Pain spiked.

Apparently I wasn't dreaming.

If I was going to escape, I needed supplies. A compass. Weapons. Some sort of plan.

And then there was the fact that I was sick. I felt my way back to my pallet just as my wobbly knees collapsed. Lying there, reattaching my rope, I was so dizzy and nauseated from even those small exertions and stresses that I retched.

Finally, curled on my side in the fetal position, I drifted off. Maybe tomorrow I'd be well enough to do something.

I WOKE to the stabbing of sunshine in my eyes and a rough hand under my arm hauling me upright.

"Come." It was the man from before. I continued to pretend I didn't understand Spanish, but his meaning was pretty clear as he untied the rope and hefted me up.

I was definitely feeling a little better today, I realized. My vision was clearer and I wasn't as dizzy—but I didn't want to be put back in that muddy pit. I dragged my feet and stumbled, my head lolling.

The guard swore impatiently and draped one of my arms over his shoulders. He had a knife in a scabbard on his belt—a modern combat knife with a molded-plastic handle, a compass embedded in the haft.

I needed that knife.

The sun was out today, and the humidity was so thick that breathing felt like snorkeling. The mud we slogged through was actually steaming. In spite of the brightness stabbing my eyes, I tried to get my bearings on the camp.

The main access seemed to be a small airstrip, one of the pistas I'd heard of, runways for the drug planes to come and go from the jungle. Clustered at one end of that runway was the encampment, a group of tents and ramshackle dwellings of scrap wood and roofing material, draped in camouflage netting beneath trees that had clearly been left to provide visual cover from the air.

I counted at least eight men in a quick survey. Two were on guard duty, but not taking it too seriously as they smoked and leaned on their rifles. The rest were playing cards or cooking in an open-sided group tent.

The guard put me in the outhouse again, which I badly needed by then. Afterward, he marched me on past my shed toward a large tent deep in the jungle shadows. We passed by the pit where I knew the other men were. All I could see was the circle of bamboo and palm fronds that covered the hole.

My guts twisted with guilt and worry over them, trapped in the unhealthy filth of that hole. I stumbled, slipping down from my guard's grasp, and as I did so I grabbed his belt.

He swore and hefted me up again, insulting my mother and sisters in Spanish, but as we got going again, his knife in its snap-on belt scabbard was deep in the cargo pocket of my filthy pants.

Compass and weapon. Check.

Though now that I had it, how long would it be until he missed it?

Too late now.

"Excuse me, sir. I brought the prisoner." My guard spoke outside the imposing canvas tent.

An interior flap was untied. A guard carrying one of our military-issued M16s stood aside after looking us over. My guard hefted me in. I kept my head lolling on my chest, sneaking glances as I was able.

The man who appeared to be in charge of this operation was sitting at a table, eating. The biodegradable tray he was scooping food from was one of our MREs. Meals Ready to Eat are not known for flavor, but this hefty, black-bearded man was shoveling in the familiar, homely beef-and-vegetable entrée like it was gourmet.

Who were these people, outfitted like our military? Had they stolen all of this, or been given it in some misguided operation?

"I brought the tall, sick one," the guard said.

"Put him on the chair," the man replied. His small, beady eyes ran over me. I was floppy and unresponsive as the door guard moved to open an aluminum folding chair. It screeched in protest as he unfolded it and further squealed as my guard dropped me onto it like a sack of rice.

"Tie him," the commander said. He opened a vacuum-packed plastic container of peaches and poured them onto the tray. The smell hit me right in my empty belly, sweet and heavy as a long-ago summer. My stomach rumbled as the guard tied my hands behind the chair back.

But he didn't tie my legs.

Head still bowed, I glanced around for a map. If I had a map and the compass, I might have a chance of getting somewhere useful.

"Prop today's paper under his chin," the commander said. "Hold his head up."

They stuck a newspaper, pulpy and curling with damp, under my chin. The guard smacked my cheek. "Look up, damn it."

A flash went off in my eyes as they took a photo. This must be the next "proof of life" installment since they cut the bone hook off my neck.

With that thought, I suddenly and vividly remembered the attack.

I'd been in the middle of lecturing. A half circle of men was seated in front of me as I talked about the three C's of evidence collection at a crime scene and the necessity of protecting the area where a crime occurred. Overhead, we heard the thrum of helicopters approaching, but that wasn't unusual. I didn't even stop talking until the tear gas shot into the tent, fired from three choppers as they landed in our airstrip area.

They mowed us down with non-lethal ammo and tear gas. A few shots were fired, but our troops clearly hadn't expected this kind of balls-out full-frontal attack. Most of the men I was instructing didn't have weapons with them—I'd left my sidearm in the tent, too.

I was on my knees, retching from the tear gas, when one of the raiders, face hidden by a gas mask, checked my uniform, apparently looking for names. LT. STEVENS was right there on a Velcro patch on my chest, right below a patch that read, contractor. Otherwise, my jungle-camo uniform was the same as the ones worn by the other U.S. men in the camp.

The man zip-tied my hands, yelling for help. I wrenched away, stumbled to my feet. One of the trainees had his weapon out and took a shot at my attacker. It drew a line of fire across my side, and I felt rather than heard someone behind me. I couldn't turn away before he slugged me on the head.

It was lights out after that, until I woke up in the pit. Now I glanced at the camp's commander from under my brows.

"Is he still sick?" the man asked, picking up the peaches and sucking them from his fingers.

"Yes. He needs help to walk."

"Well, let me know if he gets any worse. He can be our first casualty," the commander said. "We'll start killing them tomorrow. One a day until we get the money."

I controlled my response with an effort, keeping my breathing slow and my head lolling.

"They aren't paying the ransom, sir?" the tent guard asked.

"Fucking tightwad Americans," the man said. "We're going to have to show we're serious." He picked up another MRE packet. "Get him out of here and start bringing up the men from the pit."

I allowed myself to be lifted up and helped back to the shed.

There the man threw me another rice ball and refilled my water bottle before he locked me in.

They weren't paying our ransom, and I was going to die tomorrow if these thugs didn't get the money. I rolled onto my side, removed the knife, and slid it under one of the bags stacked beside me, in case my guard missed it and came back to search me.

I was going to have to escape, and if possible, bring the other men with me.

Now that I had the knife with its compass, survival was at least possible, and while I didn't have a map, I'd gotten a good look at the one on the wall behind the camp commander. Directly north of us, through a belt of jungle and what looked like some open area, was the Coco River, and on the other side, Nicaragua. I could get some help if I could just find people to alert to our situation, and hopefully the kidnappers wouldn't pursue us into another country.

It was still light out. There was no hope of escape until dark, and even then, getting the other men out was going to be difficult.

But maybe the ransom would come today.

There was nothing I could do until nightfall, so I ate the rice, drank only a little water because I planned to take the jug with me, and willed myself to sleep.

Of course, it didn't work.

Instead, I remembered Lei on the last night before I left, standing in the doorway of our bedroom, wearing nothing but a towel. I'd gone to her. Looked down into her face, hoping.

I loved that face so much it hurt.

Her big, tilted brown eyes were full of shadows and darkness, but her lush mouth was turned up to mine. I bent down and kissed her, and she responded, the kindling of our bodies against each other instant and fiery.

I'd missed her so much. We hadn't been together in two months, since she'd moved out of our room when I'd told her about the deployment. I was too stubborn to beg or try to visit her in her little hideout at the back of the house. She was too stubborn to come back to me. But now she was here, and she dropped the towel. Nothing was left between us.

All that existed was the velvet of her skin, the slickness of her mouth, her strong legs and delicious breasts and all of me over and in and around her as we strove. It was hard and harsh, wrenching and intense. Then, sweet and slow as a long last breath.

What a fool I'd been.

There were so many other things I could have done about my shit than come to this godforsaken hole. I'd wanted to punish myself. And I'd succeeded. But I'd punished her, too, and I'd seen it in the tears she shed even as we made love, sliding down her cheeks silent and desperate. We spoke no words, because words would destroy the moment. Words would remind us we were still poles apart.

Yeah. I'd punished us both, and my son, too.

But I was still alive, and I was off the booze now, and I'd faced Anchara's ghost for the last time, at least according to her. Now I just had to stay alive and get back to my family.

I'd go tonight.

I shut my eyes and waited for night to come.

LEI SLAMMED the door of her truck. She'd pulled up onto a half-moon of stony beach a short drive from Mrs. Yamaguchi's house. "So you go down here every day?" she asked.

"Yes." Mrs. Yamaguchi had slid on a pair of bright green Crocs with her cotton pants and shirt, and donned a ratty sweater for their drive to the beach. She carried a canvas shopping bag emblazoned with Hasegawa General Store, the small family-run emporium in Hana that stocked everything for the remote town from candles to cartridges. "This for my litter cleanup."

Lei followed the elderly lady as she picked her way with the aid of one of her canes across the mounds of smooth volcanic rocks polished round by the ceaseless tumble of waves on the shore below. She looked up and down the beach. No one was there but the tiny white arc of an iwa, a Hawaiian tropicbird, flying above with its distinctive pure white silhouette and long, split tail. The ocean was the gray-green of an overcast day, and off in the distance, Lei spotted an unusual red rainbow beneath storm-blown cloud. Wasn't that some sort of Hawaiian omen? She turned back, making her way through piled rocks and the mounds of driftwood clotting the beach.

Mrs. Yamaguchi was still walking. They reached a small creek coming down from one of the many nearby valleys. The creek drained out into the ocean here, bouncing and trickling across the stones and carving through them to the sand beneath.

Mrs. Yamaguchi pointed her cane at a mound of interwoven sticks, logs, and debris on the other side of the creek. "It was in there."

"I see how smart those Crocs are," Lei muttered, as the old lady waded the shallow stream flow, wearing the plastic footwear, to reach the driftwood pile while Lei was still pulling off her athletic shoes and socks. She joined the old lady a few moments later. "Where was the skull?"

Lei had already slipped some latex gloves on in the truck, so when Mrs. Yamaguchi pointed with her cane, Lei lifted the wood away, searching carefully for anything more.

"Mrs. Yamaguchi, I'm looking around this area and there's nobody. For miles. I don't see any houses in that valley either." Lei gestured up into the thickly jungled, narrow valley. "You have to tell me why you said someone would take the skull."

"There are people in that valley," Mrs. Yamaguchi said. "People who don't want you to know about them."

"But I told you the skull was old, right? It was buried. Probably an old grave that washed out in a flash flood." Lei gestured to the mountain of tangled branches and debris. "These floods rip down the valleys and clear out all the overgrown brush. Some little boy's ancient grave just finally washed away in all this."

"You think what you like. I know what I know."

"What do you mean by that?"

Mrs. Yamaguchi refused to answer and just wandered off, picking up bits of plastic and litter and putting them slowly, painfully, in her bag.

Lei tore into the pile of debris, pulling it apart and searching it carefully. She found nothing but branches, rotting grasses, old logs, leaves and twigs, and one battered coconut.

But somewhere up in that narrow valley was a gravesite and people Mrs. Yamaguchi said didn't want to be known. She photographed the area, the stream, and the valley with her phone camera. Seemed like a good time for a hike.

But first she'd have to take Mrs. Yamaguchi home and let Pono know what she was up to.

She checked the time on her phone. Twelve thirty p.m. She wasn't going to make it back from Hana in time to pick Kiet up from school. Signal was iffy out here, but hopefully on the beach she'd be able to get a call through. She connected with her father, Wayne.

"Hey, Dad. I'm out in Hana and can't get back in time to pick up Kiet. He's supposed to go to Ellen's today—would you mind?"

"No problem, Sweets. The lunch rush will be over by then." She heard the clatter and clash of dishes in the background. Wayne's Local Grindz in the Haiku Cannery Mall was doing a brisk business since he opened a few years ago. "I'll run him out there. Maybe have a cup of coffee with Ellen while I'm at it."

"I'm sure she'd like that." Lei had often wondered if the friendship that had grown up between Stevens's widowed mother and her own single father might turn to something more. "I should be home by five, though. Thanks so much."

She hung up, but didn't call Pono because Mrs. Yamaguchi was making her way back. The canvas bag was filling up with trash. "Do you do that every day, Mrs. Yamaguchi?"

"I do."

"It's amazing that there's that much trash on this beach, then," Lei said.

"Such a shame, that," the elderly lady said. "Rubbish, it washes up from the ocean. So many people, they throw any-kine stuffs in the ocean like it one big garbage dump."

"I hate that, too." Lei's most recent case had revolved around fish poaching and reef conservation. "The ocean is more fragile than people realize."

"The `aina, too," Mrs. Yamaguchi said.

That Hawaiian word for "land" was also the name of a handsome Coast Guardsman she'd met on her last case, a man whose appearance and heritage, similar to hers, had elicited something within her. A recognition. A chord of something shared, compatible, and exciting.

But she wasn't going to find out what. She didn't care what it might be. She was married.

Happily.

Okay. Maybe not happily, but married. And her husband was a captive in Central America, probably suffering right now in some hideous prison camp. On the other hand, there was Kathy Fraser, her husband's beautiful partner. Kathy knew things Stevens should have shared with his wife. She meant something to him, and he to her, and that scared Lei.

Still. It wasn't right to think about Aina Thomas and his kindness and the connection she'd felt with him. She flushed with shame for even having a thought about another man. Hopefully he'd get the message and just leave her alone, because she wasn't feeling very strong right now.

Stevens was captured, in danger. That was the priority. That, and her son. This case was just a time filler, but she might as well have a look for the gravesite since she'd driven all this way.

Lei dropped Mrs. Yamaguchi off and tried to get a signal to call Pono, but there was no reception at the Yamaguchi house. She drove back to the beach and parked on the shoulder beside the stream. She found a plastic water bottle in the back seat, along with her portable backpack crime kit.

Lei twisted her wayward hair into a ponytail and tried to call Pono again. This time the call went straight to a glitching voice mail.

"Hey, Pono. Just wanted you to know I'm taking a hike into a valley in Hana at"—she looked around for a landmark—"mile marker sixteen."

The voice mail cut off abruptly in midsentence, and when she tried to call back, it didn't connect at all.

Oh well.

She locked the truck, donned the backpack and her Kevlar, checked her weapon, pulled her MPD ball cap down over her hair, and headed into the mouth of the stream.

CHAPTER SEVEN

Darkness had finally fully come. I prepared as best I could, untying the rope, which might be useful for something else, and looping it around my waist. I snapped the knife scabbard onto my belt, drank a little water, and carrying the jug, headed into the back corner. I pressed gently on the shutter.

It didn't open.

It was too dark in the shed to really see, so I set the water jug down and felt around the edges of the window.

Yes, there was an opening in the wall. Whatever hallucinogenic state I'd been in yesterday, I wasn't so gone that this remembered window wasn't even real. But the opening was shut firmly now. Pushing on it, nothing happened. A wave of terror rippled over me, prickling the skin of my hands and erupting across my shoulders in sweat.

This was the first time I was really scared. All this time I'd been pretty sure that the best thing I could do was stay alive until rescue, that I'd be ransomed. But I'd heard it myself from the camp commander's lips—I was to be made an example of, to show how serious the kidnappers were.

I need to get out. I stifled the desire to pound and push on the window. That would draw attention.

Perhaps there was a latch of some kind.

I drew the knife from its scabbard. It was a six-inch blade of tapered, tempered steel with a serrated back and a razor-sharp blade, the tang running all the way through the molded plastic grip. It fit my hand like it was made for me.

I slid the knife down into the crack between the edge of the window and the shutter, sliding it slowly along.

It made a rasping sound against the metal that sounded like our dogs when they wanted to get in at the back door, a clawing that raised the hairs on the back of my neck.

And it caught on something.

I worked it back and forth, hoping it was a simple hook.

Hyperaware of the loud scraping noise I was making, I slid and pried, jiggled and worked. Finally, with a squeak, the latch of the shutter gave.

A draft of slightly cooler, mossy-smelling air drifted up into the shed as I lifted the shutter. At least it wasn't raining at this particular moment.

I sheathed the knife, dropped the water jug gently outside. I slowly raised the metal shutter, looking and listening. No response to my activities so far.

I used my arms to lift myself into the opening, and brought up a leg. Awkwardly, painfully, I slid my leg out over the sharp, narrow edge. Weakened as I was, it took all I had to ease myself quietly out the opening and drop onto the soft, pulpy ground outside. The smell of green, growing, and rotting things filled my nostrils as I squatted, all my senses alert.

In the dark of the creaking, clicking, squeaking jungle, several of the glowing moths flitted. I'd probably been having a hallucination yesterday. Anchara couldn't have visited me.

Thank God the shed butted up against the jungle. It would be easy to just set off into the darkness, but I had to see if I could get any of the men out of the pit.

I flattened myself against the metal wall and sidled along it, staying in the shadow of the roof overhang as I worked my way to the front of the building.

The moon was a thin blue-white flashlight in the sky, flicking on and off as clouds came and went. The deep shadow of trees provided extra cover around the shed, but ahead of me was the open area at the end of the muddy runway. Temporary shelters hunkered like turtles around a fire pit area.

I could hear voices coming from that area, snatches of conversation. The fire provided a distant glow and flickering invitation, glimpsed through the tents' fabric.

Even though things looked deserted, there had to be guards posted.

How was I going to get out into the open area to the pit, let alone figure out a way to get the men out?

Perhaps a distraction could draw attention away.

My eyes finally adjusted all they were going to, and I spotted two guards. They were armed, leaning against trees near the main open area. They didn't appear to be highly alert—their postures were relaxed, their heads turned toward the fire. One of them was on my side of the clearing, the other on the opposite side, farther away but closer to the pit.

Perhaps I could disable one of them and he would have something I could use as a distraction.

I began working my way around, keeping to the shadows, my rubber-soled hiking boots silent on the damp jungle mulch underfoot. There was no rush. I had all night. I just needed to get around the camp undetected, disable the guard, and then... That was as far ahead as I could plan.

I controlled my breathing, keeping each breath quiet and slow, and as I did I felt an extraordinary alertness flood me. My earlier weakness and sluggishness were completely gone. As I crept around the wide, rough-barked bole of a tree, I realized I hadn't felt this alive in years.

I was clearheaded, revitalized, and firing on all cylinders.

This. This was what I'd come for.

In a highly dangerous situation, with my life and the lives of others at stake, I finally felt good in my body again. This was what I'd needed and had been unable to explain to anyone.

When I got home, I had to get back to solving cases. Being the trainer behind a desk had been making all my other shit worse.

I closed the last few yards toward the guard leaning on his tree. I slid around the tree, focused on the man leaning there, his rifle carelessly propped on his leg and his chin nodding on his chest.

I grabbed him in a yoke chokehold, hauling him back into the darkness.

He thrashed, and I tightened my grip, feeling his struggles get more frantic. His legs were kicking up leaves as he writhed and kicked, so I lifted him off the ground, and that settled things rapidly.

I hoped I wouldn't have to kill him. When I felt the artery in his neck, his heart was still beating.

"Arturo! You okay, man?" came from the other guard in Spanish.

"Taking a piss," I called back in that language, coughing into my fist in case my voice didn't sound right.

I lowered the unconscious man to the ground. He was wearing a web belt with shoulder straps loaded with several grenades, ammo, and a canteen. I stripped it off him and put it on, acquiring another knife and a pistol, too. In his upper shirt pockets were a chocolate bar, a packet of sugar cookies, and a small LED flash-light on a webbing strap, meant to be worn as a headlight.

Jackpot. I was good to go into the jungle with all of this.

I gagged the man with his own neckerchief and hog-tied him with his belt. Killing him certainly would have been faster, but I didn't want to raise the stakes on this whole operation before I'd even gotten away from camp. I put Arturo's billed hat on, and holding the M16 in the same way he had, I slouched back to his surveillance spot.

"I need to piss now," the other man said.

"Go." I gestured with the weapon, and the other guard vanished into the jungle on his side of the clearing.

I was now on the opposite side of the camp than I had been, with the pit close to me on my left. Perhaps I wasn't going to have to make too big of a distraction. While the other guard was gone, I could assess the prisoners.

Feeling naked and vulnerable, knowing I was taller than the other man had been, I slouched into the open and walked casually over to the pit, hoping the dark concealed my U.S. camouflage uniform clothing. I squatted and lifted one edge of the bamboo frame with its covering of palm branches. I flicked the headlight on and shone it into the pit.

The hole was empty. Several inches of muddy water at the bottom gleamed back at me, mocking.

"Arturo! What are you doing?"

The other guard's voice was right above me. He'd approached while I was distracted. My heart stuttered in my chest and a wave of adrenaline jacked through me.

The time for stealth was over.

I shot up from my crouch with the stolen combat knife in my fist and drove it upward into the man's throat from below, burying it to the hilt in the soft triangle of flesh beneath his jaw

He dropped, clawing at his throat, emitting a horrible gargling. Warm blood, only slightly hotter than the surrounding air, pumped over my hand. I let go of the knife and grabbed the man under the armpits, hauling him out of the open area to his post against the tree, lowering him to a seated position against it.

He spasmed and lost control of his bowels, filling my nostrils with an abrupt stench. His legs sprawled and contracted. His heels drummed.

I'd forgotten how long it took for a man to die and how unpleasant it was to witness. No time for that sentimental shit. I needed the knife back. I yanked it out with a sideways gesture that opened the rest of his throat and finished things quicker, and got out of the way of the blood that followed.

I wiped the knife on the man's shoulder. Gently, I replaced his hat, which had fallen off, and tipped it forward over his face. To a casual observer, he would have appeared to have fallen asleep at his post.

Straightening up, I scanned around.

No new sounds or movements. The fire flickered. The voices continued, interspersed with snatches of laughter.

I removed the man's canteen from his belt. I took grenades, knife, and pistol and loaded up my harness belt, but I didn't need another M16. I shot the magazine, stuffed that in a pocket, and threw the weapon into the dark.

Time to find the other captives.

I tried to think logically as I assessed the camp.

The kidnappers must have decided the pit was too unhealthy, so they'd moved the prisoners. I just couldn't believe that the rest had been ransomed or rescued and I hadn't and that's why they were gone.

The men wouldn't be stashed in a tent. Too easy to break out of. And most of the clustered shapes were tents. So I just needed to find a structure that was secure and solid, and that's likely where the prisoners would be.

There was only one of those, a big sturdy-looking wooden shack, right in front of the fire. A row of men was seated in front of it, passing a bottle. Talking. A couple of them were playing cards.

Directly across from them, scanning the jungle and the open area, was another guard.

I wasn't going to be able to break out my fellow prisoners

without a major distraction, after all. I crept along toward my target, feeling the urgency to flee beating in my veins.

Every second I spent at the camp was another second closer to discovery.

I squatted in the deep cover of a tree, feeling my heart beating with heavy thuds. The fresh blood from the guard was sticky on my clothing and skin, and its coppery tang filled my nostrils. Listening to the strange sounds of the jungle around me, I deliberately calmed myself.

I shut my eyes to remember the map I'd seen in the commander's office.

Directly at the end of the runway, a couple of clicks to the north, was the great artery of the Coco River. I'd rescue the men and, using the compass, get us to the river and across it into Nicaragua, where hopefully these men wouldn't pursue us. I had no idea how to do any of it, but I hadn't known how to get this far, either.

Maybe there was some way to strike a blow against the camp while I was at it.

I opened my eyes and looked toward the far end of the runway. The three Black Hawk helicopters used to attack us were parked there, draped in camo netting.

Perfect.

I took a sip of water and chewed down the guard's chalky chocolate bar. My stomach wanted to rebel, but I needed to keep this machine fueled, because I had a lot more to do.

I crept along the edge of the jungle to the helicopters, wishing I knew how to fly one, but flying wasn't something I'd ever made time for. In a running crouch, I made it to the closest chopper, felt down the fuselage, and unscrewed the fuel cap. I took the fuel caps off all three, and then splashed fuel between them from a square green fuel container I found sitting nearby.

This was almost too easy. Something was bound to go wrong any minute. I had to hurry.

I pulled back into the jungle and took out two of the grenades I'd lifted off the guards.

I pulled the pin on one and tossed it between two of the choppers, then tossed the other one, too. It bounced and rolled between the struts of the third Black Hawk. I squatted down behind a big sheltering mahogany tree and plugged my ears with my fingers.

CHAPTER EIGHT

LEI STOOD on a smooth flat rock in the middle of the creek, scanning the banks. She'd been looking for some sort of path or trail into the deep crack of this valley from the beginning, but still hadn't spotted anything other than a thick welter of pili grass, wild ginger, kukui nut, rose apple, and mango trees forming an almost impenetrable wall of trees and foliage.

Most of these valleys had been heavily populated by Hawaiians at one time, but this one had a wild feeling, and Lei hadn't seen any of the telltale lo'i terracing that showed the remains of Hawaiians' agricultural domestication.

Perhaps it was too narrow. The walls rose claustrophobically steep and close on either side of the stream, bracketed by heavy undergrowth.

What could Mrs. Yamaguchi have been referring to? There was no sign of any human habitation here, and that in itself was unusual.

There were matted bits of grasses and dried, broken branches tangled in the underbrush along the way, giving testament to a flash flood not long ago. Probably the one that had washed the skull downstream.

"Well, someone was buried here," Lei muttered, and she resumed her rock-hopping progress up the stream as the easiest route into the valley, her eyes continually scanning the banks for any sign of the grave that had yielded the boy's skull.

The canyon made a sudden jag to the left, and the sides encroached even more, turning to nothing but a bluff of steep black lava rock with the jungle trying to get a grip on it by way of vines and grasses. Lei stooped, picking her way under a rough stone arch, and she straightened up and gasped. She moved forward several yards, awestruck by the beauty of the spot she'd stumbled upon.

A stream fell from a hundred feet of cliff directly ahead of her into a wide, calm pool surrounded by grass and kukui nut trees. The valley opened up entirely into a spacious bowl surrounded by the familiar crests of other ridges. This secret valley, cupped in the mountains like a fertile cradle, had been heavily populated at one time. Lo`i terraces, their even lines broken up by coconut and ulu breadfruit trees, ran in a stepwise pattern from the ridges down to the pond. Rock walls, fallen into disrepair and overgrown with vines and grasses, showed where Hawaiian hales had stood in a village.

And everywhere Lei looked were planted the tallest, lushest marijuana plants she'd ever seen. The hairs on Lei's neck rose, because even though no one was in sight, the unique smell of the plant and a whiff of its smoke coming from her left told her that this was not a good place to stumble upon alone, wearing a badge.

Lei sank back down behind a large boulder as she assessed the scene. This was a mega-farm of the famous Maui Wowie pakalolo she'd heard came from Hana. The crop had been carefully planted in and around already-existing trees, using them for cover from the Green Harvest helicopter patrols the DEA used to do regularly—though now, with the loosening of policies toward marijuana, they were scheduled less and less often.

A mechanical noise and movement came from one of the fields.

The noise was a pruner on an extension rod, and the boy standing next to the plants looked no more than twelve. He was dressed in camouflage green, and he was harvesting mature buds from plants that soared fifteen feet high, reaching the pruner up to clip off the dense, sticky-looking, hairy green bundles that held the most THC. The kid was careful how he pruned, and Lei could tell that the dense plants had been growing awhile and had yielded several harvests. As Lei watched, another kid joined him, gathering the buds as they dropped into a plastic barrow. A third followed, using handheld clippers to harvest in the lower areas.

The kids had come from somewhere. She had to see where, but she didn't want to be spotted. Wherever there were kids working, there had to be an adult making them work.

She didn't have long to wait. A large, dark-skinned man with a halo of heavy black dreadlocks slouched into view from a shack deep in tree shadow on the opposite side of the pond. He was wearing camouflage, too, with a green undershirt that bulged unpleasantly over a boulder of a belly. A Glock was rammed into the belt of his pants, gangster style.

The kids took one look at him and sped up.

"You boys get your quota, you can watch some TV," he said. Lei could hardly hear his words over the trickling of the stream.

He sat on a rock beside the pond and took out a large Bowie knife. The stick she thought he was holding turned out to be a stalk of sugarcane. He peeled the skin off with the knife and bit into the pulpy inner meat of the stalk.

Lei remembered the sugary crunch of raw cane fondly, but the sight before her stole the memory's sweetness. This asshole was making kids work in a pot field when they should be in school, bribing them with TV while he held a gun.

I could take him.

But he was armed, and who else was back here in the shelters?

65

There could be multiple perps, and she'd put the kids in danger if she made a premature move.

Lei slid her phone out of her pocket, checking for signal. There was none. Making sure it was on silent, she shot a picture of the man, crunching a sugarcane stalk as he watched child laborers harvest the biggest, fattest marijuana buds she'd ever seen.

It was like a third world movie happening right here on Maui.

The sun felt hot on the Kevlar vest she wore, and on the top of her head. Stealthily, Lei reached down and dipped a hand in the cool stream water, rubbed it around on her face.

She had to get back out undetected. If she could just get through the stone arch and around the corner, she could rock hop down the stream and be out of there, then come back with reinforcements and do a proper raid with SWAT and DEA.

Lei began a stealthy withdrawal, squatting low and backing her way down around the rocks. She moved carefully, still facing the boss man. She was pretty sure she would make it until she saw the dog.

A big blue-nosed pit bull trotted down from the area where Boss Man had come from. He was one of those heavily muscled dogs with a big square head, wide chest, and the kind of heavy jaws that clung to prey until the fight was over.

Lei froze, hoping like hell that the slight breeze blowing in her direction from the waterfall didn't swirl her scent over to the big dog now standing beside Boss Man. Lei continued her withdrawal, sliding backward, dropping down into the water to stay lower out of sight.

Sunlight shone on the pit bull's blue-gray coat, rippling over its muscles. Thick as a tree trunk, the dog's cropped behind wagged in a way that reminded her of her beloved Rotties. Lei took a stealthy step backward, and another. The stones beneath her soaked shoes were muddy and slick, but she was almost at the stone arch, where she'd be out of sight.

And suddenly the dog scented her, throwing his head up and

spinning to point in her direction. He let out a menacing bellow of a bark.

There was nothing to do but brazen it out.

"Maui Police Department!" Lei jumped to her feet where she stood in the stream, holding up her badge, her weapon drawn. "Call your dog, or I'll have to shoot him!"

Boss Man was on his feet, weapon in hand. He fired in her direction in answer, yelling, "Get her, Killah!"

The dog leaped into the stream and came at her like a sleek gray missile.

Lei scrambled backward on the slippery rocks, cursing as she stumbled, trying to keep the dog in view and almost losing her weapon. Then the dog was on her, too fast for her even to get a shot off as it jumped, jaws sinking into her Kevlar vest, knocking her backward into the water among the rocks. It sank its teeth into the vest and shook her with such force she tossed back and forth in the shallow water, gasping and flailing.

But she'd kept a grip on her weapon. She put it against the dog's head and pulled the trigger. The report almost deafened her.

The dog's big, muscular body relaxed abruptly, and he dropped onto her, weighty as a bag of rocks.

He didn't feel a thing. Tears started in her eyes, even as gunfire erupted from the direction of the marijuana fields. The day had finally come that she'd had to kill a dog, and she was lucky to be alive to do it.

That child-slaving dog killer. He was the one whose fault this was—he'd sent his dog to its death. Tears wouldn't stop streaming from her eyes as Lei tried to heave the pit bull off her, but its teeth were sunk into the vest and locked. She wasted precious seconds shoving the Glock between its jaws and prying them open to rid herself of the heavy body. Finally, with one glance back at the deadly valley, Lei dove through the stone arch and behind the sheltering bluff that curved downward toward the ocean.

Scrambling downstream, Lei pulled her radio off her belt,

thumbing it on to call for help, but there was no reception. She fumbled her cell phone out of the pocket of the vest and called 911, but there was no reception for that either in this remote canyon.

And so she just ran, diving into the heavy jungle beside the stream, unwilling to make herself a target by rock hopping as she had on the way up. Lei fought her way through the underbrush, blindly shoving reaching branches and heavy growth out of the way, stumbling and scrambling, her wet pants, shoes, and Kevlar vest as heavy as her heart.

CHAPTER NINE

THE EXPLOSION that rocked the jungle was more than I'd bargained for. I was very glad of the shelter of the wide, heavy trunk of the native tree as the choppers' metal exploded in all directions with the shriek of a thousand banshees. Flaming, gas-covered, melting plastic soared into the air. The blades of one of the helicopters scythed through the tents. The weapons on the birds exploded, too, and in the middle of it all, a massive round went off with a whizzing boom like the biggest of Fourth of July pyrotechnics.

As a distraction, it was superb.

The three burning birds were still firing random bits of destruction all around them as I stood, pulled my cap down, and ran purposefully toward the wooden shed through the shouting, milling hostiles.

Everywhere men were yelling and cursing, almost drowned out by the roaring, crackling flames spreading from the burning choppers. Everyone at the shack had run to see what the problem was. The shack's door was deserted, and it was sealed with a simple hasp and padlock. I looked around the side of the building, and sure enough, hanging on a hook was the key.

I unlocked the padlock, keeping my pistol ready and eyes

moving, but no one came back this way. I could hear the hostiles mustering over by the burning choppers. They'd be back in a moment.

I threw the door wide.

"This is Lieutenant Stevens. Come with me!" There were four men inside, already up and no doubt freaked out by the noise. "We're getting out of here!"

"Yes, sir!" The young man whose name began with a "K" ran toward me, and two others—Falconer and another man. One stayed back, sitting down on his pallet with his back against the wall. It was Carrigan. His polo shirt was black with filth, but his blue eyes sparked in the light of the flames.

"No. We're being ransomed."

"They're going to start killing us tomorrow. I heard it straight from the camp commander. This is your chance."

"No. Good luck, you crazy bastards."

I slammed the door on Carrigan and ran into the forest, the three other men following me. Once in the darkness of the trees, I slid the headlight on its webbing band around my forehead. "Grab each other by the belt and hang on. We need to get as far as we can from here."

Thankfully, there were no arguments to this rudimentary plan. I handed K-Man and each of the others a weapon, keeping the M16 and the compass knife for myself as we moved out. K-Man grabbed the back of my belt.

We managed a shuffling trot in the dense jungle, which was surprisingly open beneath the canopy of foliage far above, once we got away from the bushy growth around the camp. We were silent except for the crunching of sticks and leaves beneath our feet and the occasional grunt or muffled curse as someone stumbled or barked their shins in the dark. Periodically, I'd pause and check the compass, keeping us headed north.

I aimed the headlight toward the ground as best I could, navigating obstacles: a stump, a fallen log, a mound of dirt, a prickly thorned bush. Going around that, we startled some sort of ground-nesting bird, which flew up from beneath my feet with a shrill cry and a clatter of wings. K-Man cursed and pointed his pistol at it.

"No!" I pushed his weapon down. "We fire something, we might as well take out a neon sign telling where we are. We're making enough racket as it is." I took that moment to scan around us with the headlight, and the numbers of glowing animal eyes surrounding us were not reassuring. "Move out."

I stepped forward and got a nasty surprise as some sort of snake wriggled out from under my boot, lashing back to bite. Fortunately it sank its teeth into my pants, and I was able to hit it away from me with the butt of the M16.

"Everyone find some kind of stick to fend off snakes. Many here are poisonous, so take a minute to tuck your pants into your boots." I got no argument as I bent and pulled my heavy, filthy socks all the way up, wrapping my pants around my legs and tucking them into the tops of the hiking boots I'd slid my feet into on a day that seemed like a year ago.

I felt exhaustion dragging at me. Trembling racked my body. I'd tapped my resources tonight for sure. And there was no way out but through.

Fortunately, everyone but Carrigan had opted to wear the uniforms we'd been issued and some sort of boots. Only my room-mate, Falconer, had been wearing a sleeveless black tank shirt when we were captured. Even with the heat of this place, it was better to be covered up.

The men found sturdy sticks nearby with the aid of my light, and I gestured for them to gather around. "My plan is to get us to the main river in this area, the Río Coco."

Falconer was standing next to me, and he nodded. His skin was so dark that he disappeared without the light on him, the gleam of his eyes the only giveaway of his position.

"I know a little of the geography of the area." His voice was a low rumble. "We can get to Nicaragua by crossing the river."

"That's what I was thinking. They won't pursue us to that side, hopefully, and if we can make contact with some other people, we can get the hell out of here. I've been navigating with this." I held out the compass-hilted knife for Falconer to see, suppressing a flash memory of the guard's warm blood pumping over the plastic grip and my hand.

Falconer gave a brief nod of assent, and I turned away and forged forward, the headlamp holding back the darkness, the chain of men behind me a weight of trust.

CHAPTER TEN

LEI BURST out of the heavy jungle underbrush at the edge of the river, stumbling over a noose of vine. The narrow two-lane road was just ahead, and her truck, pulled over on the shoulder, an oasis of safety.

Bam! Bam! Bam!

Lei threw herself facedown to the ground behind a rock as the report of a shot was accompanied by the hiss and thunk of the round hitting a tree nearby. She smacked her shin on a protruding stone, scraped her cheek on the rough bark of a tree, and nearly knocked the wind out of herself. Rallying, the sound of pursuit unmistakable, Lei belly crawled behind the nearest cover, a large boulder surrounded by heavy undergrowth. Her breath tore through her lungs in ragged gulps as she tried to stay hidden but see where the threat was coming from.

Her only visual window was toward the road.

"Come out, cop!" A harsh bawl from the area of the stream. "Come out, and let's make a deal!"

"Yeah, right," Lei muttered under her breath. She was surrounded by heavy undergrowth and currently hidden, but it couldn't last long if they decided to beat through the bushes. The road was a nearby promise of escape—but also dangerous. The hundred or so feet across the open asphalt to her vehicle looked miles away. She ejected the clip from her weapon and checked—she had thirteen rounds.

"That your truck, cop?" The harsh voice she was sure belonged to Boss Man had drawn closer. Lei very slowly pulled her limbs in tighter behind the protective shield of the rock. The smell of moss and damp stone filled her nostrils.

A sudden burst of automatic gunfire made Lei jerk into an even smaller ball behind the rock. She lifted her head and peered out to look when it ended, and terror and rage dried her mouth—the growers had shot up her truck, blanketing the silver Tacoma with a fusillade of bullets. The alarm went off in feeble protest. The broken lights flashed and the vehicle pulsed in strangled tones, exactly like a creature dying. Another burst of gunfire, this time from the front, firing into the truck's hood, ended the alarm with a wheezing, sad little bleep.

There was a second shooter on the other side of her. Both had automatic weapons.

The growers must have a path through the jungle on the other side of her—she knew there was nothing alongside the stream. She was pinned down between them, and her means of escape was gone.

"Shit." Lei tried to calm her pounding heart and slow her breathing. Panicking wasn't going to help. Unless these perps were going to beat their way through every foot of the natural cover she was embedded in, she was safe for the moment. She heard the rumble of a car's engine coming down the road and held her breath, terrified for the unsuspecting commuters along the famous, picturesque Hana Highway.

The car, a bright red rental, meandered slowly past, a string of other cars and a van-style tour bus bringing up the rear. She could jump up and wave down a vehicle, but with the level of violence these growers were showing—what was to stop them from mowing down an innocent tourist in their effort to eliminate her? She couldn't put anyone else in danger with the armed shooters right there in the bushes.

Surely someone would notice the bullet holes riddling her vehicle and call in? Please God. Please have someone call it in.

The train of cars passed on, with no visible decrease in speed or change of behavior in response to her battered truck, as if they drove past shot-up vehicles every day.

When the road was clear, the shooters came out onto the open road. One was the big man she'd nicknamed Boss Man. He was carrying an army-issued M16, and she spotted the handgun still in the back of his pants.

The other shooter, who'd come from the jungle on the other side, was no more than a teenager. "She's not getting away now." Lei's throat closed at the excitement in the kid's demeanor. "We'll get her."

"We have to get her," Boss Man said. "Or she'll go straight back and bring in the narcos for a raid. We're on a schedule now."

The two of them stood with their backs to the truck, scanning up and down the road as if Lei were going to be crazy enough to come out. She stayed perfectly still, grateful for her army-green pants and camouflage-patterned vest. She raised her weapon, steadying it on the rock, and drew a bead on Boss Man.

Lei was a decent shot, but not great, and the distance was significant. She'd need to get him in the head or chest to keep him from firing that automatic weapon all over the area. And then she'd need to nail the kid, just as permanently. She loosened her finger on the trigger.

There had to be another way out of this.

"If she hadn't shot Killah, he'd find her for us," Boss Man said. "I'll kill that bitch myself just for that." He hooked a radio off his belt. "Eddie, get everyone out harvesting the bud. If we don't find that cop, we need to bring in everything we can and burn the rest." A long pause as "Eddie" vented, the words too garbled by static and distance to make out. Boss Man nodded. "Yeah. Pull the plug. You know what that means. And send Akira out with the rest of the ammo. We might still be able to find her."

Boss Man had begun walking down the road as he was speaking, heading for the hidden trail opening the teenager had come out of.

Lei pulled her phone out, thumbed it on. Still no bars.

"What should we do, Uncle?" the teen asked. The kid was slender, his wifebeater tank shirt hanging on a hollow-chested frame. He swung the machine gun around, his finger alarmingly loose on the trigger. "You want I should just fire all around the area? We'd probably hit her."

"Nah," Boss Man said. "I saw where she dove into the bushes. When Akira gets here, we'll grid off and search for her."

Lei's heart hammered. She had a limited amount of time to get out before she was discovered.

Staying flat on her belly, she backed stealthily into the heavy undergrowth, giving up her visibility window onto the growers. She'd run out of options now that she'd decided not to risk shooting them. She needed to get far enough away into the jungle that she could approach the road again, and flag down a car when it was safe.

As if in answer to this thought, she heard the sound of approaching cars and a muffled curse from Boss Man. He and the teen ducked out of sight.

This was Lei's chance, while they were distracted by the passing vehicles. She rose to a crouch, the Glock ready, and moved as quickly and quietly as she could, deeper into the jungle.

CHAPTER ELEVEN

I STUMBLED over something as we moved through the dark jungle at a trot. I never saw what it was, but I went down with a muffled curse, and the headlamp fell off and went out. The black was instant and total.

"Shit! You okay, LT?" K-Man had lost his grip on my belt as I went down, and I heard the rustling and muttering of the men behind him.

I rose to my hands and knees. "Hold up. I'll find the light." I patted the ground around where I'd tripped, feeling twigs under my hands. Leaves. The stiff, poky sensation of some broken branch. Something unpleasantly damp and spongy, probably a lichen of some kind. I tried not to think of the vicious smack of the snake hitting my pants as it tried to bite.

"It's got to be right here," I panted. "K-Man, can you help?"

"My name's Tim Kerry, LT," the young man who'd been my best helper said. "But K-Man is okay." I heard by the change of his voice that he'd dropped down to squat beside me.

"Let's get side by side and search a square pattern," I said. Kerry got close beside me, and we swept and patted the ground, making sure no more than a few inches separated us.

"I found it!" Kerry exclaimed. I heard him fumbling with something in the dark. My eyes had adjusted more, and now I could see the faintest gray of sky behind the lacy patterns of the leaves of the jungle far above. The moon was up, somewhere out there.

"It's not turning on, LT," the young man said, and he thrust the light to me.

I felt the unit all over, and sure enough, it was no longer turning on with the touch of a button.

"Maybe it's damaged or the battery got knocked out. Everyone, take a break." I heard by the rustling that the men had dropped where they stood. Everyone was waiting for me to get the damn headlight working.

Using touch, I located the notch in the back cover and fumbled it open with a fingernail. It seemed to be a AAA battery. I slid it out, rubbed it on my pants, reinserted it, slid the little door back up, and pressed the button.

Nothing. "Damn it. I think we're going to have to quit for tonight. We can't get anywhere without a light. Unless someone has matches, a lighter?"

"Naw, LT. They searched us and took anything that could be useful," Kerry said.

"Okay, then. Might as well get some rest. Stay close together, though, and keep your weapons handy. There could be predators out here, and not just the human kind. Let's set a watch by turns. Falconer, can you take the first round?" I trusted the competency of the big black man.

"You got it," he rumbled from beside me. I'd never heard him advance to my position.

Rustling and murmuring followed as our little group settled into the damp tree litter and underbrush where we'd halted. I lay down, curling on my side. Sleep fell over me, a thick blanket of oblivion brought on by exhaustion.

THE MAUI JUNGLE growth was thick. A combination of saplings, ferns, wild ginger, and other bushes choked the bases of java plum, mountain apple, and other bushy growth as Lei pushed forward, scanning and listening. All she could hear was the distant breeze in the tops of the trees, a swish of movement. Mynah birds did their conversational chattering, doves cooed, cardinals chirped, and there was the sound of her movement: the crack of a twig under her shoe, the whisk of wet jeans, the soft thud of her feet as she bore to the right, hoping to parallel the road.

Lei crossed the trail that led into the growers' secret valley after a quick check that it was clear, and kept going.

She wasn't sure how far to go before heading back toward the road, but the question was answered for her by an abrupt rise in the ground as she hit one of the steep valley walls.

She looked at the ridge. She'd have to go relatively straight up, at least a couple of hundred yards of climbing, and then descend the other side.

Better to go back to the road and see if she could flag down a car. She turned in the direction of the road and hurried through the underbrush as quietly as she could.

"Stop!" The teenager's reedy voice steadied as he yelled again. "Stop! I've got you!"

Lei froze. Her weapon was in her hand, held in the low ready position.

"Drop your weapon! I can't miss!" The kid's volume increased, and so did his aggression.

They were going to kill her if they captured her. There was no doubt in her mind. But right now she had her back turned to a trigger-happy kid with an automatic rifle. She had to buy time.

"Okay, okay." She dropped the pistol right in front of her.

"Get on your knees!"

She did. But he didn't say to put her hands up, so she kept them down at her sides, ready for action. She heard him crunching through the leaves, talking into his handheld radio.

"I got her, Uncle."

"Good. Hold her until I get there. If she moves, shoot her."

"Ten-four." He must be putting the radio back on his belt. Lei could imagine the automatic in his hands, pointed toward her, his finger itchy on the trigger, amped up by adrenaline and eager to prove himself. Scared to kill a cop, but determined to do what his boss wanted. Part of him not wanting to kill, the other eager to. Neither part really understood what it meant to take a human life.

Lei understood it too well.

Time slowed down, those seconds right before action unwinding one by one, sliding by like beads on a string, every sense hyperaware.

The rustle of leaves as the kid approached.

The smell of damp and mold thick in her nostrils.

Wetness as the mulch she knelt on soaked her pants and penetrated to her skin.

Shush of the wind, high overhead.

Pale, gray-streaked bark, nubby as a hand-knit sweater covering the java plum tree directly in front of her. On the left, a rising, steep tree- and debris-covered slope of the ridge. On the right, more jungle and forest.

Right behind her, a very dangerous kid.

"I've got you now." The boy's voice was gloating. Lei felt the barrel of the automatic press into the notch between her neck and skull. She drew a deep breath and coiled all her muscles tight, drawing on core strength. She'd practiced a jump from knees to feet both in the gym and on a surfboard, but this was the first time she'd tried it with a gun to her head.

Lei bounced to her feet and spun, grabbing the barrel of the automatic and tearing it out of the kid's hands. The strap caught on his shoulder and head, and he gave an inarticulate cry. She didn't have it totally free because of that, but hit him with all the leverage she could with the butt end of the rifle, nailing him in the chin.

The boy's hand scrabbled for the radio as Lei wrenched the strap off over his head and used the butt end of the rifle to whack him again, from the other direction. The kid yelped, twisting sideways. He got the radio into his hand this time, but now she had some room to maneuver. She swung the rifle with all her strength.

He dropped like an anchor. Blood streamed from his nose.

Lei took a second to scan and see if Boss Man had appeared yet, then looked at the slender, crumpled form at her feet. At least the little bastard was still alive. She hoped he deserved the break she was giving him.

She reached down to search the kid's pockets. She found a cell phone and a knife in a scabbard. No ID or wallet, but stuck out in the valley as they were, he probably had no use for those. She unbuckled his belt, flipped him, and used it to bind his legs. She put her cuffs on him behind his back, and gagged him with his T-shirt.

The whole operation had taken five minutes, and that was five minutes too long. Slipping the automatic's strap over her head, she retrieved her Glock and broke into a run through the trees, heading for the road.

CHAPTER TWELVE

FALCONER WOKE me with a squeeze on my shoulder. "Sun's up, Stevens."

"Barely." I sat up and dusted leaves off of my clothing, looking around at the deep gray shadows around us. "But enough for us to move." We woke the rest of the men and got moving quickly.

The twittering, keening, and shrieking of birds and animals brought the jungle to life around us and increased our sense of urgency. I rationed out the packet of sugar cookies I'd taken off the guard, and we each ate one and sipped water off the canteens as we walked. With enough light to see a little distance, and that light brightening by the minute, I set as fast a pace as I could in my weakened state.

I was glad we'd stopped where we had, because we had hardly gone another hundred yards before we encountered some sort of wetland slough. The tall forest gave way abruptly to shorter, bushy trees, bunchy clumps of sharp grasses—and swampy, sinking mud that dragged at our boots.

"I'm hoping this means the river's ahead." I took another compass reading. North was straight into the wetland.

"I saw some maps of the area." Falconer joined me, assessing.

"The camp organizers said to watch out for the areas around the riverbanks. Snakes and pockets of quicksand."

"Do you remember how far that stretch went? Is the river right on the other side of this?" I swiped the sweat pearling on my forehead with a muddy forearm.

"I was planning the infiltration training, and I was going to do a section in this environment, but I was working on more traditional obstacle courses as a warm-up," Falconer said. "We need to go slow if we're going to try to get through here. Probe the ground with sticks and clear any wildlife."

"Maybe we should go sideways a while," Kerry said. "There might be an area where we can get to the riverbank that's drier."

"We haven't even considered how we're getting across the river," the fourth man said. "It's a huge river."

He was a bald, barrel-chested man who worked for Security Solutions. I wondered at the kidnappers' choices. Falconer, Carrigan, and I were contractors, but Kerry was an MP, and here was a Security Solutions staffer.

"What's your name again?" I asked.

"MacDonald. Devan MacDonald."

"Do any of you have an idea why each of us was captured?"

Falconer shrugged. "I thought it was for the kidnapping insurance on us. It was in the contract."

"You have that, too?" I frowned. "So how did they know Security Solutions had that insurance? And a better question—why wasn't Security Solutions negotiating for our release?" I told them what I'd overheard from the Spanish-speaking camp commander. "He was going to start killing us the next day, starting with me. I had to take the chance to get out."

"I don't have any extra insurance, as far as I know." Kerry rubbed the back of his neck. "I do have a wealthy family back in the States, but that's supposed to be confidential."

"Let's walk and talk." Falconer had found a long, heavy stick.

"Do we want to go west awhile, then try for the river again? Or straight ahead, into the swamp?"

"Let's vote." I'd gotten them this far, but I wasn't willing to be responsible for everything that happened from this point on. The men voted to go west, and with Falconer in the lead, probing the dank puddles before us. I told them what I'd seen in the commander's tent. "So why wouldn't they pay for our release is what I'm wondering," I concluded.

"I hope Carrigan makes it," MacDonald said. "He seemed pretty confident that they were going to pay his ransom. I just didn't want to take the chance."

The heat intensified with the rising sun, and with it came insects. Tiny gnats rose in irritating clouds, and the mosquitoes were an ever-present whine. My stomach was so empty it felt like knotted rope. I was relieved to let Falconer lead. Truth was, the burst of energy that had carried me from the camp was long gone, and without food and rest to get back to full health, I wasn't sure how long I could keep up the pace.

The buzz of mosquitoes was drowned out by the distant sound of all-terrain vehicles. They sounded like motorcycles, a burring growl, but I remembered seeing several of the four wheelers parked around the commander's living area.

I should have blown them up, too.

Falconer broke into a run. "They're coming!"

I began scanning for somewhere to take cover, but once we'd turned away from the swamp, we were back in an area of more open space under the trees' canopy. The four-wheeled ATVs would be able to navigate the area easily, and I was sure we were leaving plenty of trace for them to follow.

"Let's go straight north, into the swamp. The ATVs can't follow us there." I paused to take a quick reading with the compass knife, and we turned straight left in the direction of the river, running as best we could, clambering over downed, rotting logs, around bushes, between the boles of the ever-present trees. Dank puddles filled with tea-colored water, shining with iridescent scum, became more frequent. I tried to leap over or go around them, but that wasn't always possible.

Kerry gave a sudden cry, and I whirled to see a snake, its sleek brown body lashing, attached to his pant leg. He kicked and the snake flew off, slithering away into the underbrush.

"Did he get you?" I took a second to ask.

"I don't think so."

"Some of the most toxic snakes in the world live right here," Falconer said. "And now that we're getting into the wet area, keep an eye out for crocodiles. They'll look just like logs."

The ATVs sounded louder, and I could feel the spot between my shoulder blades itching as if it were a target. The heavy undergrowth and razor-sharp grasses increased. We made a single file line again, forging forward as fast as we could, eventually ending up in water to our knees.

The sound of the ATVs ceased abruptly.

They'd probably had to abandon the vehicles once they hit the water, but that meant they were on foot, and nearby.

"Here's the compass," I told Falconer. "You lead. I'll bring up the rear and watch our backs."

Falconer took the knife and pushed on, clambering over a slimy, half-sunken log, MacDonald right behind him, Kerry next. I brought up the rear, turning every ten steps or so to scan behind us, the M16 at the ready.

I scanned constantly for crocodiles, snakes, and other hazards. I didn't want to use the rifle except as a last resort, because it would pinpoint our location for the pursuers.

I heard a splash behind us, and whirled. A log was arrowing toward us through the dark water.

But logs didn't swim. "Croc!" I yelled.

The men burst into a run as best they could. So did I, lifting my knees, floundering and pushing through the scummy brown water, heading for a large downed tree that broke the surface, a long low wall of safety. My finger tightened on the trigger of the rifle as I looked back. The croc's snout had broken the surface and its tail lashed the water as it sped toward me. I couldn't even see its tiny, slitted eyes, only the arrow shape of its pursuit.

I still didn't want to shoot it and give away our position. Now that we were in the water, there was some chance the kidnappers would lose our trail.

"Run, Stevens!" Falconer bellowed, and I knew the creature was almost on me. I dove for the huge fallen tree's stump, scrambling up onto the exposed roots. I felt a quiver through the wood and heard a thump and splash as the croc struck the log.

My soaking-wet boots scrabbled for a purchase on the slippery wood as I hauled myself higher by my arms alone, the rifle banging my back as it hung by its strap. Kerry caught me by the back of the shirt and hauled me completely out of the water. I straddled the log, panting and soaked with sweat and swamp water.

I turned just as the croc lashed its tail and surged forward, jaws agape. I yanked my leg out of the way and it hit the log, its powerful, green-brown tail propelling it upward. The short clawed legs scrabbled and huge jaws clashed. I scrambled back with a cry toward the other men. We all moved farther down the log, crawling to stay on it. I hoped the height was enough, only three feet above the surface of the water.

The crocodile fell back with a grunt and a splash. It swam back and forth a few times. We all made sure our legs were up out of reach.

"Close one, LT," Kerry said.

"Yeah." My breath was ripping through my lungs and I couldn't stop shaking. We squatted in a row on the vast length of fallen wood. It was a big log, but at some point we had to get back off and continue our miserable journey.

The croc submerged suddenly and disappeared. I scanned the water for bubbles, for anything to indicate where it had gone, but it seemed to have vanished.

"Look!" Falconer pointed. We could see a slight disturbance of the water thirty feet away, a tiny gout of bubbles, a vibration of the surface.

"He could just be waiting for us to get off this log." MacDonald gave voice to what we all feared.

I squatted on the log, shivering with damp, my belly so empty it had stopped even hurting. I scanned the water. Just because we couldn't see monsters didn't mean they weren't there.

CHAPTER THIRTEEN

LEI RAN the last few hundred feet through the stand of trees and burst out into the open on the road. Rifle at the ready, she scanned up and down the road.

No one in sight. As it often was, the two-lane, picturesque road was bordered by the jungle she'd just come from on one side and the ocean on the other.

She turned and headed back in the direction of Kahului at a run.

Lei was just rounding the hairpin turn of the road as it curved around the bluff that was the rise she'd decided not to climb when a truck came roaring around the bend. Lei tried to wave it down, but couldn't get the driver's attention as the man, clearly a local, just accelerated at the sight of her waving arms.

"Shit." She trotted up the road in the oncoming lane, looking for the next car.

The next vehicle to come along was a convertible silver Mustang, a popular rental, and the windblown, sunburned couple came to a halt at the sight of her, legs spread, badge and gun raised.

"Maui Police Department. I need this vehicle."

"Hey, what's going on?"

"Step out of the car. Now." She lowered the automatic rifle, and the guy pushed the door open and got out. "Police emergency. Both of you, in the back seat. We're going to the Hana Police Department."

The woman got out, both of them looking angry and scared as they clambered in to the back. "Sorry. Emergency. Thanks for your cooperation." Lei cranked the car around in the narrow space and laid down some rubber heading for Hana, the couple clutching each other for comfort in the back seat.

The police station was a small beige concrete block building whose color was made dingy by a film of mold. Lei showed her badge, asked for the commanding officer, and called in to Captain Omura. It ended up taking several hours to round up the necessary personnel for a raid of the growers' secret valley.

Lei called back to the house and spoke to her father, making sure Kiet was taken care of, then called Pono.

"Lei, what the hell was that message?" Pono sounded annoyed. "Thought you weren't going off by yourself anymore."

"Yeah. About that." Lei paced back and forth, tethered to the long cord of the phone on one of the Hana PD's desks. Her cell still wasn't getting coverage. "I found a lot more than I bargained for when I went up that valley looking for where the skull washed down." She described the action so far. "So I won't be back in this evening, needless to say. We're pulling together a raid."

"I could have told you not to go into one of those valleys without backup. Never know what you're going to find out there!"

"Well, so far no one's died. Except a pit bull named Killah, which was horrible." Lei shut her eyes on the memory, but told Pono what had happened.

"You know it's not your fault. His owner, that's the guy whose fault it is."

"Yeah. This perp is a piece of work. Working kids in the fields, siccing his dog on me when I warned him I was armed..." Lei pushed a hand through her tangled curls. "I can't wait to get this

90

guy, but I heard him on his radio. They're pulling the plug on the valley. Probably will be long gone when we get there."

"Well, you could come back. Let the Hana PD and SWAT take care of the raid." Pono's voice held little conviction that she'd choose that option even as Lei shook her head.

"No. That bastard shot up my truck. And I left the satellite phone I'm using to connect with Security Solutions in my vehicle. Even if I didn't need to see this through, I'd need to get back and pick up that item."

"Shot up your truck?" Pono groaned. "What's that, number three?"

"Yeah, it's totaled. I'm trying not to keep count."

"Call me when you're done. I'll see if we've got any laulau in the freezer. I can have Tiare run some over for you and the boy?"

"My dad's got us covered, but we appreciate it. Thanks, partner." Lei's chest tightened and her eyes prickled. "Thanks for looking out for me."

"Someone's got to." He hung up with a bang. Lei knew he wasn't mad at her but at her husband for leaving.

Replacing the phone in its cradle, Lei wondered what was happening to Stevens. She shut her eyes briefly. "God, please keep him safe. Please."

"Time to roll, Sergeant Texeira," the station commander said, walking by. Lei's eyes flew open and she hurried after him.

WE LET another five minutes pass in our safe spot on the log, and in those long moments of careful looking and listening, we could hear yelling and splashing in the distance.

They were coming, and they weren't happy about it.

Falconer lifted a finger to his lips, turned, and slid silently off the log on the opposite side from the croc. He barely made a splash as he entered the water. The rest of us followed in our established order, not as quiet as Falconer, but making every effort to keep the noise down as we hurried forward. I didn't mention the snake I saw slithering through the water, its arcing movement strangely beautiful.

And suddenly we'd reached the Coco River. Glimpsed through a scrim of trees, it was a vast swath of churning brown water. We stood at the edge, on a submerged bank where the river had over-flowed into the jungle in flood.

"How are we getting across?" MacDonald gestured to the forbidding stretch of water. Swimming was out of the question. The river was the chocolate-brown of churned soil, surging and swirling in eddies, and as I watched, a whole tree rolled by, spinning lazily in the current.

"No idea," Falconer said. "Stevens?"

I scanned around. "I was hoping for some dry ground. Or some other people. I heard the river was fairly well-trafficked. I thought we might find a boat. Let's pick a direction and work our way along the bank. We don't have a lot of choice." I gestured back the way we'd come. "They don't have dogs or any way to track us on foot now that we're in the water, so as long as we keep moving, quiet and out of sight, we're bound to lose them."

"Let's go east," Falconer said. "The nearest town is west, so they'll expect us to go that way. We should do the opposite of what they expect."

I was grateful for Falconer's lead. After all, he'd been hired to train the MPs in infiltration, tracking, and survival skills. Given our limited resources, we were damn lucky to have him. I hadn't had enough of a look at the map to have any idea which way was the nearest town—and though getting to civilization was appeal-ing, it wasn't likely that we'd be able to beat the kidnappers to that destination.

Hours of silent movement downstream followed as we clam-bered over obstacles, swishing through the water. I constantly turned back and kept an eye on our rear. We heard a spooky yowling cry that I was pretty sure was a jaguar, but made progress along the overflowed banks parallel to the river.

The Coco River was a steely brown expanse glimpsed through the trees. We forged on, and saw no sign of other humans until we heard the distinctive thrum of a chopper.

"Take cover." I ducked in close to a tree. The chopper, a Plexiglas-fronted Bell Jet, zoomed low along the river. The doors were open on either side and a pair of shooters armed with automatics hung over the struts.

MacDonald hadn't gotten behind a tree fast enough. His startled movement must have drawn their attention, because the next thing we knew, the murderous zing of automatic fire ripped through the trees, scattering birds and raining shredded leaves and broken branches down on us. The tree I'd sheltered behind shuddered with the impact of bullets.

"Holy crap!" Kerry exclaimed, his words drowned by the hail of fire as the chopper paused and swiveled, trying for a better angle. We endured the storm and then, abruptly, the bird lifted.

"They're reloading. Move inward!" We sloshed and splashed as fast as we could in deeper, farther from the river. "Take cover!" I yelled again, hearing the whir of blades directly overhead this time. I pressed close in to the nearest wild mahogany tree, a giant sturdy hardwood tree prized throughout the world for its quality lumber.

This time they strafed us from above, but without a clear shot at us, they gave up after a few passes and went back to the river, moving up and down, looking. Hurrying from tree to tree, we worked our way deeper into the jungle and away from the river. The water level began dropping, and I became aware of the persistent burning of my blistered, waterlogged feet chafing within my boots.

"They must have had a fourth helicopter parked somewhere. Wish I'd gotten them all. But for now we need to get out of the water," I told Falconer. I was shaking nonstop with mild hypothermia from the wetness. Even in the jungle humidity I couldn't get warm, and I tried not to think about what the water was doing to my skin.

"I'm looking for some high ground," Falconer agreed. "We can always come back to the river some other way." He pointed. "Over there." Ahead, we could see a mound of dense foliage, the long flanged leaves of wild bananas.

The thought of bananas reawakened my belly and it gave a loud growl. "Maybe there will be something to eat there."

"We can hope." We splashed forward toward the rise in ground and pushed up into the dense foliage. Falconer used the knife to hack a way into the overgrown stand of banana trees, and we climbed gratefully after him.

"Oh, shit!" Kerry shrieked. A huge, hairy brown spider had jumped onto him from the banana trees.

I knocked it off and it scuttled away. "Harmless. Most of them don't bite."

"Can I just say, once and for the record, that if I'd known the destination for this assignment was the deep jungle of Honduras, I wouldn't have taken the job?" MacDonald swiped his arm across his forehead.

"Likewise," Falconer rumbled. "I suspected Central America, because I've worked here before, but this area has never been a favorite destination. Let's get up out of the water and dry out a bit." The ground rose slowly and steadily out of the swamp, but we were getting farther and farther from the river, which had the potential to attract help and get us to civilization.

There was nothing to be done about any of it right now. Scanning around, I spotted the first bright spot of the day—a cluster of greenish yellow bananas dangling high above on a long stalk. I pointed. "Lunch break."

We managed to get the stalk down by pushing on the tree's pulpy, plantlike stalk until it leaned over enough to cut the bananas down. "I don't think we should eat too many at once," I told the men. "We haven't had anything in a while, and these aren't ripe yet. Three per person." Falconer agreed, and used the knife to cut three of the short, thick wild bananas off the stalk and hand them out.

The first one tasted like heaven, sweet and starchy and over too soon. The second was also good—but by then my stomach had begun to rebel. I stowed the third in a pocket as my belly cramped painfully. Falconer cut up the rest of the bunch and gave us each a handful.

"If we find a palm, I know how to get the heart, and that's good to eat. Bamboo, too, and ferns. There are some edible roots and other fruit here."

We stripped off our boots. I didn't want to look at my feet. I'd been feeling blisters and lesions forming on them as we moved through the water, brought on by friction on wet skin. Sure enough, all of our feet were going off to some degree, but mine were the worst. Open, oozing sores covered my feet, and sheets of skin came off the soles as I removed my soaking-wet socks.

"Jesus, LT," Kerry said.

I didn't say anything. What was there to say? I didn't want to take my wet pants off and give the clouds of buzzing mosquitoes more to feast on, so I draped the socks over a banana frond and curled up, the M16 cradled in my arms, as Falconer assigned a watch order for while we rested.

Lying on my side, curled in on myself under a few banana leaves, I noticed a gleam of water on the leaves of the jungle floor. The color sparked a memory of Lei.

The sun shone on her curly brown hair just that way in our yard at home as Lei threw a ball for the dogs. Our son ran after the ball, too, laughing. I loved that big yard, filled with fruit trees, the grass always a little too long because neither of us had time to keep it up the way we should.

My heart felt as sore as the rest of me. I shut my eyes briefly.

God, keep them safe. Just get me home. I'll never leave again. I'll never drink again. Please.

Sleep dropped over me like a black cloak, and even as it did, gratitude filled me. I was sleeping again, and that felt like heaven. Too bad I'd had to come to hell to get it.

CHAPTER FOURTEEN

THE POLICE CONVOY CRESTED A RISE, and Lei looked out the window of the SUV down the stretch of muddy road into the cup of the secret valley. Sharply pungent smoke rolled up from the pot fields.

"Contact-high alert." The SWAT leader in the front seat grinned. "They'd rather burn the product than let us get our hands on it."

Lei nodded, but she couldn't smile or joke, even with the pre-raid jitters. She wore a helmet and a new, black Kevlar vest, and she was glad to have left the blood-stained, tooth-marked one behind. On the way she'd chugged a bottle of water and eaten a couple of sticks of beef jerky one of the men had given her. Tension crawled along her nerves as the vehicles bumped through deep puddles, the fronds of wild hapu'u ferns, grass, and ginger brushing the sides of the vehicle as they crept down the rough track to the bottom of the valley.

They pulled into an empty clearing. Tire tracks showed the departure of vehicles. Camouflage netting was draped over a series of nearby metal sheds, and a path led deeper into the valley.

"Stay to the rear," the SWAT commander told her as they flung the doors open. "We're going to check for hostiles and booby traps in these buildings first."

Booby traps. That would be just like Boss Man. He would be happy to hurt them just for spite. "Yes, sir."

Lei hung back as directed. The team swept the buildings, one of the men checking for hidden trip lines and explosives. It reminded her of working with ex-partner Abe Torufu, with his big grin and steady coolness under pressure—but she didn't miss her bomb squad days. Lei felt no such cool. A restless apprehension swept over her in waves as she waited by the vehicles, her weapon ready.

Finally they gave the all clear for the sheds. Lei strode over and looked inside. Clearly used for drying and processing the marijuana, the sheds were empty now but for the thick scent of dried weed. She walked under the drying racks, bare of anything but a few twigs, and looked around outside. The area was tidy, and signs of human use had been hidden under the kukui and albizia trees that forested this area.

"I want to see where they were keeping the workers. The kids I saw. There were living areas near the fields at the stream," she told the commander.

"Will do. Let's move out." He gestured for the men to follow. They moved out down a well-worn path leading toward the source of burning. Lei was sandwiched between the SWAT members, with the booby-trap expert on point. He carried a motion detector, a powerful light, and a probe for clearing the path. As they walked along, he worked his equipment.

Lei kept her shotgun ready, scanning for movement, but there was nothing other than the last of the afternoon sun gleaming on the light green palmate leaves of the kukui trees. Clumps of six-foot pili grass provided a scary amount of cover as they progressed down toward the smoldering fields.

"Got a trip wire here," the sabotage expert said, turning to them. He was in the standard black helmet and bulletproof vest, but he wore an additional backpack of supplies. He slung it off his back and set it down.

Lei spotted the wire crossing the path once he pointed it out. It was actually a loose strand of transparent fishing line, and if the sun hadn't gleamed on it, she wouldn't have seen it at all. She moved up next to the expert, Sergeant Manolo, whose name was marked on his vest.

"Can I help? I have explosives training."

He glanced up at her. An older, weathered man, his intelligent brown eyes gleamed. "Yeah. You can hold this clamp. Keep the tension on."

Lei held the clamp steady, keeping the tension on the line, as Manolo traced it to its end, uncovering a cardboard box. She controlled her breathing and tension as he opened the box carefully. Inside, a grenade was nestled cozily in a bed of nails. The transparent filament was tied to the pin of the grenade.

Manolo cut the line. "Keep the tension on while I check the other end."

Lei felt sweat spring out under the restrictive vest. She remembered this from working on the explosives detail with Abe—endless minutes filled with danger. Patience, skill, and calm nerves were required. The bomb squad had not been a good fit.

Manolo traced the other end of the line and it was tied to a small sapling. "Done."

He cut the line. Lei dropped the clamp back into his kit, exhaling on a whoosh of breath.

"Where we've got one booby trap, we may well have more." Manolo addressed the squad leader. "This is crude, but could have been plenty effective. We need to proceed with extra caution."

The squad leader gave a brief affirmative nod. "Move out."

Manolo led the way. Lei followed him, and the rest of the team covered them, constantly checking the area with their weapons while Manolo scanned the path slowly as they proceeded. They arrived at the area of the burned fields. Most of the marijuana had burned down to smoking skeletons of the huge plants Lei had seen, but the smoke was still sharp and potent in her nostrils.

The stream with its waterfall was as beautiful as Lei remembered—and the pit bull's body lay in the water where it had fallen. Lei gulped bile, harsh and burning, at the sight. Whatever else happened today, she was going to bury that dog.

"Looks like a shelter over here," Manolo said.

"Yeah, that's where the kids appeared to be staying." Lei gestured to that side of the stream. "The boss came from a building on the opposite side. I want to check on the kids' shelter first."

"Roger that." Manolo continued his deliberate progress up the short path to the crude shack built of scrap wood and tin. They were within fifty feet of the shelter when they heard thumping and muffled cries of distress coming from inside.

Lei tightened her grip on her weapon. "Could be the child workers I saw earlier."

She started to run forward and fling the door open, but Manolo held up a fist, halting them. "Got another line. Across the door." His handheld light ran back and forth along the transparent filament draped across the doorway. "Window, too. Sergeant Texeira, let's do a perimeter check around the building."

"Roger that." Lei fell in behind Manolo as he circled slowly around the exterior. The captives must have heard them, because the frantic thumps and cries grew louder.

Lei's heart thundered, and sweat prickled along her hairline. She couldn't hate Boss Man more, a righteous rage that was hard to control.

But explosives detail was all about control.

She did her relaxation breathing and pulled in close behind Manolo as he ended the search and opened his kit at the door. She holstered her weapon and he handed her a clamp.

"Same deal as before with these. I'll trace the line, find out what kind of IED they left, and cut it. You keep the tension on."

"Got it." Lei placed the clamp he handed her on the window

line and held the line's tension as Manolo traced the strand to another grenade in a box of nails, this one tucked up under one of the roof's crude rafters. He shook his head as he deactivated the IED and removed it. "This would have really done a number on this little building."

The front door trip line was the same, but taking it down went faster now that they knew what they were dealing with.

The door was locked with a padlock. "I don't think they will have more booby traps inside," Manolo said to Lei and his captain as he got a pair of bolt cutters out of his pack. "These have the look of quick and crude devices. Something rigged to go off from inside takes longer to set up."

Lei hated to imagine the terror of being restrained and locked inside a shed that was rigged to blow up victims and rescuers alike. "He decided the boys were disposable."

"Maybe they have intel he didn't want to get out," the squad leader said.

Lei hung back as Manolo used his light to carefully check around the lintel of the closed door as he breached it, and then he gave it a tiny push. It creaked open.

CHAPTER FIFTEEN

I woke with a sticky feeling in my mouth, a mealy texture, as if the unripe bananas I'd eaten had decided to grow on the walls of my mouth. The light was dim, the sun hiding behind clouds somewhere high above. I sat up slowly, taking inventory. I had aches and pains, most specifically the ruined skin of my feet, but I felt much better than when exhaustion had pulled me under so completely.

Perhaps I was done with withdrawals.

Drawing my knees up, looking out at the dense foliage, I mentally tested the idea of a drink of good single malt.

I looked at the imaginary glass in my hand, filled with a nut-brown liquid that captured light, distilling it in warm sparks. I could feel the smell of it in my nostrils, tingling and smoky. I sipped, feeling a slight numbness on my lips. The taste was a little harsh, peaty and dark, then smooth as it moved down my throat, leaving an initial burn followed by a loosening, a wave of warmth that rippled through my body and brought relaxation.

It still appealed.

I was an alcoholic. Probably inherited the tendency, like they said you did, and the mental shit had set off the addiction. I'd known it for a while and was finally ready to really know it. I was going to have to stay off the sauce permanently. But I wasn't sick anymore, and that was a damn good thing, given the circumstances. If I could just get home, I'd never drink again.

MacDonald was on watch. "Hey, LT." His voice was low. Falconer was sleeping curled on his side. He'd covered himself with banana leaves. Kerry was closer to me, sprawled on his back. His face looked young as a teenager's as soft snores issued from his slack mouth.

"So what do you do for Security Solutions?" I whispered.

"I'm the camp's coordinator. I put the whole package together." MacDonald shuffled closer to me so we could talk quietly.

"You mean the physical camp we arrived at? Trifecta?"

"Yeah. I'm the manager. I get everything from the tents to the menus lined up. Keep supplies moving. Run everything."

"So the army doesn't have anything to do with that?"

"They provide most of the actual supplies and support staff. But I work with them, order shit, et cetera. They provided the security detail that was with us. We're doing a specialized service for them—training the MPs. In return, they pay for the services and provide infrastructure."

"Did you notice all the American supplies at the camp where they were holding us?"

"I didn't get much of a chance, between the pit and the wooden shelter. But yeah, I noticed the weapons were American."

"A lot more than that. The camp commander was even eating MREs." I contemplated my ruined feet. "How did the kidnappers know where we were? And who to take?"

MacDonald shrugged, but he looked down. He knew something.

"You work for Security Solutions. Think they have a leak?" I asked.

"Maybe." He still had his eyes down. "Could also be someone in the army brass."

"So why'd they take you?"

"All Security Solutions employees carry the same insurance you do."

"If that's the case, why isn't Security Solutions negotiating for our release?"

"That I don't know. Could be the army interfering. They'd have policy changes and we were often the last to know. Right hand doesn't know what the left is doing, all that."

I leaned closer and caught his eye. Devan MacDonald had the soft jaw and waistline of a man who spent a good deal of time behind a desk, though our recent hardship had caused a collapse of his plump cheeks. "You sure that's all that's going on there?"

"I don't know anything worth anything. But I heard something from one of the guards at the camp. I speak Spanish, so they used me as an interpreter with the other men a little bit. Anyway, it seems like there might have been a dirty army officer involved. Someone was getting a kickback from the kidnappers."

"I wouldn't be surprised, for them to be able to nail us so completely. But I can't imagine Forsythe being in on it." The polished major had made no bones about how much he disliked the location and the assignment, but he'd seemed like the kind of straight-arrow officer who was an army lifer.

"No. Not likely Forsythe. Maybe one of the sergeants." There had been Forsythe, two sergeants, and our camp's security detail.

"Think the Hondurans were in on it? The trainees?"

"Naw." MacDonald shook his head. "They were freaking the hell out when we were hit."

"Doesn't mean they weren't scared shitless for a reason. Their people were pulling off the raid. They're a trigger-happy bunch. But if the army decided they were terrorists, that would make the negotiations a lot harder."

"I just don't know, LT. There were casualties when they took us, and who knows what the kidnappers told the army when they asked for the ransom."

I wondered what the people at home had been told, too. I longed for the satellite phone I'd left that day on the charger back in the Trifecta tent. Just to be able to hear Lei's voice—she must be going crazy.

My stomach tightened. She wouldn't come over here and try to get me out, would she? I already knew the answer to that, and it almost made me retch. God forbid the army gave her any information. But she wouldn't come after me. That other time she'd gone off the reservation had cost us more than either of us wanted to admit, and she wouldn't leave Kiet.

My wife was a warrior, but she was a mother, too. She wouldn't leave our son.

The best thing I could do for both of them was to survive this and get home, sober and right in the head. But I'd settle for just surviving, at this point.

I reached into my pocket and took out the third banana. My belly should be able to deal with it after digesting the other two. I took extra time chewing, hoping to break it down more in my mouth. Falconer woke up, rustling up from under his banana leaves, and that woke Kerry.

"Think we'll be ready to get moving soon?" Kerry sat up on his elbows.

"We can't go back into that water." Falconer gestured to my feet. "Stevens's feet will go septic."

"Would be great to let our clothes and socks dry out before we got moving." I grabbed my socks off the frond they'd been draped over. They were still damp. "We have no idea how close the hostiles are, do we?"

Falconer shook his head and lifted his dark face to the sky. As if to demonstrate how helpless we were, rain began plinking down. "Shit. We can get moving, or we can make a shelter with these banana leaves and wait this out."

"Shelter. Wait for it to pass," Kerry voted, raising a hand. MacDonald nodded in agreement.

"Probably should have made the shelter first thing, but we didn't know how long we'd be here." Falconer stood and stretched, his muscular body imposing. I was damn glad he was with us. "I'll cut some leaves. Let's use the walking sticks for the frame."

In a remarkably short time Falconer had directed the erection of a fairly functional lean-to shelter, with room for us to all lie inside. The banana leaves, layered on top of each other, did a good job of sloughing the rainwater off.

The patter became a downpour, and we huddled close. I slept again.

THE DOOR CREAKED OPEN. A path of light illuminated the three young boys Lei had seen working the fields. They were restrained and gagged with duct tape. One of them had lost control of his bladder, and the smell of urine stung Lei's nose as she moved forward into the room, weapon drawn, and knelt beside the nearest child.

"You're okay now. We're going to help you. This will hurt a bit." The boy whimpered as Lei pulled the gag off the boy's mouth and the ultra-sticky tape pulled the sensitive skin of his face and lips. "Are there any other booby traps we should know about?" She squatted beside him, pulling her knife to cut the tape binding his wrists behind his back as Manolo freed the others.

"No more. Just the window and the door." The boy's voice was rusty and dry, and she gestured for one of the SWAT members to bring his canteen forward.

"Are you boys okay? Did he do anything to you?" Lei asked.

The one she'd freed nodded his head. "We're okay." But all of them were shaky and tear-streaked as they sat up and sipped from the canteen, passing it back and forth.

"We're going to check the other building," Manolo said. "We'll leave a couple of men here with you."

Lei nodded, and the two SWAT members took up stations beside the door.

Lei didn't want to overwhelm the kids with questions. "I'm going to record you, okay? So you don't have to go through the story so often." She took her phone out and thumbed on the recording feature. "What are your names?" Lei asked.

"Danny," the boy she'd freed said. "And this is Kekoa and Dexter." She asked for their last names and wrote those down, too.

"So tell me who the boss man is."

"Will he—will he be back?" Danny's eyes were huge and hollow with fear.

"He's long gone. But we need more information to catch him."

"He only let us call him Uncle," the middle boy, Kekoa, said. He was the smallest and slenderest of the three. "We're foster kids. He's our foster dad."

Lei's stomach clenched as faces of kids she'd put into the system flashed in front of her eyes. How many of them might have ended up in a situation like this?

"So how did that work?" She kept her voice soft with an effort. The other narco detective with their team returned. His partner was still looking at the fields, but the detective, a long-boned, balding man named Shepherd, came in and flipped a mattress behind the boys. A comic book fluttered from beneath it. She frowned at him.

"Can we leave that for a minute, Detective?"

The man gave a brief nod and squatted beside her. "Hey, guys. I'm Detective Shepherd. We need to know everything we can about what was going on out here."

"I don't know nothing." Dexter, the tallest kid, finally spoke. He looked a little older than the others, with peach fuzz on his upper lip. He was the one who'd lost control of his bladder, and he hunched over to hide his wet shorts.

"Why don't you start at the beginning? How you came to be here." Lei scribbled her old pen on the spiral notebook she used to take notes.

"We're fosters," the middle boy, Kekoa, repeated. "We came at different times. But we all lived in Kahului before. And we came to Hana to go to Aunty Selina's foster home. Selina Tahua." Lei wrote the name down. "So Aunty Selina, she meets the social worker and picks us up. Then she drives us out here. And Uncle, he put us in here, and we work." He shrugged thin shoulders under a filthy shirt.

"Who else was out here?"

"Two men stay with Uncle sometimes. Eddie and Akira. Two more come and help move the weed," Kekoa said.

"And Uncle, he had a helper. Tony was one of us. But he'd been out here so long, he came like he was Uncle's son." There was an envious note in Dexter's voice as he spoke. Tony must be the teen she'd left bound in the woods.

"Tell us what happened today," Lei said.

"You came." Danny pointed at her. "And you shot Killah."

"I know, and I'm sorry. I love dogs." Lei firmed her mouth to keep it from trembling. "I told Uncle to call his dog. I didn't want to hurt him."

"Killah was only Uncle's dog. He wasn't nice. One time Uncle he told Killah to stop me when I tried to run away." Danny lifted one leg of his dirty shorts. A ragged scar was visible on his thigh. "I got sick from Killah biting me. But they nevah take me fo' go hospital." As the boy talked, his pidgin grew broader. "He'd have killed you if he could."

Lei sighed, still conflicted. "Would you boys help me bury the dog after we're done talking? I don't want to leave him in the river."

"Yeah, sure," Danny said. The other boys nodded. Sounds of the team moving around the shack, photographing and making sure the marijuana fires were going out, penetrated the shack's walls.

"So we need names," Shepherd said. "Names of anyone who came down here that you might have heard or picked up." He was able to get four names from Danny and Kekoa, including that of

TOBY NEAL

the chopper pilot and a description of the bird used to transport the raw marijuana.

"So what did you boys do out here when you weren't working?" Lei asked. "Did they keep you locked in this shed?"

"Yeah," Danny said. "Uncle would bring food down once a day and a jug of water." He gestured to the gallon jug in the corner. "Once we were done working, he locked us in. We had a flashlight, but we usually fell asleep once it was dark."

"We had video games." Dexter reached in his pocket and brought out a handheld battery-operated game. "If we worked hard and got a lot done, Uncle would let us watch TV at his place." He gestured to the other bunkhouse across the stream. Stockholm syndrome, that pattern of attachment to a captor, appeared to be affecting Dexter the most.

"So I have a hard question for you boys," Lei said. "I came up this valley because I found a skull that had washed down the stream to the beach, and someone found it there. Do you know if there were any other kids, who...?" She thought of how to phrase it. "Might have disappeared?"

The boys shook their heads. "We weren't the only ones to work here," Danny said. "I mean, we were the ones working here, but we knew there were others before us. Because of Tony."

"Yes. Tony." Lei could well remember the teen she'd beaten with his rifle and left tied with his belt. Now that she saw what had happened to the other boys, she needed to have an officer go check on his location. She'd assumed Boss Man had freed him and taken the teen with him, but now she wasn't so sure. "Was Tony one of you, working?"

"No. Tony graduated. He lived in the bunkhouse with Uncle," Dexter said.

"Graduated. What did that mean?"

"Means he did something to make him a man." Kekoa's voice was a scared whisper as he contributed this.

Lei frowned. "Do you know what it was?"

"No. Uncle, he said it would be something different for each of us," Dexter said. "I get to graduate now." The boy pulled a grenade out of his pocket.

Lei's breath stopped and her heart jumped. She locked eyes with the tall, slender boy. The fear that had caused him to lose bladder control wasn't just from being tied up in a shack wired to blow. He was the final booby trap, and he was scared—and suicidal.

CHAPTER SIXTEEN

I woke sometime deep in the night, startled by something running with light insect feet across my bare arm. I shook whatever it was off.

"You okay, LT?" Kerry whispered. He was on watch, sitting up in the low shelter beside me. It was barely tall enough to accommodate him sitting cross-legged.

"Yeah. Something ran across me." I turned toward the young man, drawing myself up to kneel. "I might as well take my watch. I slept extra this afternoon."

"You seemed like you needed it. Nothing much going on, just some animal activity." He handed me the rifle. I crawled out of my nest of leaves and sat down where he'd been, bracing my back against one of the banana trees that we'd used for a corner of the crude shelter. Mere moments later, I could tell by Kerry's regular, deep breathing that he was asleep in the spot I'd vacated.

I scanned the darkness.

It was a busy darkness, filled with clicking, rustling, and far off, the squeal of something dying abruptly. My eyes adjusting, I could see the faintest lightness of moonlight high above the trees. Every now and then I'd see a gleam of something bioluminescent.

And as suddenly as if conjured, one of those glowing moths appeared, dancing around our tiny open area like a will-o'-the-wisp.

I flashed to the night I'd had the dream of Anchara. This moth or butterfly had none of the charged energy of that strange haunting—it was merely a pretty, glowing butterfly in the thick velvet darkness. Watching in that darkness, my knees drawn up and the rifle resting on them, my mind could wander.

Had Anchara really visited me? The moth had shown me a way to escape the shed, and that was undeniable. It was also true that the tormented dreams I'd had about Anchara and her death had ceased. It could just be the stress and distraction of the kidnapping causing a temporary reprieve—but I didn't think so. I usually had more of the terrible dreams, not fewer, when I was under stress.

If we could just survive this, it would all be worth it. I felt different. Free. Not just dried out by necessity. Even though I'd had to kill a man, blow up three choppers, and ruin my feet.

Lei's face rose in my mind's eye. Those serious level brows bracketing big brown eyes. I never got tired of the tiny freckles on her nose. Never got tired of tasting that lush mouth I'd missed so much while we were separated. She'd tease me if she knew what I was thinking, if she knew how often the colors of this place and its shades of brown reminded me of her.

"My English lit haole boy." She'd kiss me. "My own Shakespeare."

She expressed her feelings with her body, not her words. I loved that about her. That one night before I left hadn't been near enough. We hadn't had time to really connect in so long.

Lei had been so angry that I'd taken the Security Solutions job that she'd moved out of our room, and I'd decided not to tell her when I was leaving until the day before, hoping that would minimize the friction between us.

It hadn't. Instead, it had led to that long separation, a wasteland of missed opportunity I'd caused with my screwed-up head and the drinking. Thank God she'd decided to come back late in the night before I left. The sex had been incredible...but the taste it had left in my mouth was desperation. It was all we'd have as I left for six months—and now, all we might have, ever.

I'd been wrong not to tell Lei when I was leaving. Especially since I'd told Kathy.

Kathy had needed the date because she was covering my duties —but I'd told her a lot more than that. She was easy to be with. Smart, funny, didn't need anything from me but seemed to like me fine. Telling her things weren't good at home had been a mistake, one I hadn't realized fully until that last day.

Kathy's soft mouth turned up to mine, willing me to kiss her. I'd pushed her away, hard. She'd hit her hip on the edge of the desk and cried out, turning away in humiliation, covering her face.

"I'm sorry. It's just not like that, Kathy." I'd grabbed my bag and headed for the door. "I'm sorry."

So that was how we'd said goodbye after a great year working together. I felt like shit. I'd hurt my partner, let things go somewhere they shouldn't have gone, and that was on me. I didn't like that Kathy thought I'd go there with her. I must have done something to make her think so. Yeah, things were hard at home, but I was a long way from falling off that particular cliff.

And if Lei ever found out...I shut my eyes at the thought.

Dawn came, slowly bleeding away the dark. I heard crunching. Something heavy was moving through the underbrush nearby. Whatever was foraging in the leaves around the base of the banana trees was coming closer.

My belly pinched painfully, reminding me it was there. I shifted, coming up onto the balls of my feet into a crouch, setting the rifle down. The gun would alert any humans to our presence, and until we had some idea where we were, and where our pursuers were, it was still best not to fire it.

I drew the knife, held it in one fist, tucking the pistol into the back of my pants. The shuffle of leaves and the sound of grunting drew closer. I could make out a large shape and several smaller ones.

Feral pigs. A family of them.

Pigs meant bacon.

All we needed was one of the small ones and we could eat for days. My mouth watered and my belly clenched painfully. I rose to a half-crouch and shuffled forward, sliding my feet so that the leaves lifted rather than crunched as I got closer to the target.

I didn't want the mother. She was too big and might have tusks. No, I wanted one of those half-grown piglets rooting nearby.

I sidled around the tree and coiled to spring. I knew the moment they caught my scent by a startled squeal and a deeper, ominous one from the mother. I pounced, leaping onto one of the smaller dark shadows, leading with a downward strike of the knife and my full body weight.

All was a welter of terrified, humanlike squealing as I grappled with the surprisingly hairy, strong, writhing creature, holding it down by force and body weight. I stabbed it again, my nostrils filled with the hot-iron smell of fresh blood and my arms fully occupied with its bristly, struggling form.

The piglet's struggles lessened, but its squalling didn't. Behind me, I heard the men yelling as they woke to the drama.

I'd forgotten about the mother.

She loomed out of the murk, snorting deep in her chest, swinging her head. I could just make out curving tusks protruding from her jaws as I rolled away, clutching the dying piglet to my chest. I couldn't get my pistol out of my pants, and I rolled frantically, crashing, thrashing, kicking. I felt a searing line of fire open up my side, and my howl of pain mingled with the piglet's.

A shot rang out, so close it deafened me, and the sow squealed. Her hooves tore up the leaf litter around us as she whirled and ran into the retreating darkness after her fleeing offspring.

Falconer stared down at me. I could tell it was him by his inky, looming presence. "Got one of the babies, I see."

"Yeah." I still held the piglet, finally gone still, hugged to my chest. My breath came in shallow pants as I tried to minimize the pain in my side. "She got me, though."

"How bad?"

"Not sure." I didn't want to move, but I slowly unlocked my arms, loosening my grip on the piglet as the two other men came to stand over me.

"Good going, LT. I'll gut it and prep it for cooking. I grew up on a farm." All Kerry was thinking of was bacon.

"Stevens is injured." Falconer's comment put a damper on the excitement. "And we've given away our position. Gut the pig while I see how bad he is. Then we move to another location before we make a fire."

"You got it." Kerry took the knife from me and lifted the pig gently out of my arms. I'd begun to shake. I breathed shallow, my arm down over my injured side, keeping pressure on the wound.

"Wish that headlight worked." Falconer knelt beside me. The ashy light was still dim. "MacDonald, you've got two shirts on. Give me your undershirt."

I shut my eyes for a moment, breathing through the pain, as Falconer gently unbuttoned my uniform shirt. "Lift your arm so I can see what's going on," he said.

I gritted my teeth, shut my eyes, and lifted my arm away from my injured side.

DEXTER'S EYES had opened so wide that white surrounded the iris. He shook, a fine trembling racking his body as he held the grenade aloft in one hand, the forefinger of the other hooked through the pin. The odor of urine and the sweat of fear was so powerful Lei felt her eyes prickle.

"Dexter." Lei held his gaze. "Uncle isn't here anymore. He can't hurt you. And he can't help you either."

Shepherd's hand crept toward his weapon as his body slowly coiled, readying for action.

"Dex!" Kekoa cried. "No do dis to us!"

"Uncle already tried to kill us!" Danny appealed to the older boy. "Don't do it for him, Dex! We your friends!"

"He told me I would graduate. That he'd make a tattoo of my name on his right arm." Dexter spoke through clenched teeth and bloodless lips. One finger was hooked through the round metal ring on the pin, and the other held the grenade aloft. "I want to graduate."

"Dexter, how can you graduate when you're dead?" Lei's blood roared in her ears. Shepherd had his hand on his weapon, tight as a spring beside her. "If Uncle cared about you, he wouldn't have done this. Set you up. Made you a weapon against people who came to save you."

The boy trembled harder.

Lei extended her hand. "Give me the grenade. You're safe now." The boy's eyes flicked to her, flicked to the door. "And Killah isn't here anymore, either. I need your help to bury him."

Shepherd whipped his weapon out just as the boy's desperate gaze came back to Lei's face and he dropped the grenade into her hand. She snatched it from the boy and threw herself onto Dexter, covering him with her body. "Don't shoot! I've got him!"

Shepherd leaped to his feet, keeping his weapon on the boy. He pulled out his cuffs. "Holy hell, Texeira. Got a death wish? I almost shot you!"

Lei stood up on shaky legs. "Search all of them. I'll get rid of this." She held up the grenade, and Shepherd nodded. She turned to look at Dexter, who had fallen backward under her weight.

The boy blinked up at her, blank-eyed with shock. Shepherd cuffed the boy as Lei made her legs work to carry her to the door, where she set the grenade carefully with the other IEDs in Manolo's custody. Outside, she took a couple of breaths of fresh air.

That was a close one. She shut her eyes on the imagined moment of their death, or even of the following one, where Shepherd nailed her point-blank as she tried to save the boy. She probably shouldn't have thrown herself on Dexter, but instinct had taken over—and her instinct was to save and protect a child, no matter how misguided.

Shepherd had searched all three boys. He found a couple more video games. Dexter was the only kid carrying any kind of weapon.

"I really do need your help burying Killah," Lei told the boys. "I know you must have shovels somewhere. Come help me." Her gut told her that doing that chore would help the boys somehow—and it would help her, too.

Dexter was allowed to follow her, still cuffed, out of the shack. Kekoa and Danny showed her where they stored tools, and the three carried four shovels down to the stream, Dexter bringing up the rear.

"Where do you think we should bury him?" Lei asked the boys.

Danny pointed at the rock where Boss Man had sat. "He used to sit with Uncle over there. Watching us."

"Hope the rock doesn't block us from digging there." Lei put a hand on Dexter's thin shoulder. The SWAT and narco team were still busy gathering evidence, and Shepherd had gone to join his partner. "I'm going to take the cuffs off so you can help us dig. Don't make me sorry that I'm trusting you."

Dexter nodded, his eyes on his filthy feet in worn rubber slippers they'd found by the door of the shack. He seemed unable to speak.

The kid needed psychological treatment. Lei mentally scrolled through whom she could call to help him. The list began with Elizabeth Black, her favorite social worker with Child Welfare Services. Elizabeth was going to shit a brick when she heard what had happened to these boys while in the system—and heads were going to roll. That was a good thing.

It took Lei and the three boys to carry the dog's waterlogged body out of the stream and over to where they'd decided to dig the hole. Lei was thankful that the blood had washed down the stream, and lying on his side, the damaged part of his skull out of view, the pit bull appeared to be peacefully sleeping. Lei felt rage rise up, lifting the tiny hairs all over her body. Boss Man was a thug who used kids and animals to do his dirty work—was there anyone lower on the planet? She didn't think so.

Lei jumped onto the T-shaped blade of the shovel to get it into the soil. The exertion of digging was therapeutic for all of them, but slow going. "So how did you get those pot plants so big?" Lei asked, swiping an arm across her sweaty face. "This soil seems pretty hard. Not so good for agriculture."

"We did a lot of compost and Miracle-Gro," Kekoa said. He'd shed his shirt, and his ribs showed. Boss Man clearly hadn't been overly generous with food. "We watered every other day if it didn't rain." He explained the finer points of marijuana cultivation as they worked up a sweat.

Manolo appeared at Lei's elbow. "Need some help?"

"Yeah," Lei panted. She handed him her shovel, and just as the boys were tiring, the rest of the SWAT team showed up.

"I can tell we don't get to leave until this is done," the SWAT leader said, a smile lurking by his mouth.

"That's right, sir." Lei gazed at the man unblinking, willing him to understand her words and actions were for the boys' benefit. "We care enough to clean up after ourselves and show respect to those who deserve it."

"You get no argument from me." The team leader took the shovel from Dexter. "Take a load off, kid."

With the men working, it didn't take long to make the hole big enough for the dog, and Lei and Manolo carefully set the body into it. The boys took the shovels again and filled it in, and as the spades whacked down on the earth, packing it firmly, Lei could see that the gamble she'd taken with the kids had paid off.

This was good for them to see and do. They were moving and sweating easily now, Kekoa and Danny even flicking clods of dirt at each other. Kids were resilient. They'd be all right.

Dexter was the only one she was really worried about. He was still silent and robotic, but at least he was moving and helping.

Lei fetched a large round stone from the stream. "Boys, you each bring one, and we'll put them on his grave." When they'd each set a stone on the pile of earth, Lei set hers on top of the pile.

"Here lies Killah, a brave, strong dog who obeyed his master. He won't be forgotten, and neither will the man who caused his death." Lei looked up. "Anything you boys want to say? You never have to come back here, to this place, again."

"I'm glad to be leaving," Kekoa said. And he threw a handful of dirt on the dog's grave.

"You did what you had to do," Danny said, gazing at Lei as dirt sifted from his hand onto the pile. "And I'm glad you came."

"I wish you didn't do that shit to us," muttered Dexter, staring at the pile of stones. "I wish I never came here." Lei knew he was addressing the man whose name they knew only as Uncle.

"Let's go." The SWAT captain gestured. The team headed back up the trail, but the boys didn't move until Lei did. Her heart squeezed as she glanced back at them, their dark heads bent as they followed her up the path like ducklings.

Maybe she could be the boys' temporary foster placement. It was crazy, but why not? Other than that she was barely home with her own child, of course—but she could take it easy, stay home more, once she found out where the skull had come from.

Lei was eager to get the satellite phone out of her shot-up truck. That reminded her of Tony and where she'd left him in the forest. She caught up with the SWAT leader, the boys jogging to keep up with her.

"Excuse me, Captain? I need to go check on something."

CHAPTER SEVENTEEN

I COULD FEEL the warm trickle of blood down my side as I allowed Falconer to pull off my shirt. He'd quickly stripped off some banana leaves, and after an initial look, he pressed them down over the wound.

"No big deal. Couple of inches long, half an inch deep or so. Probably hurts like hell, but far from fatal. Keep pressure on and the bleeding will stop soon. I'll try to rig some sort of bandage. The biggest danger is going to be infection."

He didn't need to tell me that. I hissed out a breath between my teeth as he levered me up into a sitting position. "Your shirt is totally ruined with pig blood—and some of yours, too. Once I get a bandage on, you can wear MacDonald's undershirt." Falconer rummaged among the banana leaves, calling for the knife.

MacDonald brought it over. "Kerry has the pig prepped already. Once we get our shoes back on, we can get going."

"I hope you buried the guts," Falconer said. "Except the heart and liver. We can eat those raw." Even in my state of shock from injury, my stomach rumbled happily at the thought. Raw liver? Bring it on. "In fact, give it to Stevens. He needs some replacement calories after all this."

"You earned it, LT." Kerry brought me the still-warm liver, and God help me, I ate the palm-sized organ in just a few nausea-inducing bites while Falconer used flexible strips of the spines of banana leaves to tie a crude pad of leaves over my wound.

My stomach lurched, but the liver made it down. I breathed through it, refusing to gag, knowing my body needed the nourishment no matter how disgusting. Falconer tied off the strips, and once they were holding the pad of leaves in place, he and MacDonald helped maneuver the undershirt on over it. He helped me up.

"You can use my uniform shirt to carry the pig," I suggested. MacDonald nodded, taking the ruined garment and buttoning the pig's carcass into it. Using one of the shelter poles, he and Kerry slung the meat over their shoulders while I focused on getting my socks and shoes on my ruined feet.

Ten minutes later we were moving. I brought up the rear, watching out back as I'd done before, the M16 cradled loosely in one arm as I kept the other down and clamped at my side. The makeshift bandage rubbed the wound painfully and the makeshift ties of banana fiber soon frayed apart, but I didn't want to slow us down.

"Far from life endangering, except for infection," as Falconer had so dismissively said. But it hurt like a sonofabitch, and I mentally willed the blood trickling down my side to wash the bacteria from the pig's tusks out of the cut.

We were heading east now, and the going was slow, as we'd reached an area of heavier undergrowth. Tall mahogany, kapok, and Brazil nut trees still towered overhead, but now we pushed our way through stands of palm-like plants, bromeliads, and wild ginger. Vines and ferns tangled up the trunks of the trees and tripped us. Falconer continued to lead the way, checking the compass on the knife and using it to hack the vines out of the way as he needed to.

The pig weighed about fifty pounds, a significant amount in

our weakened state, and the men paused in an open area to move the pole to their other shoulders just as Falconer seized something that wasn't a vine.

He'd grabbed some sort of slender green snake. He gave a grunt of surprise and heaved it instinctively away—straight onto Kerry. The snake, about two feet long, landed on Kerry's chest. The young man yelped and grabbed at it, dropping the pole. The pig slid out of the sling into the leaves, and Kerry stumbled to one knee. The snake coiled backward and sank its teeth into his wrist.

LEI GOT a ride out to her shot-up truck with the narco team—Shepherd wanted to check the area where she'd left Tony bound in the jungle personally. They rounded the curve of the bluff where Lei had reached the road and flagged down the Mustang. It felt like a lifetime ago.

"I didn't send Hana PD out here right away because I knew Boss Man was right behind me. I just assumed he'd free the boy and take him with him, but once I saw what he'd done out at that shack..." She shook her head. "He clearly doesn't care who he hurts. Straight into the trees from here." Lei pointed as they pulled over and parked. "I'm not surprised Hana PD wanted to wait for me to come out to check on the kid's location—it was hard to describe. I was so amped up when I got out of there I hardly registered details of the car I commandeered, let alone how to describe what the exact area looked like."

Late evening was casting long shadows under the trees as Lei led the two narcotics detectives through the trees. It was a surprisingly long way inland through thick underbrush and trees, at least half a mile, by the time they found the teen.

They could see by the track of disturbed leaves that Tony had managed to wriggle twenty or so feet from where she'd left him. He was butted up against the trunk of a kukui nut tree, apparently rubbing the belt on his feet against it in an attempt to escape. His dark eyes glared at them from over the T-shirt she'd used to gag him so many hours before. Tears, snot, and dried blood from his nose covered his face.

"Hey, Tony. I see Uncle didn't take you with him." Lei folded her arms as Shepherd and his partner freed the boy's feet and took off the gag. "I'm thinking you're actually lucky he didn't put a bullet in your head. Guess he just left you to die of thirst instead."

"Screw you, bitch," Tony whispered hoarsely.

Shepherd looked at Lei. "Want I should put the gag back on him, Sergeant?"

She and the kid stared at each other for a long moment, and the boy was the first to look away. "No. He's going to mind his manners now. Aren't you, Tony?"

The boy refused to look at her, clearly not wanting to be gagged again. "I need to piss."

Lei turned and headed back toward the vehicles as Shepherd assisted with that awkward necessity. She reached the road and walked down it, arriving at her truck.

The sight of her ruined vehicle, covered from top to bottom with bullet holes, brought tears of angry exhaustion to Lei's eyes. She fumbled her key out of her pocket and unlocked the truck, then retrieved the satellite phone from her purse under the front seat. It flashed with a message.

She called the voice mail. The satellite connection worked, even out here.

"This is Lieutenant Colonel Westbrook. We have a situation to discuss. Please call me as soon as possible." Her finger hovered over Call Back, but just then Shepherd's black SUV rolled up. She wanted privacy for that call.

She tucked the phone into her filthy pants and picked up her purse, sunglasses, and Kiet's booster seat. "Can you give me a ride back to Kahului?" she asked Shepherd, carefully not looking at

Tony. The kid was sitting way in the back of the vehicle, still in cuffs.

"Man, Sergeant. They did a number on your vehicle. Automatic rounds?" Shepherd said.

"Yeah." Lei relocked her vehicle, and it gave a strangled bleep at the electronic signal.

"I'll get Impound to tow it to Kahului for you." He reached for his radio and called it in.

"It's evidence now," Lei said grimly. "At least that way I don't have to pay for my own damn tow." Out of the corner of her eye, she saw Tony duck his head. She hoped it was a little shame that made him do so, but that was probably too much to hope for. He was pretty far beneath Boss Man's thumb.

She got into the front seat beside Shepherd since his partner was already sitting in the back. "So, Tony." She turned to the boy as they reversed and got on the road. "I have to stop at Hana Police Station to make sure your friends have a foster care situation to go to. Remember them? Kekoa, Danny, and Dexter?"

Tony kept his head down but his shoulders hunched. Definitely a reaction there. Might as well get to work popping his illusions about Uncle Boss Man. "He left those boys bound and gagged in their shack, and he booby-trapped it to blow. Real nice man, your uncle."

The boy's head came up. His eyes blazed, dark and feral. "You lie!"

"Me, lie?" Lei turned to the other cops. "Detectives, did you get some photos of the scene when we first approached the shack?"

"I did, Sergeant," the partner said. "Got some right here, on my phone."

"Would you show Tony a picture of the bombs set to blow on the shack? And of the boys inside. Please." She kept her voice flat, overly polite, and he returned in kind.

"Happy to, Sergeant." He scrolled to the photos on his phone.

Lei watched Tony's face as the teen was forced to see what he didn't want to know.

"Now you understand why I was happy to see that Uncle had left you alive even though you failed him," Lei said softly. "When I left you there, I assumed he would free you when he found you, that he would take you with him. But once I saw how he treated the other boys, I realized you'd be lucky to be alive. He doesn't deserve your help."

Tony shook his head, a slight negation.

Lei persisted. "What's his name? That's all we need. His name."

Tony hung his head. "Uncle was angry I let you get away. Said I was a screw-up and always would be. Said he was leaving me there so I would learn a lesson. After a few hours I realized he was never coming back." The boy lifted his head and narrowed his eyes at Lei. "I learned my lesson—it's all your fault."

Lei sighed, turned back to face out the windshield. "Guess you just need some jail time. I tried." She lifted her feet up and rested them on the dashboard, feeling infinitely weary. "Did I or did I not try to help this boy, Detectives?"

"You did, Sergeant."

Shepherd switched on some mellow Hawaiian slack-key guitar, and Lei leaned her head on the window.

Back at Hana PD, they booked Tony Akahi on charges of attempted murder, destruction of property, and assault with a deadly weapon. The boy was stonily silent as one of the officers put him in a cruiser for the drive to Kahului.

Lei focused on the boys who remained. The three of them stood up when she went into the interview room where they'd been stashed. A pile of food wrappers and soda cans testified to their snacking while she'd been gone.

"We found Tony. He's still loyal to Uncle, even though Uncle cussed him out and left him tied up in the jungle. But that boy's brainwashed." She flapped a hand, dismissing Tony and his delusions. "It's you guys I'm concerned about. I have a friend. Her name's Elizabeth Black, and she's a social worker. She's on her way, and she has a big heart. She was so pissed when I told her about Uncle and Aunty Selina. We still need a name for Uncle. Did you ever hear him called anything?"

"No. Only 'Boss' or 'Uncle,'" Danny said.

Dexter blinked slowly. He still looked dazed, but the food appeared to have restored him a little. "His first name was Noah. I never heard his last name."

Lei touched Dexter's shoulder lightly, appreciating what it meant for the kid to give up the man's name. "Thanks. That helps. It really does."

Lei went to the door and told Shepherd to include the first name Noah in the BOLO they had out on the murderous pot grower. She came back in and shut the door. "So I have to go back to Kahului. But I want you to trust Elizabeth. She'll look out for you."

Danny grabbed her hand. "Don't go, Aunty."

Aunty. The title of respect children called women they cared for in Hawaii. Lei was being called Aunty. Her eyes prickled. She would really have to see what Elizabeth said about taking care of the boys.

Elizabeth appeared, her strong-boned face peering through the wire-laced window in the door. Lei opened it. "And here's Ms. Black now. Let me talk with her a minute."

Lei slipped out and tugged Elizabeth a few feet away from the door. Elizabeth's twin iron-gray braids hung over sturdy shoulders, emphasizing the Native American shape of her eyes and jaw, the strong look of her face.

"These boys are wounded. Traumatized," Lei said. "They were kept isolated and used as slave labor. For months. We don't know how long, exactly."

"I'm going to see those fake foster parents prosecuted to the full extent of the law," Elizabeth swore, dark eyes hard.

"Yeah, of course you are, and I'll help with that. But that doesn't help them right now. They're terrified, and they bonded to me during the rescue. Can I take them home? Just until you find placements?"

"Lei, you need that like a hole in the head. Especially with your husband overseas. What, you're going to fill your house with needy strays so you don't have to remember that? You already have a kid you haven't seen all day." Elizabeth frowned at her. "I'd consider it, if I thought you'd actually be around to take care of them."

Lei ducked her head, feeling smacked and knowing Elizabeth was right. "Fine. But you can't separate them. I'm really worried about Dexter." She filled Elizabeth in on recent events and Dexter's behavior. "I'd keep him under suicide watch."

"I have a therapeutic crisis home to put them in, where they can all stay together. Introduce me."

Lei pushed the interview room door open and went in, Elizabeth following. The boys had tidied their mess into a rubbish basket and now sat around the table with their handheld games. They dropped these and looked up apprehensively.

"Boys, this is Elizabeth Black. She's a social worker, and it's her job to make sure you're taken care of. Ms. Black, this is Kekoa, Danny, and Dexter."

The boys each stood and shook Elizabeth's hand. The social worker smiled at them, an expression so warm and luminous that it totally changed her stern face. "I'm happy to meet such incredibly brave young men. I have a place for you to stay for the next few days, and you'll all be together."

"We want to go with her." Danny pointed at Lei.

"I'm sorry, but that's not possible," Elizabeth said. "As you can see, Sergeant Texeira is a hard-working police detective. She's doing all she can to capture the man who kept you out there, and we need her to do that. But she'll stay in touch, won't she?" Elizabeth gazed at Lei.

"Absolutely. You couldn't keep me away. I'll bring my son to meet you. And maybe my dogs. They're Rottweilers, and they love kids. But for now you guys need to get ready for hot showers, soft beds, lots of food and video games." Grins spread slowly across the boys' faces at this. "Try not to have too much fun until I see you next, okay?" Lei waved goodbye, and was able to close the door, leaving them with a lighter heart.

She could add three boys to the short list of kids she was mentoring, topped by an extraordinary Filipina girl she'd busted on Oahu.

Lei finished the paperwork she had to leave at Hana Station and hopped into the SUV with Shepherd. "Please drop me off in Haiku. I'm going straight home."

On the way back, Lei used the satellite phone to call Captain Omura and brief her on the afternoon's events. "I saw the BOLO on that grower," Omura said. "Do you have a photo of the perp?"

"No, but the boys at the station are being interviewed with the social worker, and Narco is sending over a sketch artist," Lei said. "Right, Shepherd?"

The bald man nodded. The weather-beaten detective drove the windy, narrow, overgrown road with the lights and sirens on and confident vehicle handling. "He's on his way. He'll meet with the boys before they go to the crisis shelter."

"We'll get him." Once she was done and had the next day's plan lined up, she ended the call and addressed Shepherd. "Thanks for getting me home quickly. I have a really important personal call I have to make."

"Heard your husband was overseas." Shepherd glanced at her. "Something to do with that?"

"Yeah." Lei looked back out the window at the lush foliage streaming by. She liked the detective, but she didn't want to say anything more to this man she barely knew. "Today's adventure was just supposed to be a half-day cold case."

"That's what you get for hiking up into one of those Hana

valleys by yourself," Shepherd said. "Nobody in Narco would be that crazy."

"That's what my partner, Pono Kaihale, told me." Lei sighed, smoothing her springing hair back into its ponytail. The day's exertions had taken a toll. Her regular phone rang as they reached cell service again. "Sergeant Texeira."

"Hey, Lei. This is Aina Thomas." The Coast Guard officer's voice was warm, and Lei's pulse picked up. She clung to her resolve from earlier in the day not to encourage him.

"How can I help you, Petty Officer?" Lei spoke briskly, conscious of Shepherd right beside her.

"Oh. You can't talk. Gotcha. Well, I was wondering if you thought more about going out to dive that wreck in Lahaina. It would be good to keep your scuba skills up." He'd asked her to go diving not long ago.

"I appreciate the idea, but I'm up to my eyeballs in work right now. Can't possibly get away."

"Maybe another time?" He sounded so nice, so interested in her. It would be great to do something fun and relaxing with someone who liked her for herself. But no. She couldn't, not when Stevens was captive. No matter what Kathy Fraser was to her husband, she wasn't going to make the same mistake.

"Not sure it's something I can ever make time for. But thanks. You're very kind." Lei ended the call gently but firmly, wishing it hadn't been so hard to do, but meaning every word. He was kind, and she could use a little more of that in her life.

But not from an incredibly attractive man who wasn't her husband.

With the siren and lights clearing the road, the drive that usually took two hours took only one, but it was still dark when Shepherd turned into her driveway.

The dogs burst into aggressive barking at the sight of a strange vehicle as Lei keyed open the gate.

"No worries about your security," Shepherd said as the

Rottweilers circled the vehicle, menacing snarls turning to ecstatic whimpers when Lei opened the door to pet them. "Beautiful animals."

"They take care of us as much as we take care of them." Lei waved goodbye as the detective turned around and the gate rumbled shut.

Kiet had been waiting at the door until the other car left, and now he flew down the porch stairs to embrace her, burrowing his dark head into her stomach. "You're late, Mama."

"I know, little man." She hefted Kiet up and then spun him around for a few steps until he giggled. "I've never been so happy to be here." She kissed him, peppering his face with smacks until he wiggled and squirmed.

Her father, Wayne, stood in the door, backlit, his tall form and curly head a welcome sight. Warm smells, redolent of garlic and ginger, rolled out to greet her with all the love and nourishment of home.

In her pocket the satellite phone seemed to pulse urgently with news of the one she loved who should be here, too—and wasn't. She'd get to the phone call after dinner. She deserved to sit down and eat in peace, after all that had happened today.

Carrying her son, Lei went up onto the porch and into the light and good smells, the dogs at her side.

CHAPTER EIGHTEEN

KERRY SCREAMED as the snake struck his wrist a second time, but he was still holding it in his panic. Falconer tore it out of his hand and heaved it away.

The young man's blue eyes were wide and terrified. "Shit! The fucker bit me!"

"I'm sorry!" Falconer grabbed his wrist. "Let me see."

MacDonald resettled the pig in its carrying rig as Falconer inspected the oozing bite marks on Kerry's wrist. "Need to get this poison out if we can. I need to make a cut on the marks and suck the venom out. Okay?"

Kerry nodded mutely, eyes huge. Falconer tugged the young man down, and they both knelt. He braced Kerry's wrist on his knee. "This bite is really close to your vein. I hope it didn't go right in." He carefully stabbed the point of the knife into the holes. Kerry shut his eyes, tightened his jaw, and swore. Falconer put his mouth over the cuts and sucked, spat. Sucked, spat.

MacDonald looked away into the jungle, took the M16 from me. "I'll keep watch."

He looked like he was going to puke, his face pale and greasy. I felt that way, too, especially when Falconer looked up at me and touched his lips. They were bloody as a vampire's.

"My mouth feels numb. That's not good. Give me some water." I grabbed Kerry's canteen off his belt and handed it to Falconer. He rinsed his mouth, spat, looked back down at the wrist clamped in his hands. Blood welled sluggishly from the cuts. Kerry lowered his head to his knees, his arm extended across the other man's knees as if in appeal. All I could see was the young man's bent back and ruffled blond hair.

"I'll try again." Falconer's voice was hoarse. The poison was affecting his vocal cords. I shuffled over to Kerry, reached down to touch his neck, feeling his pulse.

The man's heart was racing at trip-hammer speed, but his skin was cold and clammy. "You okay, Kerry?"

He didn't answer.

Falconer dug in with the knife again. More blood flowed. More sucking and spitting, now interspersed with rinsing his mouth and pouring water over Kerry's wrist.

Suddenly Kerry leaned to the side and retched. Nothing much came up. Shudders racked the young man's body. I moved in, squatting beside him, and draped an arm over him, holding him tight. I remembered how he'd held me the same way in the pit, keeping me warm and steady with his body heat.

"Relax, Kerry. Deep breaths. Calm your heart rate down." I didn't want to tell him that panicking would speed the poison's route to his heart. Falconer's grip tightened on Kerry's arm, refusing to let go of it. He redoubled his efforts to get the poison out.

But Kerry died anyway, suddenly and without a word—a slight stiffening, which I felt jolt through his body. Then he went limp, slumping in my arms like a puppet with its strings cut. I felt his neck for a pulse.

There was none.

LEI WAITED to call Westbrook until after they had eaten the dinner her father had made and she'd hugged her father goodbye. She settled Kiet in front of some cartoons. She badly needed a shower, but she needed to know what the army liaison had to say first.

"Mama has to make a phone call. I'll be in the office, okay?" She pressed a kiss on the little boy's thick hair, remembering the other boys she hadn't been able to bring home.

"Okay. But come right back." Kiet put his thumb back in his mouth. He hadn't sucked it since he was three, and she knew her son was going to end up in bed with her again. Kiet hadn't adjusted well to Stevens's departure. She had to keep any further stresses out of his life.

Elizabeth was right. Lei could hardly take care of those who really needed her, let alone three psychologically damaged foster kids—and what effect would they have on Kiet? There was no way to know, and she needed to keep the boy on his routine.

She carried the satellite phone into the back office room and called the number Westbrook had left.

He picked up. "It's a bit late, Sergeant Texeira," the army officer said by way of greeting. "I left that message this morning."

"I'm sorry. I had an intense case. The phone was in my truck, and it got shot up with automatic weapons fire. Took a while before I could retrieve it."

"You should join the army. At least it's not your own vehicle getting shot up," the officer said with perfect composure. Lei gave a little snort of laughter.

"Couldn't be more hazardous than what I went through today. What is this news you have for me?"

"It's not good, I'm afraid." The man's voice sobered. "We got proof of life and an increased ransom demand."

"I thought you were paying the ransom." Lei frowned, her chest tightening with stress.

"We—there was a glitch with that. But things are progressing. We've got the kidnappers' location."

"Rescue ops often go wrong." Lei kept her voice calm with difficulty. "What is this proof of life?"

"I really can't say. But it shows that the hostage is alive, and like I said, plans are moving forward."

"The hostage? Only one hostage sent proof of life?" Lei was shrill.

"This call was a courtesy to keep you informed. The next time you hear from me will be when I have something to report that applies directly to your husband." Westbrook hung up, a soft click that felt utterly final.

She'd pissed him off with her questions, but now she was really alarmed. A rescue operation in a Central American country had too many ways it could go wrong. She set the Security Solutions phone down and picked up her regular cell phone, calling her tech friend Sophie Ang.

"Lei. I'm glad you called." Sophie's slightly husky, accented voice was tense. "I was going to contact you when I had this all put together, but it's been hard to tell what's really going on."

"I just got a phone call from Westbrook. Said they had another proof of life, but only for one hostage. And that they were mounting a rescue op."

Sophie hissed a breath. Lei had seen her do that before—Sophie's angled brows pulled down, full mouth pinched, brown eyes narrowed. "So that's what all this chatter is about. I've been doing a little hacking. Just looking, not messing with anything out there. I opened a file about the kidnapping. It appears that the army and Security Solutions weren't on the same page about paying the ransom. Security Solutions wanted to. According to their memo, 'That's what we have insurance for.' The army is sick of getting hit, especially down in Central America, and wants to find a way to send a message to kidnappers and rescue the victims at the same time. Your proof of life? It's an ear from a contractor named Carrigan. They sent video of it getting cut off, and the ear was sent to the rescue team."

"Oh my God," Lei whispered.

A knock came from the office door. "Mama? I'm scared." Kiet's voice sounded shaky.

Lei felt shaky, too. "Let me know the minute you know anything more. Kiet needs me right now, but I have to decide what to do."

"Don't do anything stupid!" Sophie exclaimed, but Lei ended the call.

There must be something she could do.

Lei went to the office door and unlocked it, dropping to embrace Kiet. "What's the matter, little man?"

"You were going to come back and watch TV with me." His lip quivered. Lei smoothed his glossy hair out of dark green eyes and her hand drifted down his soft cheek. What would a child she and Stevens might have look like when the one Anchara had given them was so beautiful?

"Just a half hour of TV. Then bath and bed." She took his hand. "What was interesting in school today?"

"Nothing." He put his thumb sulkily back in his mouth as they went into the living room and settled on the couch. He snuggled close, and she put an arm over him. She stroked his hair as they watched some Cartoon Network, and then she ran a bath for him.

He didn't want to get into the bath without her there, so Lei occupied herself cleaning, scrubbing, and spritzing the neglected sink and toilet while he took his bath, splashing happily as long as she stayed in the room.

She was going to have to talk to her longtime psychologist colleague, Dr. Wilson, about the problems Kiet was having. If their son found out Stevens was in trouble...Lei couldn't even complete the thought.

Eventually she got the boy down for the night in their big king-sized bed and was able to take her own shower. But she didn't have the energy for anything more than getting into bed with him, her hair still damp.

What a day.

Maybe tomorrow more things would become clear, like what she could do to help Stevens. Desperate as she felt about his situation, she couldn't think of one thing she could do that would help —and leaving Kiet was out of the question right now with his anxiety so flared up.

She could still pray.

On her back, her hands folded, she gazed up at the stucco ceiling. The plaster had been brushed on with a flat, spade-like implement. She remembered the day they'd done it. The house had been filled with friends helping them complete this last bit of work to make the place ready for occupation. A radio playing Hawaiian music had accompanied the mellow backbeat of friendly voices echoing slightly in the unfurnished space.

Lei had still been raw with sorrow over losing their baby and had worked back here in the bedroom alone, leaning up off of a ladder to swipe the stucco onto the ceiling, getting blobs of the hard white plaster in her hair.

Stevens had come in, tugged on her leg. "Take a break."

"I'm almost done." Lei was at the corner of the room. A couple more swipes. She shaped the ceiling material into a heart.

She pointed. "See? Done."

He laughed and tugged her leg again. "Come down here." Smiling, she descended the ladder and stowed the trowel.

He framed her face, hot from her exertions, in his big hands. She loved gazing into his crystal-blue eyes. "I like it. Sure you don't want to do the whole ceiling in hearts?"

"That would be cheesy."

He plucked a piece of stucco out of her hair. "And you are many things, but never cheesy."

He pulled her close, wrapping long arms around her. She fit just right against him, her head tilted and tucked in the notch between his neck and shoulder. They were both warm from working, and she breathed in his unique, slightly spicy scent. He kissed her, sweet and deep, a kiss filled with all the hopes he had for the new house. She'd answered the kiss with her own: dreams of peace, plenty, and family.

The kissing went on a while.

Pono had knocked on the doorframe and interrupted them. "At least shut da door if you goin' get up to dat kine," her partner drawled, his pidgin heavy with teasing.

Now, in the almost-dark of the bedroom, Lei could just see the fragile tracery of the heart in the stucco of the ceiling.

"God, bring him home," she whispered aloud. "Please, just bring him home."

CHAPTER NINETEEN

KERRY'S SKIN felt cold and rubbery and his body was floppy as I held him. Nausea swept through me at the tragedy. Kerry had been like a little brother, helping me and looking out for me from the first day I woke up in the pit. Here one moment, gone the next. Jesus, take him in your arms. I stroked Kerry's hair. It still felt alive, silky and resilient under my fingertips.

"Stop," I told Falconer, who was still sucking and spitting. "He's gone. Wash your mouth out really good."

Falconer let go of the young man's wrist, now swollen and red. Kerry's arm dropped limply onto the leaves. Falconer's face was a statue in carved ebony, expressionless and set. He lifted the canteen, sipped, swirled the water in his mouth, and spat.

Did it again.

"He's dead?" MacDonald's voice was charged with horror as he returned from his short walk. "Holy crap! He was alive five minutes ago!"

"That was one of those snakes whose venom is a paralytic," Falconer whispered. "I can tell because even a tiny amount has made my mouth numb."

"Get it all out," I told him. "We need you alive."

He hung his head, then nodded briefly and took another pull off the canteen.

"Son of a bitch! What the hell just happened here?" A burst of panicked adrenaline seemed to have hit MacDonald. "The kid's gone? Just like that? How do people live here?" He threw an arm wide in frustration. "This place! It's the ninth ring of hell!"

"People have lived here for thousands of years. We just don't know how to," I said.

MacDonald stomped back and forth, muttering furiously, swinging the rifle as he tried to assimilate what had just happened. Falconer and I sat numbly. I felt bad for the big black man. He'd saved us half a dozen times already, and the one time he tosses a snake, it nails one of us.

"It wasn't your fault. It was an accident."

"Doesn't matter how it happened. He's still dead." Falconer retched. I watched the man closely to see if he was going to succumb to the poison as well. Finally he stopped dry-heaving, sat back on his heels, and covered his face with his hands.

MacDonald had a lot more energy than I did right now, and he could put it to use. "We need to bury the body as best we can. Use the stick to dig. I'll take anything useful off the body," I told him.

Falconer stood and picked up his walking stick. The two men found an open area and began digging, gouging the pointed ends of the sticks into the soil to soften it, then scraping it away. It was going to take a while and burn a lot of time and energy, but just leaving our companion to rot was out of the question.

I removed Kerry's dog tags and a cross on a silver chain from around his neck. If we made it to safety, his family would treasure these. I rolled his body over and unbuttoned his shirt. Crude as it was, we needed everything we could use, beginning with the shirt. I took it off, and then tore strips from his undershirt. I was able to shed the banana-leaf dressing and tie the rags around my wound, which was still oozing and angry-looking.

I took off Kerry's belt. "Do we need his boots? Pants?" I asked the other men.

Both shook their heads and went on with their grim chore.

"We might as well make our fire and cook." The thought of eating made me queasy, but we needed to be practical. "We've been here a while, and we'll be here a while longer."

"You know how to start a fire?" Falconer tipped his head, assessing.

"I know the bow method. I just need the knife and some dry wood."

"That'll do. I'll help if you run into problems."

I stood and shuffled through the damp leaves, picking up a pile of sticks and finding a small log. It seemed the driest of the lot, but I needed it bone-dry.

Perhaps some fiber would help. I could make the string for the bow out of fiber, too.

I picked a green branch and peeled it, bent it into a two-foot bow and tied a narrow strip of fabric off Kerry's pants to it as the string. Whittling a bowl-like hollow into the log, I set aside the dry shavings and mixed them with cut-up cotton fibers from Kerry's clothing. Finally, I found a sturdy stick, carved a sharp point, peeled the damp bark off it, and then, using the bow, began spinning the stick in the bowl of the log. The tinder piled around the point of the spinning stick would provide fuel for the spark and heat as it developed.

Falconer and MacDonald moved loosened soil out of the area they'd dug with their hands. Falconer got up and came over to inspect my rig. "Not bad," he said, as I began the spinning.

He returned to the hole and I kept going.

The tiniest breeze moved down on us through a hole in the thick canopy far above. I was sweating freely as I worked the bow. It was tricky to hold the log, work the bow, and not lose balance of some part of the rig. After five or so minutes I could feel heat

145

being generated by the friction of the stick's spinning point in the bottom of the bowl.

Falconer sniffed. "I smell smoke." He came to check my progress again. We both watched the spinning point of the stick. My shoulders had begun to cramp, and he must have noticed because he reached out and took the bow. "You go help dig. Just don't open up your side."

I surrendered the bow and he continued the spinning without missing a stroke. It was essential that, once started, the motion and friction be maintained. Falconer had come in at just the right time, with fresh energy.

MacDonald was loosening soil out at the edge of the pit as I joined him. "If you can keep digging the soil, I'll scoop it out," I said, and he nodded.

Looking at MacDonald was like watching a human figure melt, as the man's pudginess disappeared, leaving bags and folds behind. MacDonald's plump, rosy cheeks had imploded into pale flaps of skin that hung off craggy cheekbones. He didn't look better thin.

He stabbed the soil with the stick, and I scooped.

"Do you think Falconer meant to throw the snake on Kerry?" MacDonald whispered.

I frowned. "You're joking, right?"

"Maybe he's not leading us in the right direction," MacDonald said. "Maybe he wants something."

I rocked back on my heels, forgetting my injury for a moment. I clutched my side with a groan. "You're paranoid."

"His kind always has another agenda."

"His kind?" I hissed. "You mean—what, exactly?"

"He's black." MacDonald had the grace to flush a little.

"Yeah, and you're an asshole," I snarled. "Shut the hell up, man."

"Something wrong?" Sweat gleamed on Falconer's forehead and muscular arms as he looked up at us, but the man was a machine. He didn't slow for a minute.

"Nothing. This guy's just not thinking straight after what happened." I narrowed my eyes at MacDonald. "Feel free to leave. Good luck making it fifty feet without us."

"Sorry." MacDonald spat after he said it, and it came a little close to me. If I hadn't been in danger of opening up my wound, I'd have taken him down right there.

"I'm gonna remember what you said," I hissed quietly. "If you give Falconer any shit, you aren't coming out of this alive. Get me? We'll just leave you behind." I didn't like what I was seeing come out of the camp manager.

"Now who's paranoid?" MacDonald hissed, but he shut up after that. We worked faster. Anger was fuel.

"Got it!" Falconer exclaimed. A tiny blossom of flame bloomed in the bowl of the log. "Help me feed it!"

I'd made a pile of tinder and sticks beside the fire rig, and I came to help Falconer strengthen the flame. Gradually we got the fire to accept damp sticks, though it smoked sluggishly.

"We need a bigger log," Falconer said. "This fire is never going to get big enough to cook anything without more fuel. You stay here and keep it going. MacDonald, let's get some more wood."

I narrowed my eyes at MacDonald. He tightened his mouth, dropping the digging stick. The two of them moved off as I nursed the tender flame, keeping it alive but trying not to blow so hard it went out.

I glanced over at Kerry's face for the first time since the young man had been bitten. I hadn't been able to do anything but focus on one area of his body at a time before.

His neck, checking his pulse.

His mangled wrist, as Falconer made a vain effort to keep the poison from making it to Kerry's heart.

The sad mechanics of rifling Kerry's pockets and removing his clothing had helped keep me from really seeing him.

Now, in this moment alone, I could really look at the man's face. Lying on his back, his eyes closed, Kerry looked young and peaceful, sprawled as if he'd fallen asleep—but his bloody wrist, resting against the forest floor, was already crawling with ants.

I restrained the impulse to brush them away. They couldn't hurt him now.

I swallowed the grief and regret locked in my throat.

I found more sticks, scooped the leaves away, and dug around the small glow of flame, preparing for a bigger fire. It wasn't long before I heard the sounds of the other men's approach. MacDonald and Falconer returned, hauling a good-sized fallen log, bristly with protruding branches.

"This was under another windfall," Falconer panted. "So it's mostly dry."

I handed over the knife, and Falconer hacked off the dry branches, feeding them into the flame. With the addition of the extra fuel, the fire stabilized and we were able to eventually work in the larger log.

"I'll make a rack for us to roast the pig. If you could finish…" Falconer gestured to the hole and the body.

I stood, and MacDonald and I got back to work, chiseling out another three inches from the bottom of the pit. I uncovered a rock in the soil—but when I went to throw it out, I noticed a shape to it. Dimples with regularity, two points on one side. I sat back on my heels and brushed the dirt off.

I was holding a small stone carving, no bigger than the palm of Kiet's hand. By the pointed ears, I thought it must be a jaguar's head, though it was so stylized as to not look like any cat my Western mind had seen. I dimly remembered reading an article about the recent discovery of a lost city in the Honduran jungle. I held it up. "Look. I think it's a jaguar head."

"What is it?" MacDonald frowned, reaching for the artifact. He frowned. "It's the devil. See the horns?" He pointed to the jaguar's ears. As if it had been conjured by the carving, we heard a yowling cry, not that far off, which I was pretty sure came from a real jaguar.

We smelled the stink of burning hair as Falconer got the pig up on a rack he'd built over the fire.

"Sorry about the smell," he said. "If I skin it, we'll lose a lot of the nutrition in the cooking process."

"I've never cooked a whole pig before. I grew up in LA. I was twelve before I realized that meat didn't come wrapped in plastic from a meat factory," I said. "MacDonald, give me back that carving."

"It will bring bad luck. Might even attract the jaguar." MacDonald tightened his mouth. He still looked pale and sweaty, and his blue eyes skittered away from mine, but he thrust the carving into my hand.

"I heard that jaguars were endangered and very shy." I slid the stone into my pocket. "I don't believe that shit about luck and the devil. But I do think we've got this hole as deep as we're going to be able to. Let's do this."

One on each side, MacDonald and I moved Kerry's body into the hole. We'd been able to get down only eighteen inches or so into the root-bound soil, but that would have to do. We laid Kerry on his back and twisted his body at the hips. We folded his knees so that he fit into the five-foot hole. He was already stiffening slightly at the joints with the beginning of rigor.

The pig cooked merrily, with a delicious odor that was sure to attract every predator for miles around. Falconer joined us, and using our hands, we moved the soil back over Kerry. All three of us patted it down, smoothing it. MacDonald suddenly gave a harsh sob.

"This isn't right," he muttered. Tears slid down his pallid cheeks. "This isn't right."

"It isn't," I agreed. "And it could be any of us. This jungle is home to some of the most venomous snakes in the world."

I watched MacDonald fight down the angry words he wanted to say condemning Falconer. I knew that helpless feeling of waste and rage, the desire for revenge, the need to blame. I'd been through all that too many times. I simply weathered those feelings now, waiting for them to pass. But MacDonald wasn't experienced in death. This was probably his first real emergency situation, and he didn't know how to handle it.

Blaming Falconer wasn't the way to handle it.

We tamped the soil down. Falconer found a puddle of trapped rainwater in a bird's-nest fern. In the cuplike center of the plant, we washed the dirt off our hands as best we could.

Falconer turned the pig. The fat dripped off of it, sizzling on the wood beneath. I wished that we didn't have to lose one drop, but perhaps we could gnaw on the wood later. I almost smiled at the thought, but that didn't feel right with Kerry's body cooling in a grave mere feet away.

"Damn it," I muttered, taking off my boots and socks. No, nothing about this situation was right.

My ruined feet had not liked the hike in the boots. The blisters and contusions from the other day were oozing, red and raw. I extended my feet to the fire to dry, hanging the filthy socks off the end of the stick piercing the pig. "Sorry about that. I have to get them as dry as I can."

Falconer made a dismissive gesture. "No worries."

We might as well learn a little more about each other while we waited for the meat to cook—talking might ease the tensions since Kerry had died so abruptly.

"What brought you to this godforsaken jungle?" I asked MacDonald. "Got a family at home?"

MacDonald shook his head. His loose cheeks wobbled. "Nah. I have a girlfriend, but we were saving for a house and a big wedding. I thought this would speed that up." He made a gesture that took in the dense, heavy jungle, soporifically hot now that the sun was out. A cloud of gnats broke up and reformed as his arm cut through them. "So you know something about the snakes here, Falconer? Is that why you threw a deadly one on Kerry?"

Falconer looked up from where he squatted, turning the pig on its wooden spit. "It was a reflex. An accident."

"We talked about this already." I narrowed my eyes warningly at MacDonald. "We're damn lucky to have someone with Falconer's skills leading the way."

"I don't know about that." MacDonald's cheeks flushed a dull red. "Seems like things are getting worse out here rather than better. You're injured, and he's got the knife. And the pig."

Falconer stood to his feet, a slow, menacing uncoiling. "Is this what you meant by MacDonald's thinking being messed up by what happened, Stevens?"

"Yeah. MacDonald seems to be having a mental breakdown." I lowered my hand to rest on the pistol, tucked in my waistband. But MacDonald was holding the machine gun. One burst from the M16 and he'd have the whole pig, and everything else, to himself. "But I'm sure all he needs is something to eat." As if to increase our longing, a drip of fat burst into flame with a smell so powerful I felt it, hot and delicious, on the insides of my nostrils. "Perhaps there's something ready enough that you could hack a piece off for him, Falconer."

Falconer's eyes rested on the rifle in the other man's hands and then he turned to the pig. "That can be arranged." He used the knife to carve into the haunch. Drippings of fat and juice splattered on the wood, making it flare and smoke. The smell reminded me of every campfire I'd sat around as a Boy Scout with a pork dog bursting on a stick—but better.

A plant with large, paddle-shaped leaves grew nearby, and I picked several leaves, layering them into a crude plate. Falconer set a large section of meat, moist and still pink, but by far the most delicious-looking thing I'd ever seen, on the leaves. Using both hands, he carried it to MacDonald.

I held my breath as MacDonald watched Falconer approach, the weapon ready. When Falconer stood before him, tall and calm, meeting his eyes, MacDonald realized that to take the meat, he had to set the gun down.

He did, leaning it against a nearby tree and taking the meat from Falconer. He didn't thank the other man. While MacDonald's hands were full, I leaned over and snatched the rifle.

"I'll just carry this for a while."

Falconer walked back to the fire and flipped the pig again. Both of us tried to ignore the sights and sounds of MacDonald's frenzied attack on the piece of meat. It didn't sound pretty, and I wasn't surprised when he suddenly stopped eating, breathing heavily.

"I'll have to kill you if you puke that up." Falconer didn't look at the man as he said this, just added more wood to the fire.

MacDonald managed not to puke. I gazed out at the jungle, scanning for danger and waiting for the meat to cook the rest of the way.

There wasn't any movement, but shifting shades of green and brown as far as I could see. A few buzzing flies, fat and hovering, had found us along with the gnats and mosquitoes. Far off in the treetops, I could hear a troop of monkeys screaming and whooping. A tiny wind shushed in the leaves above us. The smell of roasting pork was heavy perfume in my nostrils.

Falconer eventually served us and tamped the fire, and finally I sank my teeth into the crispy hind leg he'd given me. Nothing had ever tasted as good as the sweet, tender, juicy, perfectly done piece of meat I ate down to the bone. I gnawed slowly, pausing every few bites to savor and make sure my stomach was able to handle the rich food.

MacDonald lay down on his back, belching ominously now and again, but he seemed to have fallen into a stupor—an improvement over his aggressive, paranoid state of mind.

After we ate, Falconer rewrapped the remaining meat in the shirt. "I'll carry this with you, MacDonald."

The other man grunted.

"We should get on our way. See how far we can make it while there's still daylight," Falconer said.

"Sounds good." I had finished eating, thrown the bones far out into the bushes. As Falconer packed the meat into its crude carrying sling, I fashioned a cross of two sticks and a piece of vine. I anchored it in the middle of the grave. "Does anyone want to say a few words over Kerry before we go?"

"I do." Falconer walked over to stand next to me. He bent his head and prayed aloud, his big square hands folded. "Our Father, who art in heaven, hallowed be thy name." The familiar words of the Lord's Prayer in his deep mellow voice were calming to me. I closed my eyes to listen.

MacDonald clawed his way out of the food coma enough to sit up and bow his head. "You were a good man, Kerry. I swear I'll get you justice."

I didn't like his words. It was my turn, and I worked the cross a little deeper into the soil and spoke casually, as if Kerry were right with us.

"You were brave and kind, Tim." He'd told me his first name, but this was the first time I'd used it. "I wish you'd had longer on this earth, because I can tell you were the kind of man who had the makings of a hero. You never spoke a harsh word, even at the end. You worked hard, carried your load, and helped others. The world needs more like you, Tim Kerry."

I patted the soil gently, as if covering the young man for the night with a blanket. It comforted me to imagine that was what I was doing. I stood slowly, keeping my arm tight against my injured side.

"Can you take some sort of heading for this spot, Falconer? So we can send a team to come find Kerry and bring him home when we get out of here."

Falconer looked at the compass and nodded. "I'll mark a tree." With the knife, he slashed a deep X. And that was all we could do.

MacDonald was still breathing heavily, his face greasy, but he picked up the carrying pole without complaining and put it on his shoulder. Falconer took the lead with the compass. I hung the rifle by its strap over my shoulder and took one last look around the tiny clearing where we'd fought a life-and-death battle, and lost.

I forced my ruined feet to move, and followed the others.

CHAPTER TWENTY

FALCONER KEPT us on an eastward heading as we pushed through the jungle. "I'm going to angle us back toward the river. We'll have to go around any serious water, though."

We had to go around other kinds of obstacles, too. Fallen, rotting logs covered with orange lichen and sprouting with ferns. Half-grown trees, coming up in clumps and pushing toward the sun, were too dense to navigate between. Mounds of debris from downed trees slowed our progress even more. Now keeping an eye out for snakes was even more of a priority.

Something huge and black burst out of the bushes in a flurry of breaking branches. MacDonald yelped, and my finger tightened on the trigger of the rifle as it snorted, bolting away. I still had the safety on, and was glad as the creature broke into a lumbering gallop, running away from us. It was even larger than the sow we'd surprised, hairy and black, but it didn't look like any kind of predator. "What the hell!"

"A tapir," Falconer said. "Really rare."

Something hit the back of my head with a solid thunk. I whirled, swinging the rifle around at the threat. A black-and-white monkey gave a shriek from the tops of the trees. Several more monkeys joined him. The creatures threw green nuts, twigs, and leaves at us, screaming an alarm that we'd breached their kingdom.

"Give me the weapon! Demons! Demons are attacking us!" MacDonald yelled. His eyes were ringed with white like a panicked horse. He lunged at me, grabbing for the rifle. I spun away.

"No! Damn it, man. They're just monkeys!" I wasn't about to give MacDonald the gun so he could waste ammo shooting at the obnoxious creatures. MacDonald made a grab for the pistol in my waistband. I barely leaped back in time. I cracked him in the face with the rifle butt. "Back off!"

MacDonald reeled back, hands to his bloody nose, but then jumped at me again, scratching and clawing. "Demons! Obeying the devil!" he screamed.

MacDonald had officially gone nuts.

Falconer caught him from behind and lifted the man right off his feet, choking him into unconsciousness in just a few struggling moments. He lowered MacDonald to the forest floor.

"I think he's snapped." I knelt next to MacDonald, taking his pulse. It was fast but regular. "This is the last thing we need."

"Especially with all this going on." Falconer gestured to the shrieking monkeys. A nut cracked down on Falconer's back, and he swore. "I'm tempted to shoot one. We could eat it."

"Not a bad idea. A bird in the hand. I bet that would scare them off, too." I handed Falconer the automatic and pulled my pistol, aiming up at the monkeys.

But I wasn't hungry enough or desperate enough to pull the trigger. The monkeys were just too humanlike, brown eyes gleaming with intelligence from their furry faces as they speculated loudly about us among themselves. I lowered the weapon. "Don't want to give away our location. Let's restrain MacDonald and see what's going on with him when he comes around."

Falconer nodded. He used the knife to rip a strip of material off the old shirt the pork was wrapped in. He tied MacDonald's hands in front of him. I tested the bonds, making sure they were loose enough but that he couldn't get out of them.

MacDonald came around, his eyelids fluttering. The monkeys had begun to settle, but one still heaved a nut just as he woke up. He screamed at the sight of the animal in the trees far above, and his cry brought the monkeys swarming back, shrieking and pelting again.

I smacked MacDonald on the cheek. "Shut up, man! You're agitating them."

"We're in hell!" MacDonald said. "And he's the devil!" He lifted his bound hands to point at Falconer. "He's trying to kill us!"

I tipped my head in the direction of the shirt, and Falconer nodded briefly, cutting off another strip. This one he handed to me, and I gagged MacDonald. He continued to moan and emit muffled cries.

"I guess I have to lead," I told Falconer. "Since you're the devil."

The big black man shook his head. "Great timing for him to lose his marbles."

"I need to get a direction." Falconer handed me the knife, and I looked at the compass on the haft to get a heading. As we ignored the monkeys, they lost interest and eventually swung easily away between the trees. Falconer bent to help MacDonald stand, but the man rolled away, grunting in terror, from his touch.

"He might run off in the state he's in." I frowned, looking down at the man. He'd shut his eyes, and beads of sweat ran down his pale face. "Devan MacDonald. Listen to me." He opened his eyes, but there was no recognition in them. I turned back to Falconer. "Gonna have to tie him to me. If he runs off, he's going to die for sure."

Falconer nodded. "Maybe some vine could work." I cut a length of the tough, fibrous vine we'd been tripping on so frequently. I tied one end of it through MacDonald's wrist restraints and the other to my belt. "Okay, here we go."

He seemed to settle after that, muttering and moaning into his gag but following me. Falconer brought up the rear, carrying the meat, his pistol at the ready.

It was slow going. I hadn't realized how much effort it took to push through the undergrowth, watching for snakes and other hazards, and how easily we got off track without the compass being constantly watched.

After fifteen minutes or so, I stopped. "I'll follow you," I told Falconer. "You lead." I could feel my wound weeping damply, a wetness at my side. I handed Falconer the knife, and he moved past MacDonald to get in front of me.

MacDonald reared back at the sight of Falconer, snapping the vine, and lumbered away, his cries terrified but mercifully muted by the gag. I tried to pursue, but my wound pulsed at the exertion, and I halted, hunched over and sweating.

"Let him go. I'm tired of this shit," Falconer said.

"We can't! He's bound and he's off his nut. He'll die for sure. Please. Get him."

Falconer rolled his eyes, but he ran after MacDonald at an efficient trot. I'd have to remember to recommend him for some kind of medal. I squatted down, panting, and shook my head. Who knew what would set someone off? MacDonald had seemed so normal.

It seemed to take forever for Falconer to reappear. He'd tied a vine around MacDonald's neck to lead him, because every few feet the man would rear back, trying to get away.

"This is getting old," Falconer said ominously, and slapped the vine into my hand. He pushed forward through the underbrush, frustration in every movement.

"Come on, Devan. We're gonna get through this, but you have to cooperate. We have to follow Falconer." I gave a tug, and MacDonald complied, stumbling but obedient.

We caught up with Falconer as he was taking a heading on the compass knife. "The river's that way." He pointed. "We've run out of the luxury of taking our time. Between your wound and MacDonald's breakdown, we need to get out of here sooner rather than later."

"Agreed. Even if we end up back in the water."

He gave a curt nod, and we struck out in the new direction.

LEI SAT down in one of the visitor chairs in front of Captain Omura's desk the next morning. Wayne had driven her to work and Kiet to school, and she'd given up on her hair, settling for restraint and twisting it into a ball at the back of her head with a rubber band. She and Kiet had both slept badly and then woken up late, and with that rough start, she was just happy she'd been able to get Kiet to school on time.

"I need a full catch-up on yesterday's events." Omura flipped through their file. The captain's makeup was immaculate and her nails were glossy red—but she hadn't had to get a fussy kindergartener to school before work like Lei had.

"Me too." Pono arrived, carrying two chipped MPD mugs. He plunked one down in front of Lei. "I put creamer in for you. Because I'm a good partner like that."

Lei picked up the mug. Chunks of white powder floated in the heavy brew. She stirred it with the little red plastic stir stick he'd thoughtfully included. "Thanks, bro. Yeah, that little field trip into the valley turned out to be more than I bargained for."

Omura leveled a shiny fingernail at her. "What were you thinking, going up into that valley alone?"

"I was thinking that skull washed down from a deserted, overgrown little canyon, and I'd just have a look for any recently flooded areas and stretch my legs before I drove all the way back to Kahului. I tried to call Pono." Lei sipped her coffee and made a face.

"And I got about every third word of your message. If you

159

hadn't called in later, I'd never have tracked you out there," Pono said.

"Yes, you would. I started with Mrs. Yamaguchi, who found the skull. She'd have told you what I was doing." Lei described her talk with the elderly Hana resident. "And then I thought, a little hike before that long drive back was a good idea. But everything went to hell once I got inside that secret valley." She described the pot fields, the foster boys working, Boss Man, and the pit bull's attack. "Hell is too good for that bastard," she finished. "Any luck on the BOLO we called in?"

"Not so far. He's gone to ground. But I have the coconut wireless fired up for any rumors. Someone knows him. A lot of some-ones, for him to move that much Maui Wowie pakalolo." Pono's network of confidential informants was legendary in the Maui Police Department. Her partner took a gulp of his coffee and smacked his lips in apparent enjoyment. "I thought I'd poke around with the tax maps, see who owns that property. That could generate a lead."

"Hold on a minute." Captain Omura's forehead was smooth as porcelain, her hair as black and glossy as the first day Lei had met her. Did Cherry Joy Omura do Botox? No. Omura was just natu-rally sweatless, poreless, wrinkle-free perfection. Lei wished she could hate her for it as the captain went on. "This is a narcotics case. Your only part is finding out something about the skull."

"Well, the foster boys that were working the place don't know anything, but if Noah Whatshisname had them, he's had others. He had a way of "graduating" the child slaves into adult service for him." Lei described the teen she'd restrained and then rescued, and then the grenade scare one of the boys had perpetrated. "Tony wouldn't talk yesterday, but a night in jail might have softened him up. Pono, you should tell Detective Shepherd that idea about the TMK maps."

"Okay. You go down and interview that kid, see if he knows about any other kids he worked with who might have disappeared.

This kid Tony might be willing to talk about that, even if he's not willing to throw his boss under the bus. But be sure to coordinate with the narco detectives working this. Not too much interviewing the kid. I can hear the defense attorneys now, talking about Stockholm and trauma effects on a young mind." Omura sat back. "Keep me informed. Speaking of, is there any news on Stevens?"

"Nothing yet." Lei didn't want to deal with Pono and Omura's questions and exclamations, when what did she really know? Only that Stevens was still in danger and that there was nothing she could do to help him.

"Well, I called Dr. Wilson and let her know you were involved in a shooting incident. She'll be contacting you to do your debrief sometime today."

"Oh, good." Lei thought of her son's adjustment issues. "I have a lot to talk with her about."

"You're the only person I get that from when I tell them they have to talk to the psychologist." Omura smiled. "But it means she does a good job."

"She has spooky eyes." Pono shuddered. "She can see the inside of my head."

"Her eyes are just—very intelligent." Lei defended her former therapist. "And very blue. I've gotten used to blue eyes." Her eyes filled, and she looked away, blinking. "I better get going."

"Keep me informed. Of everything," Omura said. Lei sketched a salute and hurried out the door, Pono in her wake.

CHAPTER TWENTY-ONE

THE VEGETATION LIGHTENED up beneath the jungle canopy, which made moving forward easier, but it seemed a long, stumbling, slow and uncertain way before we reached an edge to the tree line.

"Looks like some cultivation ahead." Falconer squatted and took cover behind one of the native kapok trees. Ahead of us, the jungle had been cleared away. Rows of corn blocked visibility to what I assumed was the river beyond. "Let's watch a little while. See if we spot any people."

I tugged MacDonald's leash. He sat on the ground behind me, watching Falconer's hunched, vigilant shape.

The light waned as evening approached. In spite of the pain throbbing in my side and feet, I enjoyed the sight of layered cumulous clouds in a sky streaked with the salmon of sunset after the smothering dim green of the jungle. It took me straight back to life on Maui, where days began with a sky festival and ended with a fireworks celebration—an ever-changing panorama of brilliant layered clouds playing around the great purple volcano that held down one end of the island: Haleakala, House of the Sun. A stab of homesickness hit me somewhere in the chest. "Please, God. Just get me home."

"What?" Falconer turned to me, alert.

"Nothing," I murmured. "What's the plan?"

"I don't see anyone. So let's just keep moving forward across these fields and find the river. The corn is close to harvest. They're bound to be watching the fields, to keep birds and animals away, and maybe we can get help."

"Farmers should be safe to approach," I agreed.

We moved out of the shelter of the trees into the rows of corn. Unlike corn in the United States, these plants were short, only chest-high. The ears were smaller, and the stalks denser with them. I picked one as we passed through the rustling stalks, stripping the husk off and biting into the raw cob.

The kernels were juicy, sweet, and starchy. I touched Falconer's back to stop him. "These are good. Let's pick a few."

"Not too many. We don't want to piss off the farmers."

I nodded agreement and caught MacDonald's eye. He looked blank, checked out, but I addressed him as if he understood. "Will you be quiet if I take the gag off?"

He didn't answer. I removed the cloth, and he licked dry lips gratefully as the gag fell away. I handed him the cob I'd already peeled. "Here. Eat." He took it and bit into it.

I picked several more ears, and Falconer and I each ate one. The starchy sweet goodness broke across my teeth, delicious, but after only a few bites, I felt my stomach rebelling. "Maybe we shouldn't eat too much."

"Agreed." We stowed the extra ears in our pockets and continued on.

The river, when we reached it, was dramatically different from the previous day. Chocolate-brown roiling had been replaced by a broad swath of brownish green. Boils and swirls still marked it, showing the speed and power of the water, but the foam and trees of flood were gone.

Falconer scanned the banks. Someone, the farmers probably, had shored the area up with stones to keep the muddy banks from eroding. A small dock had been built behind a sheltering curve in the bank.

"There." I pointed. "Let's wait there for someone to come along. Someone is taking care of this corn, and I don't think they're coming from the jungle."

"Agreed. We should eat the rest of this pork before it spoils."

A mango tree sheltered the dock, and the three of us squatted beneath the tree. Remarkably, my appetite was back, as if the starchy corn had been some sort of accelerant. MacDonald and I dug into the pork chunks Falconer hacked off for us, and with no difficulty, the three of us polished off the last of the pig.

I rinsed my hands in the deep jade water swirling around the legs of the pier. The color of it reminded me of my son's eyes. I missed him with a sudden ache that dried my mouth and made my eyes prickle. I hoped the little man was doing okay. The voice mail he'd left for me before we were taken was etched on my memory as he told me he wanted me to come home and that he loved me. His piping voice had been wobbly.

Kiet was a sensitive kid. I had always wondered if his mother's traumatic death, resulting in his abrupt birth, had done a number on his nervous system. He was alert to changes and, though a happy and loving boy, he liked to make sure we were both there and that everything was routine. If things got too stressful, he had night terrors, sitting up in bed and screaming, but still asleep. They were a terrifying experience as a parent, though the pediatrician had assured us that some kids just had them and he'd grow out of it.

Lei was a patient, loving, and physically hands-on mom. She was instinctively good with Kiet, but didn't hesitate to ask for help when she didn't know how to handle something that came up. Her fears about her past making her a bad parent had been unfounded —as I'd known they'd be. Her own childhood abuse had made her extra sensitive, if anything.

People assumed Kiet was our natural child—but I knew that

someday we'd have to tell him about his birth mother. I'd dreaded it, until now.

Swishing my hands in the green water, I was willing to believe I'd seen Anchara's ghost here in Honduras—and we'd made some kind of peace. I wasn't apprehensive about telling Kiet about her anymore. I'd have the words I'd need when the time came. I was deeply grateful to Anchara. She'd given me Kiet. He was all she'd cared about in the last moments of her life.

Back under the mango tree, I addressed Falconer. "Let's take turns watching and getting some rest. It's getting dark. I doubt the farmers will be coming back until tomorrow."

"I want to check out your ribs."

I'd been afraid he was going to say that. Frankly, I worried about what we'd find when we took off the crude bandage.

"No point. We have no way to clean it or do anything about it, and right now it's at least covered. I'll deal with it when we've got some way to treat it."

Falconer gave me a long look, then nodded. "You rest. But tie him up before you do."

MacDonald was already lying on the ground on his back, snoring in the humid, deepening twilight. I tied the vine attached to his wrists to one of the pilings and lay down, bunching the smelly shirt that had wrapped the pig into a crude pillow and stuffing it under my head.

I fell asleep like falling down a well, and was thankful for the oblivion.

"I'm coming with you to interview Tony the teen hood." Pono caught up with Lei as they left Omura's office.

"What about our other cases?"

"Nothing too critical happening. We have that tourist floater that's probably accidental, and the two overdoses. Kinda in between big ones right now. Got to admit, I never expected your cold case to get so hot."

"Me neither. I need to call down to the jail and get him moved to an interview room, and follow up with Dr. Gregory about the age of the skull. It could turn out to be unrelated to the pot farm."

"That would be good to rule out."

Back at their cubicle, Pono booted up his e-mail while Lei worked the phone. She called Detective Shepherd and invited him and his partner to sit in so they didn't duplicate efforts. "I just want to ask Tony about this one thing—the skull," Lei told him.

"Glad you called. We were going to pull him this afternoon," Shepherd said. "We've been trying to track Noah No-name this morning. We had some supposed sightings on the tip line, but nothing's panning out. Can you push your interview back to then? Because I have some Hana PD officers going out to pick up the female foster parent, Selina Tahua. I'm hoping she's willing to snitch on Noah in return for reduced charges."

"That sounds good. I'll wait to hear from you. In the meantime, I can go visit the other foster boys, see if anything new emerges," Lei said.

"I'll let you know as soon as I get anything on Selina Tahua."

"Excellent. Speaking of, my partner had an idea." Lei told him about looking up the TMK map of the property where the pot farm was located. "That place was so well-established. There must be some connection between the landowner and Noah. He couldn't squat for long in that valley without permission."

"Good lead," Shepherd said. "I hear your partner, Pono, has a great CI network, too."

"Yeah, and he's put the word out." Lei turned to smile at her partner, the phone wedged between her chin and shoulder. "He'll call you if one of his people gets something."

Pono's dark eyes gleamed like polished kukui nuts as he nodded.

"Appreciate it." Shepherd hung up.

167

TOBY NEAL

Lei called Elizabeth Black next. She got the location of the boys' crisis home and permission for a visit. "They keep asking for you, so I'm glad you called," Elizabeth said.

"Have they talked any more about the fake foster parents?"

"We did a bare-bones intake interview, but my priority was getting them moved and settled. The foster family at the transition home says they're doing okay, except for Dexter. He's hardly talking, won't get out of bed. I have a psychologist going out later on today."

"Okay. Thanks. And, by the way, you were right to tell me no about taking the boys home. I've got my hands full with my son and with Stevens gone. But it makes me think we might try foster parenting someday." Lei hadn't realized that was what she was concluding until the words came out of her mouth.

"I think you'd be wonderful at that. But you are also a workaholic. The two may not be compatible," Elizabeth said. "Still, seasons change in people's lives. Makes me smile to think about you as a foster mom."

"Makes me smile, too." Lei ended the call thoughtfully. If she and Stevens never had their own child, perhaps this was a way they could expand their family. The idea comforted her, warm as sliding her feet through sun-warmed sand.

"I thought we were going to interview that Tony kid." Pono glanced up from his monitor.

"Later. I'm visiting the foster boys while Shepherd follows up with Selina Tahua, the fake foster parent." Lei stood. "Want to come?"

"Nah. I'll work on our other cases. Call me when it's time to go to the jail."

"Coward. You're afraid you'll end up bringing one of those boys home."

"Exactly right. Tiare's banned me from going to the Humane Society, too—we already have five former fighting cocks and three dogs."

168

"Glad I'm not the only one." Lei squeezed Pono's bulky shoulder affectionately.

Out at the truck Pono had loaned her, Lei checked the satellite phone. No news on Stevens. She turned on the vehicle with a sigh and programmed her GPS to the boys' foster home address.

The house was a modest concrete block ranch in Kahului's warren of residential streets. An avocado tree shaded a yard dry as the California foothills. A mailbox painted in a black-and-white cow pattern proclaimed the address, and Lei pulled up and parked behind a couple of bikes lying in the driveway behind a minivan.

Lei approached through the garage, where a pile of rubber slippers beside the mat proclaimed the main entrance to the house. She knocked.

A short, round Filipina woman appeared, wiping her hands on a dish towel. Delicious smells wafted through the door—chicken, pineapple, and spices. "Can I help you?"

"Hi. I'm Sergeant Texeira." Lei held up her badge. "I came to see the boys who arrived last night?"

"Aunty!" Danny's smiling face nudged under the woman's elbow, bringing an answering grin to Lei's face. "You came!"

"Welcome to our home," the woman said, opening the screen door to Lei. "Philomena Butaga. Elizabeth speaks highly of you. I see you were expected. Danny, go tell the other boys they have a visitor."

The boy trotted off. Butaga extended a dimpled hand to Lei, and she shook the woman's hand. "Thanks. I think highly of Elizabeth, too. Are the boys doing all right?"

"As well as can be expected. My husband and I keep our home available for those first tough days after kids are removed. We have low expectations. I just try to get them cooking, eating, and sleeping. Our goal is to stabilize them, let them know there are kind people and plenty in the world."

Danny and Kekoa returned. Lei could tell they wanted to hug her, but they hung back. She opened her arms. "I sure missed you guys." They came then and pressed against her, their arms crossing over one another's. "Where's Dexter?" Lei asked over their heads.

"He's in bed. He's not talking." Kekoa's voice came out muffled as his lean brown face pressed against her sternum. Lei remembered how good it had felt to finally hug someone, her Aunty Rosario, after she'd been rescued by Child Protective Services from the house where her mother had died. That the boys had attached to her so intensely was a weighty gift.

"Let's go see him."

"Yeah, and when you boys get back, I could sure use some help with this adobo." Butaga stirred a pot on the stove.

Danny towed Lei down a dimly lit, linoleum-tiled hall. The boys were between ten and thirteen years old, but their behavior was that of younger children—a product of their enslavement and trauma.

Dexter was lying on the bottom mattress of a pair of bunk beds, his back turned to the room. A TV, DVD player, and game system dominated one side of the small room, and nests of blankets on the floor showed what the boys had been doing before Lei's arrival.

"Didn't I tell you straight?" Lei pointed at the game system. "Soft beds, lots of food, and all the video games you could want."

Dexter heard her voice and rolled over. His dark eyes, meeting hers, were expressionless. She dropped to her knees beside his bunk and stroked his rough black hair off his forehead. "Hey, buddy. You okay?"

He shook his head.

"It's normal not to feel okay after what happened. After what Uncle did to you." It was important to acknowledge what the boys had been through without dramatizing it. "I smell Aunty Philomena cooking adobo." Lei sniffed theatrically. "I know the smell of good adobo anywhere. She told me she needs help. Can you boys go help her? I want to talk to Dexter for a minute."

"Okay. But when we get back, you have to play video games with us," Danny said.

"Deal."

The other two boys left, and Lei sat beside Dexter's bunk. "My friend Elizabeth said she was sending someone to talk to you. I know you may not want to, but you should tell them what happened. It helps."

Dexter's brown eyes were blank as old pennies. Lei drew a breath, let it out. "I know a little what you are going through. I was rescued and went to a crisis home, like this one, when I was younger than you."

His gaze flicked over her, lingering on the badge clipped on her belt and her sidearm in its shoulder holster. She read disbelief in that look.

"It's true. My mom was on drugs, and she had a bad boyfriend. He—did things to me." Dexter blinked once, long and slow. "Yeah. It was bad. And then he left my mom, and she was so upset that she blamed me. Beat me up with a hanger and put me in the garage with no food. Then she went in the living room, shot herself up with heroin, and died."

Dexter slowly sat up.

"How did you get out?" His voice was scratchy from disuse.

"I was in there two days. I called for help and banged on the door, but no one came. I ate cat food. Went in the litter box."

Dexter wrinkled his nose. "Gross. We had an outhouse at least."

Lei nodded. "Finally I got so hungry that I broke a window over the sink and crawled out. When I went inside the house, I found my mom's body." Lei's words stuck in her throat, and she cleared it. Tell your tale, Dr. Wilson had said. Tell it enough times, and it stops hurting. Tell it when it will help you or someone else.

"Was it scary?" Dexter frowned. "I've never seen a body."

"It was scary. And very sad." Lei couldn't suppress the flash of memory: her mother, Maylene Matsumoto Texeira, slumped against the coffee table, lips blue and foamy, legs sprawled, already beginning to smell. She felt her lips tremble.

He nodded. "My mom does drugs, too. That's why I got taken away to foster."

"Drugs hurt a lot of people. I'm sorry your mom is in that scene." Lei swallowed, pushed on. "So after I found Mom, I called my aunty in California for help. She was too far away to come because I was on Oahu, so I had to go with the cops when they came to the house. They brought me to a place like this. I stayed with a nice haole family until my aunty came and got me and she became my foster mom. The family were good people. They cleaned me up, bought me new clothes, fed me lots of food. But I kept waiting for something bad to happen."

Dexter nodded. "Uncle could come find me. He'll know I didn't throw the grenade like I was supposed to."

"We're going to catch Uncle Noah, Dexter. And when we do..." Lei drew a quick, hard breath. "I wouldn't want to be him. You know that man who hurt me when I was a kid?"

Dexter nodded, eyes wide.

"He went to jail, for a very long time. And when he got out, someone shot him."

"Whoa," he whispered.

"Yeah. So don't worry about Uncle anymore. We're going to get him and put him away where he can't hurt anybody." She stood. "I think Aunty Philomena might need more help with that adobo. What do you think?"

Dexter got out of bed. His ribs were visible through the thin tank shirt as he stood up. "I'm still hungry. I hope she doesn't get mad that I'm eating so much."

"I think you've come to the right place for eating plenny kine. And it's a long way from cat food."

Dexter smiled. It was quick and almost gone before she saw it, but it was real. The boy followed her down the hall, back to the kitchen, where the other boys were chopping vegetables.

"Got another helper here," Lei said.

The boys helped with the huge pan of chicken, vegetable, and pineapple adobo Philomena was making. Lei looked on, sipping a Coke the bustling woman handed her. Finally, when the rice was cooking in the meal's final phase, Lei went back to the bedroom with the boys for a few rounds of Halo.

Her phone rang in the pocket of her pants. She paused her character, which was immediately and gleefully annihilated by the boys. "Texeira here."

"We have intel from Selina Tahua. Got a location of a hideout in Kaupo." Shepherd's voice was tense with excitement as he named a remote, tiny settlement south of Hana. "You and Pono come on the raid. We need two more."

"On it." Lei jumped to her feet. She handed Dexter, who'd been passively watching, her controller. "Keep my character in the game, will you? I have to go catch some real-life bad guys."

"Uncle Noah?" Dexter asked, voice wobbling.

"I hope so." She waved goodbye to the boys and hurried through the house.

Butaga waylaid her in the kitchen. "You're a magician. Dexter's eating and talking!"

"He was worried to eat too much."

"Oh, so sad he would think so. I told him he could eat all he wanted. Speaking of, I made you some adobo fo' take home. Here, take this." Butaga thrust a Tupperware container into Lei's hands.

"Mahalo!" Lei gave the woman a quick hug. "The boys are in good hands here. I hope my visit helped." And she flew down the steps toward her truck, adobo dish in one hand and phone in the other as she called Pono with the change of plans.

CHAPTER TWENTY-TWO

I woke to the throbbing of my ribs in the silver light of dawn. The river gleamed nearby, ripples revealing its ever-shifting power beneath the glossy surface, like the muscles of a snake beneath its skin.

I was shaky, my eyes dry and hot as expended brass. Anxiety clenched my gut. The wound was definitely infected. We had to get help today. I sat up carefully, but couldn't stifle a moan. The whites of Falconer's eyes gleamed in the dim morning as he turned his gaze to me.

"You didn't wake me up for a watch," I accused.

"You needed the rest more than I did."

I had no response to this. He handed me a shucked ear of corn.

"Keep your strength up."

I was only able to eat a couple of bites. "You take the rest." He ate it without speaking. I scanned the river, hoping for some sign of other humans. A whimper from MacDonald indicated that the man was waking up, but when I looked at his face, he didn't appear to recognize me.

Mist swirled off the river's surface, and as if conjured from wishful thinking, I heard the putt-putt of an outboard. A long wooden pirogue appeared with a man at the back, steering a small outboard. A second man near the front wielded a paddle.

Falconer stood. "We should keep the weapons out of sight for now. Don't want them to think we're hostile."

"Agreed." I laid the M16 down, tossing the shirt over it, but kept the pistol in my waistband. Falconer kept his similarly placed.

The pirogue came directly to the dock. Falconer approached the men, his hands open and raised halfway in a universal gesture of nonthreatening entreaty.

"We need help." His Spanish was slow and careful. "We are American. We have injured men and need to get to a hospital."

A spate of excited Spanish patois met this. The first man in the canoe jumped out onto the dock and tied the hand-hewn craft to one of the wooden pilings. The men were brown and stocky, wearing worn pants and mud-spattered shirts. I'd begun to think everything was mud-colored in this country.

Falconer tried to slow down the patter of speech, but when the men reached back into the canoe for machetes and a pile of burlap bags, Falconer shook his head and pointed to us.

More Spanish. More gesturing. Falconer wasn't winning whatever argument was going on.

I breathed shallowly. Tremors racked me. I looked over at MacDonald. He was awake, but stared vacantly at the sky, where sun-brushed clouds heralded a day that was doubtless going to be hotter than a carpet steamer.

But at least it wasn't currently raining.

We were a fine pair, MacDonald and I. Poor Falconer.

Falconer returned. He was carrying a sack and a machete. "They came to harvest the corn that's ripe this morning. They can't take the time to run us back before they pick the corn. They told me I can harvest with them to pay for the ride across the river."

"I should help." I moved, pulling my legs in under me to stand, but pain rendered me breathless. He shook his head impatiently.

"No. I'll go help them. I need you to keep an eye on

MacDonald—we can't leave him. I gotta go. The sooner we harvest the corn, the sooner we'll be out of here."

I dropped back. The three men, Falconer towering behind the smaller, native men, disappeared into the field.

Dark memories came and went as I fell into a doze. Knowing I was delirious didn't help.

I relived the moment when I found my mother passed out in Kahului. Her blond hair protruded from a sleeping bag next to a dumpster. I'd thought she was dead, but she was only drunk and dehydrated. That had been her rock bottom and, eventually, the beginning of a new life.

And here I was, sick with infection and out of my head, on a riverbank in Honduras, my ruined feet encased in rotting wet leather, body failing. The tiny part of my mind that was still conscious hoped like hell this was my bottom.

Another memory. My brother, Jared. Stronger than me this time, leading the way, pulling my shirt and crawling just ahead of me as I choked on smoke and dragged our beloved dog by her collar, barely escaping the burning house.

Sitting beside Lei in the hospital bed after she'd lost the baby. She turned to me, freckles like flecks of dried blood on her pale skin, her hand in mine clammy. Her eyes begged, and I shut mine because I couldn't bear it.

"Baby?" she asked. I shook my head. She wailed as she turned away, a cry I was too numb to give.

Wasn't there anything good I could remember?

Kiet's eyes were the deep green of the algae-rich pond Jared, I, and our dad used to fish in the summers growing up. Kiet hugging me, his sweet breath on my cheek, his arms and legs tight around me. Kiet snuggling against me on the couch. Laughing as I threw a ball with him in the yard. Sprawled on his back, sleeping in the same pose I did—one arm up behind his pillow, the other down along his side.

Lei coming to the door of our darkened room the night before I left, wearing nothing but a towel, a hesitant but determined expression in her shadowed eyes. I went to her, hoping. The kiss said everything, and the heat between us burned up the dross, the wasted time, the misunderstandings and grief.

My family was waiting for me. I just had to make it home.

I woke when water splashed on my face. My eyes felt like marbles on an iron griddle. "Get up and onto the boat." Falconer slapped me again with a hand trailed in river water. "We're going to Nicaragua."

KAUPO IS the first sign of human habitation in miles of wide open, barren, wind-twisted coastline after the outpost of Ulupalakua Ranch. The area reminded Lei of those vast sweeps of empty country in California that she and Stevens had traveled through when they'd gone to Yosemite for their honeymoon. She'd done this drive a few times as a day trip with Stevens and Kiet, going fishing at hidden rocky beaches in places only locals knew called Black Point and Plenny Kiawe, enjoying the swoop and meander of the narrow, two-lane road.

Now, following Shepherd's SUV in Pono's jacked-up purple truck, sirens and lights off and radio silent in case Noah was monitoring the police band, the hour-long drive was long and stressful. Lei filled her Glock's clip and a second one, loading them with fifteen rounds each. That done, she prepped two pump-action shotguns as Pono, jaw bunched and meaty hands tight on the wheel, navigated the road at high speed.

They hit a cattle guard and levitated. The box of shotgun shells flew off Lei's lap, hit the dash, and tinkled all over the front of the cab.

"Shit!" Lei unbuckled her belt and bent forward to retrieve the shells just as they hit a curve. Unbuckled, Lei flew forward and smacked her head on the dash. "Pono! At least let me get to the raid before I get killed!" Lei hauled herself back into the seat and buckled up.

"Sorry." The tiny replica war helmet dangling from Pono's rearview mirror swayed and spun wildly. "I sure hope this is good intel. Long way out here for a dry run."

"Shepherd seemed sure he's at this location. Some Hana PD are meeting us out there. We have to get this guy."

"You seem pretty invested."

"If you'd seen those boys, you would be, too." Lei picked up a shell, rammed it into the chamber, and stowed the box of ammo behind her seat. "This guy is the worst scum we've dealt with in a while."

Pono inclined his head in silent agreement. They reached the tiny settlement of Kaupo, little more than a small general store with the look of a shoe box left too long in the elements, and a few dilapidated houses—the wild beauty of the deserted strip of coast-line continued, unbroken, miles farther on. An almost invisible, overgrown track led off the main road and headed toward the foothills, and Shepherd turned there. They followed, bumping over potholes hidden by overgrown grass, broken-down fencing made from cut guava wood testifying to the area's history in cattle ranching.

The road branched, and they took the left. Now wild ginger lined the narrow dirt track, leaning in with heavy, fragrant bouquets of silky orange flowers and long, sword-like leaves. The smell of ginger wafted headily through the truck as they pulled up in an open area where several trucks were parked. In the distance, up a slight hill, Lei could see a small house shingled in silver cedar and an unpainted barn.

One of the black SUVs contained four Hana PD officers, who leaped out at the sight of them. Lei put on her helmet and tightened down her Kevlar, handing Pono his shotgun and hefting her own. The sharp tang of gun oil and steel replaced that of wild ginger blossoms. The others were similarly armed as they gathered behind the vehicles. Lei breathed deliberately, consciously calming pre-raid jitters.

"Let's fan out in pairs and approach the house." Shepherd gestured right and left. The men nodded, and as they bent and moved forward through knee-deep grass, even the eight of them, armored and armed, felt inadequate against open, unprotected space and higher-ground defensible positions as they headed for the house and barn.

Lei and Pono hung back a bit. Lei scanned the area, her breath echoing inside the helmet, which as usual felt hot and restrictive but comforting, too, a layer of protection that dulled her hyper-alert senses.

The first shot from the house knocked one of the Hana PD officers down, and they all dropped to the ground. The knee-deep grass restricted vision but also provided a layer of cover. Lei belly crawled rapidly forward to a large boulder. She pulled up behind it, rested the shotgun on top, and aimed for the windows.

The report, as she fired, was always louder than she remembered. The kick of the shotgun smacked her padded shoulder, and the glass window disappeared with a distant tinkle.

"Check the officer back there. I'll cover you," she told Pono, who'd come up beside her. He nodded, anonymous and menacing in his helmet and body armor. He crawled to the downed officer, who'd rolled on his side, moaning.

"The vest took the shot. He's okay," Pono said into the general comm unit. He grabbed the back of the man's vest and tugged him along through the grass to shelter behind the boulder.

Shepherd and the others were working their way closer to the buildings as Lei and Pono bent over the injured man, pulling off his helmet and loosening the bulletproof vest. He drew gasping breaths as they got the covering open. A swollen red area marked the middle of his chest where the Kevlar had stopped the round.

"You're okay," she told him. "Got a story for the grandkids now." The man had the look of a grocery store meat cutter, stocky and muscular with a friendly face that had gone pale with the loss of breath. "Just get your lungs moving again. Take it easy."

Pono gestured that he was moving in, and Lei rose back up, sighting on movement in one of the windows and firing as her partner crawled toward the house.

The rest of the team had reached the house. Shepherd was at the door, he and his partner hitting it with a small door cannon as the other officers fanned along the sides, ready to breach.

There was an abrupt roar of mechanical sound from the barn. Someone was in there and was firing up a getaway vehicle. Only Lei was in a position to intercept. She was by far the closest to the big, weathered wood structure.

Lei glanced down at the injured man. He was breathing again, color coming back into his cheeks. He'd be okay. "Moving to intercept at the barn," she said into the comm. She stood up and ran for the sound coming from the outbuilding.

CHAPTER TWENTY-THREE

I MANAGED to get into the pirogue with Falconer on one side and one of the native men on the other, but it was a tricky business. I was weak, burning with fever, and my ribs throbbed with every beat of my heart. The boat was long but tippy, and I ended up in the bow, lying on my back.

MacDonald screamed when Falconer approached him. Falconer turned back to the men and explained in halting Spanish, tapping his forehead and making a circle, so they knew MacDonald was off his nut. One of the native men finally had to take the vine rope around MacDonald's neck and lead him to the boat.

"Talk to him, Stevens. Tell him we're going to safety," Falconer said.

It was close to the middle of the day by the way the sun looked overhead, a fireball in a bleached denim sky. I'd been lying there, staring up at it. Probably not a good plan. I struggled to sit up, and the pirogue tipped in the water.

"Get in, Devan. These men are taking us to safety." MacDonald looked at the canoe blankly, but when the native man tugged on the makeshift rope, he stepped in, stabilizing himself with his hands on the gunwales. He sat by my feet, staring straight ahead.

The two men and Falconer then loaded in the bags of corn. I dozed in and out, but whenever I was aware of what was going on, I was alarmed by how close to the surface of the river the pirogue had sunk.

The native men didn't seem concerned, though, and in a few minutes, the steersman fired up the outboard and his compatriot picked up the paddle. We moved away from the dock. One of my hands, resting on the rough, hand-carved gunnel, trailed into the water, and the feel of it woke me up again.

We were in the middle of the river where the current was strongest. I could see green-brown eddies and mini-whirlpools, and the pirogue slid downstream faster than it moved forward, an indication of the strength of the water's flow. Logs and branches floated in the current, spinning lazily. I turned my head to see the far bank—more jungle, an impenetrable swath of green.

"Where do these men live?" I asked Falconer.

"In a village a few clicks downriver. They are Miskito people. Though this river divides Nicaragua and Honduras, the Miskito have always lived in this area, and they farm wherever the land is good and will support a crop."

I knew I'd have been interested in this on another day, when I wasn't racked with pain and fever, delirium kept at bay by the feel of the cool water on my hand. I was the only one facing backward, and a log seemed to be caught in our wake. It floated twenty or so feet behind, but no one else noticed.

Falconer touched MacDonald. "Move forward, man. We need to distribute our weight a little better."

The effect was instantaneous. MacDonald shrieked, a high, thin wail, and shot to his feet.

The canoe rocked wildly. Water sloshed in from both sides as the craft tilted back and forth. Everyone yelled in alarm, and

MacDonald lost his balance. Arms windmilling, he pitched backward into the river.

Shouts accompanied the splash that followed his fall. He disappeared, bobbing up in seconds and looking around wildly for the boat.

"Here!" Falconer extended the paddle, but MacDonald saw who was holding it and turned with a guttural cry and struck out, splashing in the opposite direction. He made no headway. The river was a freight train of power, and we were as ineffective as leaves floating on the surface of it.

MacDonald spotted the log that had been caught in our wake and stroked toward it. "No!" I yelled, realizing that the small, gleaming bumps near the front of the log weren't knots in the wood, but eyes.

MacDonald recognized that, too. He didn't have enough breath to scream, but he turned in the water, splashing toward me, just as the crocodile submerged. It yanked him powerfully from beneath the water, and he disappeared.

He surfaced again, flailing.

"Help me!" he screamed. His mouth was still open, his hand reaching toward the paddle he'd rejected, when he was jerked beneath the water again. The surface roiled with activity for an endless moment, and then the river smoothed out, leaving not a ripple or a bubble.

The native men burst into exclamations. Falconer handed the paddle over at the second one's imperative command. The outboard clicked into gear, revving as much as it could, and now we were moving as fast as our heavily laden craft would go.

The men spoke a blend of native language and Spanish, and I was able to pick up that once a croc had a kill, it attracted others. Our low-slung boat was far from secure.

I had sat up in the midst of MacDonald's struggle, unaware of it, and now fire in my side brought me low, groaning. My heart flopped like a fish in a barrel, and I was slick with sweat and horror.

"He's just—gone." Falconer was still scanning the water for any sign of MacDonald. "I knew that crocs pulled prey under to drown, but that..." He shook his head. "God, I wish I hadn't touched him."

"It's not your fault he decided you were the devil." I forced the words past dry lips. Facing backward, I couldn't see where we were going, but the canoe slowed as the steersman throttled back, and I felt a gentle thud as the canoe pulled up at a dock. The second man got out and secured the boat with a rope. Falconer and the steersman handed up the bags of corn they'd harvested, and it was finally time to move me.

I had no desire to end up in the swirling brown water that ebbed and flowed around the pilings of the dock, so I tried to help, turning toward the dock, getting my feet under me, and allowing Falconer to put his shoulder under one arm and lift me up, though the movement ripped through me with such agony that I retched. Falconer managed to hand me off to the men on the dock, who'd been joined by more villagers. They were short and stocky and wore Western clothing. Waves of their Spanish/Miskito dialect swirled around me, incomprehensible and thick as the river's water.

Spots spun in my vision, narrowed to a black point, and winked out.

A BURST of gunfire from the direction of the house indicated ongoing action there, but Lei couldn't pay attention to that. She had to intercept whoever was trying to escape from the barn. She circled the corner of the large weathered structure, out of the sight line of the house. The barn's main door faced the house, but Lei doubted whoever was in the vehicle inside was going to try to escape past the seven heavily armed cops surrounding the dwelling.

"There must be another exit," she muttered, and as if in answer, she heard the squeal of long-unused hinges on the side of the barn farthest from her.

Lei sidled along the splintery, rough wood, her jeans whisking, her feet tangling in the overgrown grass. She reached the corner as she heard the vehicle rev, engine rough and growling. It was either a motorbike or a quad, and neither option was good.

Another loud burst of sound, and a four-wheeled all-terrain vehicle shot out the door.

Lei pumped the shotgun, took aim, and fired at the quad. The vehicle hit an obstacle, a boulder hidden by the long grass, just as Lei's round blew out one of the tires.

The quad flipped spectacularly, landing upside down.

Lei ran forward, shotgun ready, tripping over hidden rocks and tussocks of thick, bunchy grass. She approached the ATV. Its engine ran unevenly, a gargling like a broken garbage disposal as the large nubbly tires rotated. As she reached it, the engine cut out abruptly. She heard a moan coming from beneath the machine.

Lei turned toward the house and yelled, "Need help over here!"

She dropped the shotgun and threw her shoulder against one of the lazily spinning tires, trying to push it back over, but it wasn't until Pono had joined her that their combined weight was enough to tip the heavy ATV over onto its side, freeing the man beneath.

Uncle Noah stared up at them. His eyes bulged with petechial hemorrhaging and his mouth opened and closed as he tried to get air into his crushed chest. Lei could see a depression marking his clothing where the handlebars had compressed his rib cage, breaking bones and crushing his lungs. His chest was caved in where it should have been elevated.

The man's gaze was frantic and terrified as he tried vainly to breathe. A trickle of blood ran from his gulping mouth. Pono dropped to his knees beside the pot grower, opening his shirt to assess the damage. "Take it easy. Help's on the way."

Lei heard the wail of distant ambulance sirens coming their way. She picked up her shotgun and walked back toward the fallen police officer. He was someone who deserved her support. She didn't want to share Uncle Noah's last moments.

The firefight was over at the house. Shepherd and his partner guided two handcuffed prisoners down the rotted wooden steps.

"Get your man?" Shepherd threw a thumb toward the barn.

"Uncle Noah is down." Lei lifted the fallen officer to a sitting position. "Pono is being the Good Samaritan."

The ambulance bounced up the rugged, overgrown road, and shortly two EMTs ran to assist. Pono came around the barn. Lei looked up at him, alert. He met her gaze with a steady one of his own.

"No need to hurry," he told the EMTs. "The one behind the barn is dead."

Lei let out a breath she hadn't known she was holding.

CHAPTER TWENTY-FOUR

THE NEXT TIME I woke I was in a different place. A ceiling was above me, and I could see by red and orange flickering that there was a fire nearby. I was lying on a cot of some sort. I couldn't move, and when I slowly lifted my head, I was naked except for clean underwear. I'd been washed—I smelled like unfamiliar chemicals. My gaze panned around. There was an IV running into my hand, and my arms and legs were tied down to the cot with strips of material.

Lifting my head had taken all the strength I had. I lowered it again, heavy as a bowling ball. It seemed strange that I was naked and tied. Perhaps there was some medical reason. Shutting my eyes was a tremendous relief. Bloodred patterns flickered behind my eyelids—the fire. I felt its warmth, and relaxed.

I was safe. And clean. Maybe even getting medical attention, though the pain in my side hadn't abated.

"You awake, Stevens?" Falconer's voice. I didn't bother to open my eyes.

"Maybe," I muttered. I felt limp as week-old lettuce, and shivers still racked me periodically. A cool cloth wiped my face, neck, shoulders.

"They have you on an antibiotic IV. You've still got a fever, though," Falconer said. "I think we got here just in time."

"Thanks, man. You saved my life."

An odd sort of pause. Falconer didn't answer. I used all my strength to pry my gummy eyelids open and lift my head.

Falconer, dressed in clean fatigues, was at the door of the room. He jumped back from the closed door where he'd been listening.

"Hostiles coming." He grabbed a metal chair and propped it under the door handle. "Shit. I was really hoping once we got to the Nicaragua side, the kidnappers wouldn't pursue us. I left my weapons in the room the villagers put me in. Shit."

"Untie me," I croaked.

Falconer was too busy looking for a way to arm himself. He ransacked the meager room with its multiple cots, unable to find anything but a pair of scissors. He unhooked the bag of liquid hanging beside me from the metal pole, laying the bag on my chest. "This will do."

"Untie me." I said it louder. "I can move. I think."

The handle of the door rattled and rattled. The boom of someone kicking the door echoed through the room. I heaved myself sideways in the cot, trying to flip it over. That did nothing but send a lance of fire through me, and a sharp yelp of pain burst from my lips.

Falconer, standing by the door, the pole raised, seemed to realize that he'd left me tied and helpless. He turned toward me just as they fired on the door from the other side.

The shotgun blast sounded like a cannon in the enclosed space. Like some horrible cartoon come to life, the round tore a hole in the wood and pierced Falconer from behind. The shell blew through his midsection, spattering me with his blood, and embedded itself in the wall above my head.

Falconer dropped the metal pole. His hands clutched his abdomen. His very dark eyes, wide and ringed with white, met mine. He gave a little head shake, an ironic acknowledgment at having come this far only to die now.

"No!" I screamed. The door flew inward. Camouflage-dressed soldiers ran in as Falconer dropped to his knees, blood pouring between his fingers. He looked down at his hands and slowly tipped over onto his side.

The captain from the camp we'd escaped from so long ago entered the room, striding with a swagger. His soldiers stood over my bed, guns pointed down at me, as the captain walked over to Falconer. He gazed at the giant wound in the man's belly. Falconer looked up at him.

"Gut shot. You will die slow and terrible," he said in Spanish. "I will give you mercy."

Falconer shut his eyes and nodded, once. The captain pulled his pistol and shot Falconer in the head. Falconer jerked, and relaxed. The smell of blood filled the room, powerful as ammonia in my nostrils.

"No!" I thrashed, but I couldn't get free of the bindings. My weakness, helplessness, and agony overwhelmed me, along with disgust and horror. My vision faded to gray, then booted back up into focus again.

The captain's face loomed close as he looked me over. He was unshaven and greasy with sweat, and in his eyes I saw a debate: Was it better to keep me alive or kill me? There wasn't a thing I could do about any of it. I welcomed the familiar darkness that closed over my head.

IT WAS MUCH LATER when Lei, Pono beside her, Shepherd bringing up the rear, sat down at a battered Formica table in the jail's adolescent visiting room. The smell of Cheetos and grape soda filled the room, emanating from a trash can near the door. The table was gouged with initials and cusswords. She briefly wondered where the table had come from—no sharp objects were allowed in the room.

Tony entered with a juvenile officer. He wore cuffs, a zip-front orange overall, and fragile bravado. "What you cops want? I nevah goin' talk."

Lei reminded him of his rights, which the juvenile officer duly noted. "Uncle Noah is dead," Lei said. "He can neither protect you nor hurt you any longer."

Tony's color ebbed until it was the shade of badly tanned leather. His eyes held the hopelessness of someone who hasn't a friend or loved one in the world. Though this kid might be too far gone for redemption, he was no more than sixteen—too young to have no one who cared.

"Do you have a family, Tony?" Lei felt sorry for him in spite of herself.

"Not anymore. Uncle was my family." Tony dropped into the molded plastic chair like a sandbag.

"We're trying to find people you're related to. You went to Uncle from foster care. You and your brother." Elizabeth had tracked Tony's foster placement and disappearance to eight years ago, when he and his brother, Luke, had gone to Selina Tahua's— and supposedly run away, never to be seen again. "Where's your brother, Luke, Tony?"

Tony looked down at his hands in the cuffs. He had a little meat on his bones, compared to the three boys at Philomena Bugata's, and that reminder pricked Lei's anger. "You want proof Uncle Noah is dead?" She took out her phone, scrolled to a picture.

Lei held the phone up so that the boy could see it. Uncle Noah's eyes were open, bloodshot and bulging, but fixed in death. Blood filled his open mouth. His chest was dented in rather than curved. Tony gasped and covered his face.

Lei flicked the phone off. "He died trying to escape when his quad flipped. He left you to die in the jungle, Tony. We just want to know what happened to your brother." She unslung her backpack, set it on the table. She'd stopped by the morgue on her way here, and now she took out a Ziploc bag containing the small skull, stained red from iron-rich soil. "Is this your brother, Luke, Tony?"

Tony gave a cry. "No one was supposed to dig him up! He was peaceful there!" He lunged across the table and snatched the skull, hugging it to his chest. "Luke. I'm sorry. I'm sorry!" He cried, harsh dry sobs.

Pono glanced sidewise at Lei. She could feel disapproval rolling off him in waves. He thought she was being too harsh.

"Who killed Luke, Tony?" she asked.

"Nobody. Luke—he got sick." Tony gestured to his abdominal area. "Super sick. Bad pain in his stomach. He was puking and crying in pain. He got really hot. Uncle, he wouldn't take him to the hospital. Said Luke was weak, that he would talk and tell about the farm. And then Luke died." Tony hung his head, cradling the skull in his arms. "I'm so sorry, Luke."

"So you buried him back there."

"We buried him by the stream. He used to love the stream, playing in the water after we were done working."

"Tony, we need to know about the farm." Shepherd came around the table with his chair to sit beside the boy. "Uncle's dead, so there's no reason to protect him any longer. But we still need to know about how his operation worked and any people still out there who worked for him."

Tony bobbed his head. "Yeah. I can tell you that."

Lei and Pono stood. "We need Luke back," Lei said. "We'll take good care of him until your family can be located to bury him properly."

The teen held the skull in both hands and tenderly kissed it on the forehead through the plastic. He handed the skull back to her. Lei took it and met the boy's gaze with her own.

"Luke led me to you. He wanted you boys to be found. And freed." She'd never been more certain of anything.

Tony's eyes filled with tears. She felt his gaze on her back as she and Pono quietly exited. She slid the skull into her backpack. Pono reached out a hand. "I'll take that by the morgue for safe-keeping. You get home to that boy of yours."

Lei smiled, handing over the backpack. "Pono Kaihale, touching a child's bones. Never thought I'd see the day."

Pono wrapped thick tattooed arms over the backpack in something a lot like a hug. "I think you're right about Luke finding a way to get help for his brother and the other kids. It's time I got over being chicken about kid cases. Solving them is how we can help."

They parted ways at the entrance, Pono to return the skull to the morgue and the special drawer where Dr. Gregory stored such treasures, and Lei to get home to her boy.

As she got into her borrowed truck, one of the phones in her pocket rang.

CHAPTER TWENTY-FIVE

THIS TIME WHEN I WOKE, it was to a bright light, blinding, in one of my eyes. Somewhere off in the distance, muffled voices called my name.

I wanted to respond. I told my eyes to open, my hand to lift, my mouth to form words, but nothing happened. I was trapped inside my body. It felt like lying in a wooden coffin, confining and tight, and the coffin was lined with nails.

That eyelid was let go, and then the other one lifted. The bright light bored into my brain, rousing me. Still I couldn't respond, though I heard them call my name again. The voices were close and immediate.

The light went away. My eye fell shut. I drifted and disappeared again.

The crocodile had stuffed MacDonald under a log at the bottom of the river. He was bloated and bobbed up and down with the gases of decay, finally just as the croc liked a body to be for eating.

"Let him go," I begged. Water filled my mouth, but I could breathe fine. Some part of me was aware I was dreaming when MacDonald opened his milky eyes to look at me.

"We're in hell, Stevens. Don't you know that? None of this is real."

"I'm not supposed to end up in hell. I prayed that sinner's prayer. I thought I was going to heaven," I told MacDonald.

"Obviously it didn't work." MacDonald shook his head.

I swam over and tried to pull the man from under the log, but the croc lashed its tail and knocked me away. The current caught me and carried me, and the croc sank its teeth into MacDonald's swollen side.

The current carried me away from that horror show. The water was dark, thick, and gritty, but I was coming up, up, up from the bottom. My nose filled with a stinging scent that felt like a spear to my brain. I broke the surface and gave a gasp.

"I think he might be coming around." My eyelid was pried open again. The light blasted. The other eye was tried. "No. Pupils aren't responding." An unfamiliar voice, American, was speaking. Was I home? Rescued?

I couldn't open my eyes or respond. The container of my body held me tight and pinioned as an iron maiden.

"We need him awake by tomorrow when the ransom comes through." This was a familiar male voice, crisp and authoritative. I knew this person, but not well. I'd recognize him if I saw him, but no name would come through the sludge at the bottom of the river and attach to his voice. I felt something land on me, heard the shuffling of paper. "Another proof-of-life photo for today. It would be better if he wasn't lying there looking like a corpse."

"Nothing I can do," the first voice said. A flash of light. The paper object was removed from my bedclothes. "I'll administer some more stimulant medication later. But maybe it's just as well if he stays unconscious. He can't tell what he doesn't know."

"True."

My eyelids opened a crack, at last obeying a neurological command. I registered a uniformed man with an upright bearing exiting the room. I shut my eyes again.

Something was wrong here. I wasn't rescued. These were not the voices I should be hearing at a hospital somewhere in Nicaragua.

I heard the sound of footsteps retreating. Silence surrounded me, broken only by the beep of a monitor.

I tried to backtrack mentally and reconstruct what had happened. We'd been attacked. I'd woken up in the pit, sick, along with four others. I'd been so sick, probably from exposure and withdrawals, that they'd put me in the shed. Anchara had appeared, and forgiven me, and showed me the way out, and I'd escaped. Tied up one guard and killed another. Blown up three helicopters. Broken out three of the men who'd chosen to come. We'd gone miles through the jungle, and one by one my companions had been killed. I'd ended up in Nicaragua in a remote village, recaptured by the captain of the kidnappers.

And now I was here.

Was here the same place as where the captain had killed Falconer and taken me?

I dragged my eyes open again.

The room was different from the one I remembered in the Nicaraguan village—it was a tent. Large and heavy-duty, but still a tent. I could make out metal support poles in the corners, and above the rip-stop material of the roof, lacy tree patterns. The sounds of the jungle were present—a howler monkey, somewhere far off. The shriek of a bird, the shushing of a small wind in the tops of the trees.

Perhaps the captain had turned me over to these Americans? If so, why had they taken a proof-of-life photo and then said what they had? They'd talked about me as if I were a captive. They were Americans, but talked like kidnappers, propping a newspaper on me and taking that picture.

My hands wouldn't move, but I could feel them now, feel the fabric under them, feel the small pain that was an IV going into the back of the left one. I wiggled my feet and they responded, lifting and moving the sheet, but when I tried to slide them back and forth, I couldn't.

I hoisted myself a little higher in the bed, making my sore head swim, and looked down. My hands were tied to the metal bed frame with wide strips of fabric. The source of the pain in my side became apparent now: A short plastic catheter, inserted into my rib area, drained pus and blood into a plastic container that reeked of sweet, putrid infection.

The sight made me want to retch, but the clenching of my hollow belly was way too painful. I breathed carefully, with my mouth open, to keep from smelling it until the reflex passed. These small efforts exhausted me, and I shut my eyes, sinking back into a gray half-sleep.

Sometime later I woke again to hear someone moving around the bed. Remembering what he'd said about stimulant medication, I decided to let whoever it was know I was awake. Perhaps I'd misheard earlier, or been dreaming. I wanted to think so, and knew this for the weakness it was.

I opened my eyes. A brown-skinned man in scrubs and a mask was checking the drain at my side. "Water," I croaked. "Agua, por favor."

The man looked up, eyes crinkled and friendly over his green mask. "So you woke up at last. Welcome back, Lieutenant Stevens. I'm Dr. Aquinas. I'll get you water in a moment. Let me finish changing this dressing. We're almost ready to remove the drain."

I turned my head slightly to see what he was doing, but that made me dizzy. Pain descended, a vise around my temples. I groaned and shut my eyes.

"Head hurt? Don't move it. You've been out a long time, and that was a serious head injury."

Head injury? I didn't remember having a head injury. Just the cut from the pig's tusk and my ruined feet. I blinked, looking at my far-off feet. I wiggled them. They felt fine, but my eyes were gritty. Everything felt stiff, like I was fighting through an onset of rigor mortis. I tried speaking. "Where am I?" My voice sounded like a rusty hinge.

"You've been very ill. Almost died, in fact. But we did some surgery, and you've been on an antibiotic drip, and it looks like you're going to make it."

"Why am I tied?"

Dr. Aquinas prodded the flesh around the drain. Again, he didn't answer my question. "This really seems to be better. I think I'll take the drain out." He pulled up the tape, and I bit the inside of my cheek to keep from moaning as the adhesive pulled my skin.

"Ready?" He pulled the drain quickly from the wound, a feeling like a saber flaying my flesh to the bone. I screamed, or would have if my voice were working—the sound that came out was the short, sharp squawk of a chicken being stomped on. "There. Got some nice fresh blood coming out now. I have to pack the wound. This is gonna hurt."

It sure as hell did. I writhed against my bonds and bit my lips as he stuffed the wound with sterile gauze tape, leaving a wick protruding.

"Still got some drainage here. Perhaps we can take this packing out in the next day or so." Dr. Aquinas stripped off his gloves and straightened up. "I'll give you a little something so you can rest now. You just came out of a coma, so the priority is to take it easy."

"A coma? How long have I been here? I have questions..."

"And I don't have the answers for you. I'm just here for your medical care." Dr. Aquinas avoided my eyes. He injected something into my IV. "Sweet dreams."

"No, man. I just woke up!" I tugged at the restraints, hating that I was bound, knowing that I was still a prisoner. Darkness dragged me under, and it felt like the crocodile pulling MacDonald down to the bottom of the river.

LEI REACHED the truck she was borrowing from a relative of Pono's, and pulled her vibrating cell phone out of her pocket. "Dr. Wilson! I was wondering when we could talk."

"Yes, Captain Omura told me about recent events. I'm on Oahu, but I thought we could perhaps do your post-shoot debrief over the phone."

"That could work." Lei got into the vehicle and turned it on, cranking up the AC. The blast of warm air from the vents smelled of the mustiness of the truck's interior, something sweet and melted in the backseat, and a note of wet dog. She frowned. Her sense of smell was not usually this good. There was only one other time when it had been this sharp—that time she'd been pregnant.

Could that one night with Stevens before his departure have...? But no. She'd been through the roller coaster of hope and disappointment way too often to wish now. "I'm hoping to get a call from the army anytime now, that they've negotiated the prisoners' release."

"Yes, Omura briefed me on the situation." Dr. Wilson's tone was concerned. "I heard Michael was captured."

"Yeah. They haven't told me much. I haven't been able to do anything to help him, and it's so frustrating." Lei blew out a breath. "I had Sophie look into the situation over there a little bit, and it's not reassuring. The army and Security Solutions seem to be having some disagreement on how to handle the kidnapping. I'm worried." She clenched and unclenched a hand on the warm plastic of the steering wheel. "First of all, that the army might do some crazy thing like a raid on the prisoners' location. And then, even when we get him back, that he's worse from this. Not better."

A long pause. "I didn't agree with his idea of curing himself by going overseas," Dr. Wilson said softly. "But as you know, he didn't ask me."

"I know." Lei pushed a hand into her disordered curls. "He didn't ask me either."

"So how are you handling the stress?"

"Staying busy with work."

Dr. Wilson snorted. "That's not exactly a news flash, my girl."

Lei laughed ruefully. "I have to keep moving. Because as soon as I stop, I think of all that could go wrong." She sighed. "But I got a really hot case that started out as a cold one, and that's how I got into a couple of shooting situations." She described what had happened with the child's skull that Mrs. Yamaguchi had found and how it had led to the discovery in Hana and the raid in Kaupo.

"I walked away when I saw that Noah the child-slaving dog killer was dying," Lei finished. "I feel a little guilty for leaving Pono to hold his hand until it was over, but I just didn't have it in me to witness that man's passing."

"How responsible for his death were you?"

"I don't know. I shot his tire, but it was the quad hitting a rock at high speed that caused it to flip. So I don't think I had anything to do with it, really. I was proud of myself for not plugging him in the back after what he did to those boys." Lei described the man's psychological manipulation of the boys and the damage it had done. "I'd love it if you could take a look at Dexter. I'm going to be involved with these boys into the future."

Dr. Wilson sighed. "Of course I will. But isn't someone working with him?"

"Yes. But I trust you."

"And I receive that as the compliment it is. I'll coordinate with your friend Elizabeth Black and make sure everything that can be done is being done. Speaking of boys, how's Kiet doing?"

"Not well. I almost called you earlier this week." Lei described Kiet's insecurity. "Is it okay that we're sleeping in the big bed together? He's really regressed. Sucking his thumb, won't let me out of his sight. It's really worrying me."

"Kiet's a sensitive kid and he senses something is wrong. I would spend as much time as you can with him. Keep him with familiar family members and maintain the same routine each day.

You have to put some extra energy into reassuring him that, though his father's absent, his world continues and his needs will be met."

"I've been doing all that. I just feel guilty I'm away so much. Especially when I was thinking I'd like to take those foster boys home." Lei explained her impulse. "But Elizabeth nixed it, and she was right."

"There was a time you wouldn't have agreed," Dr. Wilson said. "But you've learned to trust a few others. And your instincts with Kiet are solid."

"Speaking of, I better head home." Lei switched her phone to Bluetooth and put the truck in gear. "I'll call you as soon as I know anything about Michael. They're probably going to bring him to Oahu, so maybe we can all meet there."

"I'll count on that, and pray it's soon," Dr. Wilson said, and Lei ended the call. She got on the road, her mind drifting to the possibility of reuniting with Stevens on Oahu as her eyes took in the coconut palms swaying in Maui's usual wind along Hana Highway.

As if conjured by Lei's wishing, the Security Solutions satellite phone rang on the seat beside her.

CHAPTER TWENTY-SIX

THE NEXT TIME I woke up might have been hours or days later. I had no sense of time anymore—it was elastic and illusory—but what I did know was that I was being moved. Overhead, I saw the lacy patterns of trees, then sky—that milky blue that heralded a hot day. I heard the roar of engines, smelled the harsh burn of diesel ahead.

I was still tied, I discovered when I tried to move my arms. I tipped my head back a little, and by rolling my eyes back, I looked up the body of one of the men carrying my stretcher. There was a triangle of beard stubble beneath his chin. He was one of the Hondurans by his skin tone and height.

"He's awake," the man said in Spanish, looking down at me.

"That's okay. We're almost there." I recognized Aquinas's voice, panting with exertion as he carried the other end of the stretcher. We'd reached a helicopter. I recognized its American designation as they stowed the stretcher on a detachable medical transport rack.

"You're going home, Lieutenant." Aquinas and the other man still wore their medical masks, and I wondered why.

"How long was I out?" I asked. Aquinas shook his head, tightening down a strap over my stretcher. He locked the IV pole into place.

From the front of the helicopter two pilots looked back at me, their pale faces and crew cuts identifying them as American. Aquinas slammed the door and sat down in a jump seat beside me as the other bearer jogged away.

"We've got you now, Lieutenant. Sit back and enjoy the ride," one of the pilots said, and the roar of the rotors drowned out any question or thought I might have had.

Just to be awake felt good. The bird rose in the air. Tremors from the engine jostled me, but it felt soothing in a weird way. I hadn't felt mechanical motion in a long time—something that was a part of my everyday life at home. Sharp smells, of fuel and straining metal, filled my nostrils, along with the roar of the engine.

I still wasn't sure what to think about Aquinas. Was he one of the kidnappers? He'd sounded American, though his coloring was consistent with Latino ancestry. But why was he traveling with me now? And who had that American in the uniform been?

All this thinking was making my head ache. I could feel that I was stronger and that I wasn't feverish anymore. There was a lot to be grateful for. I didn't have to have all the answers now.

Eventually the thrum of the engines translated to soporific, enough for me to drowse off, but I woke when we touched down on the ground. The door of the helicopter flew back, and a couple of uniformed medics jumped in. Aquinas hopped out and walked away.

"Good to see you awake, Lieutenant," one of them said, checking the IV. "We're moving you into a medical tent until we fly you out tomorrow."

"Okay." My voice still sounded scratchy and unused. I lifted my head to see where they were taking me and spotted a cluster of hangars, planes, and heavy-duty tents, all in camouflage. Wherever we had arrived was a military facility. My heart thudded heavily with anxiety as the medics lifted me down and stowed my stretcher on a rolling gurney.

"Can you guys take these restraints off?" I asked as they stowed my IV bag. "I'm not going anywhere now that I'm rescued."

"Of course, sir." One of the men pulled a combat knife from his belt and cut the bindings at my hands. He lifted the sheet and cut the ones at my feet, tucking the sheet back around them.

I asked what I thought they'd know. "Where are we?"

"Capital of Honduras. Tegucigalpa," the medic who'd helped me said.

"Tegucigalpa." It was pronounced pretty much like it was spelled. "So...I'm going where?"

"Back to the States. You've been negotiated." The young man grinned. "Hear you had a short but eventful time in Honduras."

"You have no idea." I was headed for home. Gratitude swept over me. "I'm still not sure how I got from Nicaragua to where I was rescued."

"Nicaragua, sir? You must be mistaken." The medic put a blood pressure cuff on me and pumped it up.

"The kidnappers captured me in Nicaragua. In a village over there." I saw the glance the man gave the other medic. Then he looked back down at me.

"Well, you're going home now. Just take it easy."

Somehow his words had the opposite effect on me. I had questions—and they weren't being answered.

I'd just have to be patient. I shut my eyes and tried to relax.

LEI'S HANDS were clumsy as she fumbled with the satellite phone, looking for a place to pull the truck over. The number in the little window was unfamiliar, but she got the truck pulled to the shoulder and put the phone to her ear.

"This is Sergeant Texeira."

"Westbrook here. Good news! We've negotiated the release of the prisoners."

"Oh my God!" A ripple of joyful excitement lifted the hairs all along Lei's arms. She shut her eyes against the prickle of tears. "When can I see him?"

Westbrook's voice sobered. "There have been some complications. Your husband was pretty severely injured and is still recovering. He'll be shipped to Tripler Army Hospital on Oahu. So you'll have to wait for that, but we anticipate his return in a few days." He cleared his throat. "And I think you'll appreciate that there's a clause in his contract that cancels it, with full payment for the term of contract, in the case of kidnapping or injury. In his situation, both occurred, so he'll be getting a bonus."

"I don't care about that!" Excitement had disappeared the minute Westbrook said "severely injured," leaving an ash of anxiety in Lei's mouth. "How badly was he hurt?"

"We don't know yet. We've transferred the funds to ensure the men's safety, but we don't know what condition they're in. We were told to send medical personnel and special transport for one of the prisoners, and when we asked which one and why, they said it was Lieutenant Stevens, but didn't tell us the extent of his injuries."

"Okay." Lei restrained her exclamations and questions with difficulty, remembering how Westbrook had shut her down in the past. "So he's in transit?"

"Yes. But it's a long way from Central America, so it'll be at least two days until he's at Tripler."

"Doesn't matter. I'll go to Oahu to wait for him."

"He will need to be questioned. Debriefed. Some psychological assessments," Westbrook said.

"Of course. But I know Michael. The thing that will help him most is to see his family as soon as possible." Even as she said the words, Lei wondered. Stevens hadn't been acting like his family was the most important thing in his life before his departure.

"I'm sure that's true. Just thought you should know there will be some protocols to follow," Westbrook said.

Lei said goodbye and ended the call, setting the phone beside her on the seat. She leaned her head on the steering wheel. "Thank you, God. Thank you so much for bringing him back to me." She straightened up, put the truck in gear, and drove home.

Jared was at the house, tossing a ball for Kiet, when she pulled up. His tall, dark-haired form was so similar to her husband's that it gave her a twinge. Her son barely looked up as he swung at Jared's soft, slow pitch with earnest effort, tongue trapped in the corner of his mouth. The little boy connected and the softball shot past Jared, who made a halfhearted effort to catch it in his glove.

Conan, who'd been waiting for just such an opportunity, bolted after the ball, the big Rottweiler's powerful haunches launching him forward in great leaps.

Lei could feel a smile stretching her face, so wide it hurt, as she got out of the truck. Jared grinned back at her, that quality of charisma he radiated giving his expression an extra dollop of charm. "Hey, sis! You're looking like you got good news."

"I did." Lei waited until both of them were looking at her, and then she opened her arms to Kiet. "I'm so happy, little man. Daddy's coming home!"

CHAPTER TWENTY-SEVEN

KIET RAN up the cement walkway to Lei's grandfather Soga's house as she paid off the driver who'd given them a ride from the airport. Soga Matsumoto opened the door wide, his normally stern face cracked down the middle with the big grin he reserved for his great-grandson. "My boy!" he exclaimed.

"Grandfather!" Kiet embraced Soga tightly around the waist. Lei hurried up the tiny walkway to throw her hug in over her son's.

"Grandfather, it's so good to see you." She breathed in his scent, flavored with a hint of glue and sandalwood. He must have been working on the floating lanterns he made every year for the Shinnyo temple's famous annual floating lantern ceremony on Memorial Day.

"Your husband is returning. Such a good thing, and I get a visit out of it." He released them abruptly, as was his way, and turned, opening the front door. "Come in. Your room is ready."

Since Lei had reconnected with her grandfather while she was in the FBI, their relationship had grown deeper. He'd greeted Kiet's surprise arrival with delight, and though she'd seen him eye her waistline speculatively, he never asked about more children, something for which Lei was grateful.

She followed Soga through the sparsely furnished house to the guest room he'd renamed "their" room. She turned into the room to drop off her bag as Soga led Kiet out to his workshop, one of her son's favorite places in the world.

Lei took a moment to flop backward on the queen-sized bed with its silky spread. It had been another full, eventful day before she'd been able to get away from work. The cold-case mystery that had begun with a small battered skull had turned out to be one of the most emotional but satisfying cases she'd worked in a long time.

Elizabeth Black had called Lei to report that the three foster boys had been kept together to minimize their attachment trauma, and a stable long-term home had been found that would keep them together.

Lei had finished all her paperwork and reports on the raid at the hideout in Kaupo. Tony had been released for a day to direct a team to retrieve his brother's remains, which were now slated to be reburied in a county-owned grave plot. Luke and Tony's parents were deceased, so Lei planned to attend the burial with the teen, who would be given a day pass for the occasion.

Lei had taken family leave to come here and deal with Stevens's situation. Lying on the bed, her eyes shut, she remembered the quick visit she and Kiet had made to the boys' new foster home on the way to the airport.

She'd called ahead this time, and the long-term foster mother, a large Hawaiian woman with a face creased from smiling, opened the door to them. Clad in a hibiscus-covered aloha shirt and capris, an air-dried clay plumeria decorating her braid, she smiled warmly at Lei.

"Welcome. I'm Aunty Belinda."

"Sergeant Lei Texeira. Mahalo for keeping the boys together and taking them all." Kiet liked to hang back and observe in new situations, so Lei squeezed his shoulder and pushed him forward gently. "This is my son, Kiet. Say hello to Aunty Belinda."

"Hello, Aunty," Kiet repeated obediently, but he still pressed back against Lei.

Lei heard the thunder of approaching footsteps. The doorway filled with all three boys, tall, medium, and short. Their cheeks already looked fuller and eyes brighter since she'd seen them last.

"Aunty Lei!" As usual, Danny was the most forthcoming and affectionate, stepping past Kiet to embrace her. "You came to visit us at our new house!"

"I told you. You're part of my ohana now. This is my son, Kiet. Kiet, this is Danny, Kekoa, and Dexter." Lei put her hands back on the little boy's shoulders. "You're going to have some hanai brothers now."

"What's hanai?" Kiet asked.

"Means Hawaiian-kine adopted," Danny said. "So we going be brothers."

Kekoa squatted a little, down to the younger boy's height. "Kiet, you like video games?"

Lei and Stevens limited his consumption of that kind of electronic media even more than TV, so Kiet's whole body came alive as he replied. "Yeah!"

"Mario Brothers?" Danny cocked his head.

"Mario Kart is my favorite," Kiet said.

"We got 'em." Danny gestured. "Come see." Kiet shot after Danny and Kekoa, leaving Lei with Dexter, standing in the doorway. Aunty Belinda opened the door wider.

"Come in. We getting mosquitoes already."

"Oh, shoots, I'm sorry." Lei hurried across the threshold into a spacious living room lined with worn couches. A big-screen TV made the far wall into a movie theater. "Can I talk to Dexter a minute? Privately?"

"Sure. I was just getting lunch ready. You and your boy like something fo' eat?" Aunty Belinda asked over her shoulder.

"No thanks. We can't stay long. We're on our way to the airport."

The woman nodded as she left. Lei smiled at the tallest of the boys. A lock of disorderly black hair hung over one of his eyes. She resisted the urge to stroke it back. "You're looking better, Dexter."

He nodded, though he still made no move to approach her. "Let's sit for a minute." Lei gestured to the right angle formed by the couches. "Did that doctor guy Elizabeth sent come visit you?"

"Yeah." Dexter sat next to Lei and hung his hands between his knees. "I talked to him."

"Did it help?" She did reach out now, slowly, as if petting a feral cat. She pushed the errant lock back and smiled. "You should cut your hair. You have nice eyes. The girls will love you when you get back to school."

He ducked his head, and the tops of his ears went red. "I haven't been in school for so long. They're going to think I'm dumb."

Lei coughed to get her voice working again, but it still sounded thick with emotion when she said, "Anyone meeting you can tell you're not dumb. How long were you at the farm?"

"Two years, I think. I was eleven, almost twelve when I got there. We had no calendar, but we had two Christmases out there. Uncle brought us presents at Christmas." He picked at the arm of the worn, tweedy couch.

"So you're going to be fourteen soon?"

"Yeah."

Aunty Belinda returned with a cutting board covered with slices of mango, papaya, and pineapple. "Aunty Belinda, did you know you've got a birthday boy here?"

"No! When's your special day?"

Dexter told her the date, in another week, and she clapped her hands. "Perfect. We'll get the whole ohana together. And maybe your parents can come, too."

"I'm not sure I want to see them." Dexter looked at Lei anxiously. "They never tried to find me or get me back."

"Oh, now, we don't know that," Aunty Belinda said. "They're still investigating the whole thing and how it happened, where your folks have been. We won't know anything for a while. But you wouldn't say no to more presents, right?"

Dexter shook his head. He appeared to be thinking it over as he eyed the tray of fruit.

Lei picked up a savory-smelling pineapple spear and took a bite. The sweet, tart, flavorful taste burst across her tongue. She shut her eyes to savor it. "Aunty—this pineapple. So sweet, so ono!"

"Thank you. My husband, he works for Maui Land and Pineapple. The employees always leave a little bit at the edge of the field after the harvest to get fully ripe, so they can take home a few to the families."

Dexter, encouraged, picked up some pineapple, too. Aunty handed them each a paper towel to blot up the drips.

"Would you like me and Kiet to come to your birthday?" Lei asked. "I'd really like to."

"Yes, please," Dexter whispered. "You folks come."

"Okay, we will." Lei wiped her hands on the paper towel. "I hate to go, but we have to catch a plane."

Now, lying on the bed on Oahu, she wondered what would be going on a week from now. Would Stevens be ready or able to come home? In any case, she had to be back on Maui for Luke's burial and Dexter's birthday. She had an ohana that needed her.

CHAPTER TWENTY-EIGHT

I SLEPT a lot on the trip home, and through the transitions, there was no one to ask my many questions—just a series of uniformed medics at each plane or way station. On the last big transport plane, finally able to sit up for short periods, I glimpsed the turquoise of Pearl Harbor out the windows and knew I was almost home. I was still on a gurney and an antibiotic drip when they brought me off that plane and onto an ambulance in Honolulu.

Honolulu Airport has a unique smell: the sharp reek of hot asphalt, the tang of metal, and the lush perfume of plumeria. The breeze, not as stifling and humid as it was in Honduras, blew across me as they wheeled me over the tarmac, and I enjoyed a brief exposure to the sun and wind before the transport to Tripler.

I still felt weak and shaky, headache beating a dull timpani in the background of my thoughts, but I couldn't wait to talk to someone and find out when my family would be notified about my rescue.

They put me in a single room with no windows, the orderlies transferring me briskly from the gurney to a hospital bed, hooking up all the monitors, and leaving. The door had a small, wire-threaded window in it, and the sound it made when it closed was the definite snick of a lock.

This wasn't what I'd expected. Not that I'd known what to expect.

A nurse entered, small and tidy in Hawaiian-print scrubs, shiny black hair, and tawny-brown skin showing her Filipina ancestry as much as her pretty white smile as she greeted me. "Welcome to Tripler Army Hospital, Lieutenant Stevens. I'm Abbie, and I'll be taking care of you during the day. Dr. Revas is on his way to give you a thorough physical exam."

"Okay." I tried to control my impatience as she took my blood pressure, pumping up the handheld bulb. "I need to talk to someone, though. About what happened. I have a lot of questions."

"I'm sure you do." Abbie peeled off the blood pressure cuff. "But I can't help you with that. What would you like for lunch? We have some menu choices." She handed me a white card with the menu options on it.

"You know what? I need to speak to someone now. I've been waiting ever since Honduras. I need to know what's happening. I don't care what's for lunch." I felt my voice escalating, and just then the door opened again and admitted a small, tan-colored man with the lithe build and quick, darting movements of a mongoose.

"He's agitated," Abbie said. I ground my teeth.

"Hello, Lieutenant. I'm Dr. Revas." The man leaned forward so abruptly I started back. His small, bright eyes reminded me even more of a mongoose. "I need to check your head injury dressing and infection dressing. But first, a quick exam of your visual reflexes."

"When am I going to be debriefed?" I knew I was growling and couldn't seem to help it. "I have a right to know what the hell is going on."

"Why are you so concerned, Lieutenant? Surely you know you're safe, back in Honolulu." Revas flicked on a tiny penlight, peered into my eyes.

"Of course I know that. But something isn't right. My feet should be—infected. Ruined from being wet in boots for days. The last time I saw them, they were disgusting. I can feel them, and they feel fine."

"Hmm." Revas nodded to Abbie, who loosened the bedclothes and lifted them off of my feet. "They look fine to me."

My feet were pale and soft, as if they hadn't been out of bed in weeks. My heart sped up on a burst of panic. How long had I been sick? It must have been weeks for my feet to be recovered this way. Dr. Revas and Abbie exchanged a glance, and the nurse covered my feet up again as Revas made a note on the clipboard he was holding.

"What? What does it mean? How long was I sick?" My voice climbed. "How was I rescued from the captain in Nicaragua?"

"Calm down, Lieutenant. You're safe now," Abbie soothed, patting me. I bit my lip to keep from lashing out in fury. The pain helped ground me. Too late, I realized Dr. Revas had used Abbie's distraction to inject something into my IV.

"Shit, no! Not more sleeping. I want answers! I want to speak to my wife!" I tugged on Abbie's sleeve, frantic, but the dark pulled me under again.

THE NEXT TIME I woke up, the room was dim. There was no way to tell what day or time it was. My bed had been lowered most of the way, and when I tried to move, I discovered I was restrained again.

"Damn it!" I indulged in a stream of profanity, venting my rage and helplessness. There was something wrong here. Something going on. I shouldn't be tied up and stashed away like this.

Panting, I subsided, my head and side stabbing with pain. I needed to think, to use the limited information I had to figure out where I was, what was going on, and how to get out.

I looked around the room more carefully.

Other than my wheeled hospital bed, there was a wall-mounted cot folded up for storage. A steel toilet in one corner. A sink, with low, rounded knobs. The walls were covered with thick, oatmeal-colored carpet. The door looked securely locked, and I knew the look of a wire-gridded security-glass window.

I was in the psychiatric unit.

I felt panic rise in a wave. I breathed through the urge to thrash and fight my bindings.

I'd been put here for a reason. Something wasn't right. Maybe I knew something I didn't know I knew. Maybe the company or the army were worried about my adjustment back to the States after the ordeal—though shooting me up with tranquilizers and leaving me in an isolation unit, bound to a bed, didn't seem very therapeutic.

I lowered my head, which was aching again, to assess my own physical state. I was definitely better. The IV was gone, and I could feel by moving that the wound in my side was closing. Other than the ache of my head, I felt fine.

The lights came up, softly. A knock came from the door—clearly just a courtesy, as I heard locks ratchet back. A familiar face appeared, and I strained to sit up.

"Dr. Wilson! Thank God. Can you get these damn restraints off me?"

"Michael. So good to see you." Dr. Wilson was wearing a white lab coat over her usual floral wrap dress, and her blue eyes, while smiling, looked worried. "I'm here to assess you."

"Assess what? I've been looking for someone to debrief me, tell me what the heck's been going on since they took me by helicopter out of Honduras, but no one will answer my questions, and now they're treating me like I'm crazy!" I tried to lower my voice. "Please take these off me. Surely you don't think I'd hurt you."

Caprice Wilson smiled and shook her head, her creamy blond hair glinting in the artificial light. She bent close. "Of course not. Let me just check these."

She leaned close as she unbuckled one of the leather straps. Her breath, smelling faintly of minty toothpaste, tickled the hair of my ear. "We're being monitored. I had to pull all sorts of strings to get in to see you. Stay very calm and I'll answer everything I can," she whispered.

I gave a slight nod. She unbuckled the restraints and pushed a lever that raised the back of the bed.

"Need some water?" There was a paper cup on the sink. I nodded, suppressing my questions. I trusted Dr. Wilson totally. She'd been my wife's therapist before we met, and had proved herself a friend and colleague over the years since.

She filled the cup of water and brought it to me. I sipped. "Thanks."

There was nowhere for her to sit, so she rested a hip on the edge of the bed. "What do you remember, Michael?"

Her voice was low, hypnotic. I knew she was doing some sort of mind juju on me, but this was Dr. Wilson. I trusted her. I shook my head carefully. "It's a long story. A lot happened. Shouldn't I be debriefing with one of the army guys?"

"They're taping this interview. Since the staff reported you were agitated, I asked if I could do your main debrief and assess your current state of mind."

"I'm glad it's you. Thanks. Do you want the long or the short version?"

"I've been thoroughly briefed on the events and timeline of the kidnapping, so give me your short version first. Then I can help you with any knowledge gaps you might be missing."

"Well, then, you can tell me how long I was sick. Because something's not adding up." I pulled the sheet aside and showed her my feet. "My feet should be wrecked. And I had an injury to my side, but not my head. I mean, someone clocked me on the head when we were taken, but that didn't slow me down. I don't know how my feet have had time to heal."

Dr. Wilson looked at me for a long minute with those blue eyes

Lei had often said could get a stone to talk. I shut my mouth stubbornly and waited for her answer.

"I need to hear your short version first before I tell you what I know," she finally said.

"Okay. Well, I was teaching my seminar in one of the tents at Camp Trifecta in Honduras, location classified, when three armed choppers attacked us, using non-lethal ammo and tear gas. I tried to put up a fight, was hit and knocked out. They knew just who to grab. When I came to, I was in a pit." I shuddered at the memory. "I was sick, and water was coming in from a palm frond thatch over the hole, and I got sicker." I told how the four other men, calling for help, had gotten me out of the pit and I was put in a storage shed and eventually escaped. "I stole a compass knife off one of the guards, got out of the shed, disabled two more guards, blew up the choppers as a distraction, and broke out the rest of the men who wanted to escape. One man, Carrigan, in charge of tech, opted to stay at the camp." Telling the story made it sound pretty extreme, and Dr. Wilson's face was still, set in unreadable lines. I sped up the narrative. "Three men chose to escape with me, because I'd heard the captain at the camp say he was going to begin killing us the next day. MacDonald, Falconer, Kerry, and I struck out into the jungle. I had a headlight from one of the guards." I described our journey and how we ditched pursuit, and how, one by one, my companions were killed.

"I got injured killing a baby pig. The mother slashed me with her tusks." I indicated the strapping around my ribs. "My wound festered, and after Falconer and I made it across the Coco River to Nicaragua, he got some villagers to tend to my injuries and we thought we were home free. But the captain must have bribed people to look for us, because they found us there. He shot Falconer." I gulped, remembering the man's death. "Falconer deserves a medal. He saved my life. Brave to the end."

Dr. Wilson plucked at the cloth on the bed. "When did you get your head injury?"

"I don't know. Perhaps the captain inflicted it in Nicaragua. I passed out after Falconer was shot. Then I woke up somewhere else." I lowered my voice. "There was one thing that was odd."

I gestured, and she leaned close. I whispered into the curve of her ear, "I thought I was with Americans, and they were trying to wake me up. For some reason I was unable to respond. But I could hear them talking. They posed a newspaper against me for a proof-of-life photo. I finally got my eyes open and heard a voice I knew. American, I'd swear it. But then they left. When I next woke, only one of them—Dr. Aquinas, he called himself—was there. He accompanied me on the rescue helicopter to Tegucigalpa. He sounded American but looked Latino. Then I was brought here."

"And your feet?"

I shook my head. "I don't know how my feet had time to heal."

"That's a remarkable story, Michael." Dr. Wilson straightened up, looked me in the eye, and spoke clearly. "And I'm sorry to tell you, not a word of it is true."

CHAPTER TWENTY-NINE

SOGA HAD TAKEN Kiet to visit a woman friend who had a dog with puppies, and Lei knew her son was delighted to be out with his grandfather. Sitting in Soga's living room, afternoon light falling in a lance across the enameled coffee table, Lei phoned Sophie Ang, her tech friend.

"Sophie, I'm here in Honolulu. Stevens is in the hospital." She sketched the recent events of her husband's return. "I'm getting the runaround about seeing him. Supposedly he's getting cleared, debriefed, yada, yada, but no one will tell me where he is or let me see him. Can we meet for coffee? I want to know about all the players involved with the kidnapping. Did you find out anything more?"

"As a matter of fact, I did." Sophie's slight accent thickened in excitement. "There's been a lot of chatter on the accounts I've been monitoring. Let's meet." She named a coffee shop, and Lei grabbed her grandfather's car keys off the wall board and headed out.

At the crowded coffee shop, Lei sipped an extra-foamy latte, gazing at her friend. Sophie Ang had a face like Nefertiti, and Lei wished she weren't jealous of the woman's height and sleek, muscular build, not to mention her tech skills. Sophie glanced up at Lei from the tablet computer she worked like an abacus.

"It seemed to me like these kidnappings were happening a little too often. I thought there must be a leak, intel on rich targets getting out to kidnappers. Someone, somewhere is getting a kickback. I found a couple of names that have been present at all the kidnappings in that part of the world." Sophie tilted the tablet to show Lei a couple of pictures. "There are others, too, but these two were at all the kidnapping sites in the last five years."

"Why haven't they been taken in?"

"Because, from what I can gather, there has been zero evidence linking them to anything."

"How can I get this information to—someone?" Lei frowned. "It seems pretty thin. I don't want to endanger Michael further. He's so vulnerable." Lei's eyes filled at the thought of her husband laid low. "He was pretty severely injured. He's lucky to be alive, from what I can gather. I think there could be a bigger agenda going on, and I've got nowhere to go with my questions and concerns."

"Sounds like something for the FBI to probe." Sophie gave a smile that showed all her perfect white teeth. "I'll let you know what I find. It's always tough dealing with the military. They have their own system for everything—but I should be able to run an alert up the flagpole through the involvement of Security Solutions, which is a civilian business." She frowned, looking Lei over. "You don't look good, Lei. Is something wrong?"

"Besides my husband being kidnapped and injured overseas? No, just a heavy case right before I got here. Took a few emotional lumps on that, too. But it all ended well." She described the skull case.

"You and your troubled teens. And dogs. You had to talk me into getting Ginger." Sophie had adopted a rowdy and loving yellow Lab from the Humane Society on Lei's recommendation. "Best thing I ever did. Well, I'll be in touch."

"Let's go visit Marcella and the baby together as soon as possible," Lei said. Her FBI-agent friend had given birth not long ago, and Lei was eager to see baby Jonas again. Just thinking of his new-baby smell brought a tingle to her breasts. She frowned at the odd sensation.

"Sounds like a plan. I want to get started looking into this." Sophie stood. "I'll call you as soon as I know something more."

"Thanks." Lei gave the other woman a quick hug. "I'll see you soon." She looked down at her buzzing phone. "It's the army. I have to take this."

Sophie waved and left, her lithe body cutting through the crowded coffee shop like a shark through water as Lei put the phone to her ear.

"This is Sergeant Texeira."

"Lieutenant Colonel Westbrook. I'm calling regarding your husband."

"Yes. I'm here on Oahu, but no one will tell me anything about what's going on with him."

"There have been complications. Meet me in the hospital lobby in an hour." Westbrook ended the call.

Lei's hands prickled as she ran out of the coffee shop. She had just enough time for a quick stop at the drugstore. It was time she knew what was going on with her body.

DR. WILSON HAD JUST TOLD me I was lying. I sucked in a breath as sharply as if punched in the gut, staring at her. "What the hell are you saying?"

Her eyes flicked to the corner of the room, then back to mine. I understood that she was signaling me that her words were for the benefit of others as well as myself.

225

"You were, indeed, attacked while teaching class. In the course of the attack, you were bashed on the head by one of the kidnappers after putting up a fight, and suffered a skull fracture. You were also shot, resulting in the wound in your side, which passed between your ribs. You were in a coma for the entire period of your captivity."

I felt the blood drain out of my face. I reached up, feeling the heavy bandage around my head. "No. Not possible."

"It's true. Dr. Aquinas is the medical officer attached to your camp. He was also kidnapped by the Hondurans who held you and the other prisoners. His job was to keep you alive, which was a challenge, as the gunshot injury in your side developed into a life-threatening infection."

I kept shaking my head, but that hurt. "And the other men?"

"Safe and sound. All of you are here at the hospital getting checked out and debriefed before returning to your families. Your transport took longer."

I felt light-headed. "I saw them die." How could all that happened have been in my head?

Dr. Wilson slid off the bed, went to the door, and knocked. It opened. She spoke out into the hall, and I heard an affirmative mumble.

"I'm so sorry you went through all that, Michael. I don't know what to tell you, except that none of it happened but the first attack. I think the best way to convince you is to show you."

I rubbed my hands over my face. The skin felt rubbery and numb. "Am I crazy?" I whispered. "Is this why I'm here?"

"No. You're not crazy. You just—had a vivid dreaming experience during your coma."

If it had been anyone other than Dr. Wilson telling me this, I wouldn't have believed her. "Does Lei know I'm back?"

"Yes. She's here in Honolulu, waiting to get clearance to see you. We need to go through a few more hoops to make sure you're okay." Dr. Wilson steadied me as I swung my legs to the side of the bed. I stood, apparently for the first time in a couple of weeks.

My legs almost crumpled. A wave of dizziness had me clutching the much smaller woman beside me. The door opened, and Falconer came in. He took three giant steps and caught me before I brought both of us to the ground.

"Falconer! You're really alive!" The big black man heaved me up onto the bed, his mouth set in a familiar reserve that hid his true nature—generous and brave as hell.

"I hear you're talkin' crazy, Stevens. You lucky dog. Spent the whole time we were captive sleeping in a comfy bed while we were trapped in a box."

"Not a pit?"

"No pit. Just hot, buggy, and bored as hell in a deserted old barracks building."

"Great to see you awake, LT. You had us worried." Young Tim Kerry entered, grinning. He was thinner than I remembered when I first met him at Camp Trifecta, but whole and alive. My eyes filled at the sight of him. I rubbed them with a thumb and forefinger, pretending they were itchy.

A third man came forward to my bed, hand extended. His cheeks were plump and rosy, his blue eyes friendly. "Don't believe we met formally, but I saw you around the camp before we were captured. Devan MacDonald, camp manager. Glad to see you up."

"Great to meet you," I murmured. My last sight of MacDonald had been the croc biting into his bloated body. I rubbed my eyes again.

Falconer fussed around the bed. "Why do they have you stuck back here in the loony-tune section?"

"I still can't believe you're alive." I couldn't help reaching out to squeeze Falconer's shoulder. Emotionally, he felt like a brother to me. So did Kerry. I looked around at the three of them. "I had this vivid dream while I was in the coma. We escaped the kidnappers. All kinds of shit happened. Falconer kept us alive—but never mind." I shook my head and immediately regretted that motion. "Dr. Wilson, I believe you now. This explains why my feet are fine."

Falconer swung my legs back onto the bed and pulled the sheet up over them. "We'll have a beer when you're out of here, and you can tell me all about it." He cracked a smile, a flash of lightning in his ebony face, and lifted a hand as he left. I watched the three of them go. I finally let the tears overflow.

It was still hard to believe that the men I thought I'd known were entirely the product of a head injury. Dr. Wilson patted my shoulder, drawing my attention back to her.

"I have some cognitive exercises to take you through."

We did those for a while: memory exercises, puzzle exercises, word associations. I began to tire, my memory slipping, and I badly needed to go to the bathroom. "Can we take a break?"

"Of course." She hopped off the bed with an athletic grace that reminded me of Lei with a sharp pang. "I'll go tell the Security Solutions and the army people you're more oriented now. I'm also authorizing you to be moved to a regular room."

"Thanks. It sucks to get back and be treated like a head case. I just needed to know what was going on."

"Speaking of head case." Caprice Wilson leveled a finger and those steely blue eyes at me. "We're going to discuss the reasons you took this job in the first place. We're not done talking." She left. I managed to get my wobbly ass to the toilet in the corner, relieving myself with my bandaged head leaning on the wall.

The whole damn escape had been imaginary. How screwed up was that? I thought back over the many unforgettable moments as we'd made our way through the jungle—beginning with Anchara appearing as a glowing moth, assuming human form, then showing me the way out.

I should have realized then that none of it was real.

But it had seemed so real, right down to mosquito bites I still felt an urge to scratch. Could I have been mistaken about Aquinas and the uniformed man, too? When did I really wake up?

Were there parts of my adventure that really had happened?

I groped my way back to the bed and fell into an exhausted doze, resting up before the next round of questioning.

CHAPTER THIRTY

LIEUTENANT COLONEL WESTBROOK, dapper in his brass-encrusted uniform, greeted Lei formally in the hospital lobby, but Dr. Wilson embraced Lei with the light, firm hug Lei had become used to in the years they'd known each other. She smelled of jasmine perfume and a tiny tang of anxious perspiration that Lei's sensitive nose picked up in spite of the psychologist's bright smile.

"Well, I have good news and bad news." Dr. Wilson drew Lei over to a corner seating unit in the hospital's bustling lobby. "Michael's in the psychiatric unit."

"Why is he there?" Lei tried to keep her voice even, worry making it sharp.

Dr. Wilson looked around, as if checking for someone over-hearing them, but there was no one else in the well-worn area with its teetering stack of Insights for Children and battered National Geographic magazines. Westbrook tugged at his jacket. "I heard he's confused and disoriented."

Dr. Wilson frowned at the army officer. "He is, but there's something more going on. I was listed as one of Michael's health care team on his Security Solutions application, and I also provide return debriefing for their staffers, but no one called me about

Michael's arrival. I heard about it accidentally from some other staff people, and when I came to investigate, found he'd been locked up in an isolation unit with a diagnosis of severe brain injury, massive systemic infection, and psychosis."

Lei clutched the arm of the cheap settee she was sitting on. "What?" Her head swam. Her vision telescoped. "Is he going to live?"

Dr. Wilson patted Lei's leg sharply, and the touch brought Lei back into her body.

"Here's where the good news and bad news come in. He did have a severe head trauma. He was in a coma the whole time he was kidnapped, according to the men who returned. They saw him go down after a blow to the head, and he was shot then, too. He was kept in a bed under medical care while they were imprisoned in a nearby structure. The staff here at Tripler apparently initially thought he was psychotic because he has a very different version of events."

Lei focused on breathing and keeping the urge to vomit in check as Dr. Wilson repeated the broad brushstrokes of Michael's version of the ordeal. "I had to conclude that he had a very vivid lucid dream during his coma. But the upshot is, he's going to have a long road to recovery. He's had some cognitive damage to his short-term memory and processing speed. I'm hopeful that's only temporary. The infection is dealt with, and he's recovering from that. I've changed his diagnosis to traumatic brain injury only, and I'm having him moved from the isolation unit—but I can't help feeling someone wants to cover something up, to silence and discredit Michael somehow."

"You think there was an insider in Security Solutions or the army who was involved with the kidnapping?" Lei asked.

"There might be. Michael has some information he tried to communicate privately, though he was pretty overwhelmed to find out he didn't really survive killing wild pigs and fighting crocodiles in the jungle."

"Oh my God. I don't know which is worse—that he went through all that in his head, or if he really had."

"I don't know either, to be honest. He wasn't in the best shape mental-health-wise going into all this." They gazed at each other for a long moment. Lying between them was a long friendship and history of knowing the passionate, loyal, dedicated—and damaged —man Lei had married. "We just have to move forward and hope for the best."

"When can I see him?"

"Not until he's been debriefed with the brass from Security Solutions and the army. I'll text you when his assessments and interviews are done," Dr. Wilson said.

"We have that scheduled for first thing tomorrow morning, if he's in shape for it," Westbrook said. The army officer fiddled with his cuffs, clearly uncomfortable. "I'm sure this will all work out just fine, Sergeant. Try to relax. We'll get your husband back to you in short order." And to Lei's surprise, he sketched her a brief salute before turning crisply and exiting the room.

"I think he feels bad about what happened." Dr. Wilson gazed after the officer's upright form as the hospital doors whisked shut behind him.

"Thank God you're on the situation," Lei said, impulsively leaning over to hug the petite psychologist. "Don't let anyone give you any shit. Including Michael. And please, hurry. I can't wait to see him."

"Will do." Dr. Wilson pulled back from Lei's arms. "I'd better get back to him. I want to oversee his move to a different room."

"See you soon," Lei said to Dr. Wilson's retreating back.

I DRIFTED IN THAT GRAY, dreamlike state between sleep and waking, ticking over the threads of truth and fiction, sorting and sifting. Once, when I was a child, I'd visited my mom's parents in the Midwest. There was some angst between them that was never spoken of, and we never went again—but now I was back in my grandfather's barn, my nose filled with the sweet, musty, dense smell of hay.

Mounds of it, loose, lay waiting to be forked into a wheelbarrow. A ladder led to a huge loft, piled high with more golden green bricks of tightly packed hay. Shafts of sunlight shone through knotholes in the old wooden structure, bright and substantial as gold bars. My grandfather stood before me, tall and rawboned, in a pair of overalls. I recognized his piercing, light blue eyes—I saw them every day in the mirror. He always had a toothpick in the corner of his seamed mouth. Today he took the toothpick out and tossed it into the pile of hay.

"Ten dollars to whichever of you boys finds it first," he said. "Nothing like your first lesson in finding a needle in a haystack."

I remembered diving enthusiastically into the hay pile with Jared, galvanized by the quest to get that "needle." After what seemed like hours of burrowing, winnowing, and sorting, we'd had to give up on earning the princely sum of ten dollars.

I felt like that now. The truth was somewhere in my head, elusive, blending with so much else. Deep in the snarl of confusion that was my mind, there was something important I needed to know, and share.

I did have a few things I was going to carry forward from this head-trip adventure—I had to go back to solving active cases. While I'd been good as a trainer, I needed the physical and mental challenge of being on the streets as a detective. Maybe my role could be modified to working cases as a mentor to new detectives.

Yeah, I'd like that, and it would be active enough to keep me feeling alive.

And I still believed I'd met Anchara in that shed and she'd decided to stop haunting me. I hadn't had a single tormented vision of her death since she'd appeared to me, and I usually had some flashback involving her every day.

I pictured that first drink—the ice cubes in the brown liquid. The smell, opening my nostrils. The taste. The feeling of warmth as the liquor made a path to my stomach. I could think about it, and while it still appealed, it didn't fill me with longing for oblivion like before. I wasn't going to drink anymore, and I felt confident I'd be able to follow through with that resolve. Alcohol's hold on me was broken, too.

The sound of the door unlocking brought me fully awake, and I tossed the sheet off my legs and sat up straighter, surprised to see Dr. Aquinas. He was in civilian clothing: a blue polo shirt and chinos. He wasn't wearing the surgical mask I'd always seen him in before.

"Hey. I remember you," I said. "Dr. Aquinas."

He smiled pleasantly, turning to the man following him. "Told you he was more conscious than he even knew he was."

Major Forsythe, from Camp Trifecta, followed him in. The major turned and shut the door deliberately.

I frowned. "What's this about? Is this my debrief interview?"

"Yes, it is," Dr. Aquinas said. "Just relax."

I was expecting the debrief, but I was damned sick of hearing I needed to relax. I tightened my abs, coiling my energy, every sense alert. My gut told me these two weren't here for any good reason.

Major Forsythe came and stood close, looking down at me. He was spit-polished to a regulation shine, and his eyes on me were river-stone cold. "This is part of your exit debrief. What do you remember?" he barked.

As soon as I heard Forsythe's voice, I knew this was the man who'd posed the newspaper against me and taken a proof-of-life picture. This was the officer whose back I'd seen exiting the room.

This was the needle I'd been looking for. I tried to keep that recognition out of my face and voice.

"I don't remember much, sir. I just learned from Dr. Wilson that I went on a whole mind trip during the coma. I thought I escaped. Blew up some choppers, fought snakes and crocs." I had no difficulty chuckling weakly and flapping a trembling hand. "I think I'm pretty fucked up."

Both of them stared at me speculatively. They were making up their minds on whether I was too far gone to be credible, or if I was a loose end that needed clipping off. Forsythe glanced at Aquinas and lifted his chin slightly. That was all the warning I had, but it was enough.

CHAPTER THIRTY-ONE

I THREW myself off the bed on the opposite side from the doctor, landing in a crouch as Aquinas plunged a syringe into the pillow where I'd just been. The hospital gown bagged and flew open, exposing my backside as I landed—but that was the least of my worries.

Forsythe cursed. "It has to look like natural causes."

Adrenaline pumped through me. I'd killed guards, blown up helicopters, fought crocs, snakes, and the elements. I wasn't going to be slaughtered like a veal calf in its fattening stall.

I threw my weight against the metal rail of the wheeled bed, hoping like hell it wasn't locked in place—and it wasn't. The unexpected vigor and direction of my attack knocked Forsythe and Aquinas off-balance, and I rammed them both backward, pushing with all I had until I'd pinned them against the wall with the bed. I threw the brake on to lock it in place and ran to the door, pounding on it and deepening my voice authoritatively.

"Need help with this patient!"

Aquinas crawled up and out from behind the bed and leaped on me from behind, the needle in his fist. We did a nightmare chicken dance as he climbed my back, arms around my shoulders and legs around my waist, trying to stab me with whatever was in that deadly syringe.

The door flew open and two orderlies stood there, faces blank with surprise as I slammed Aquinas back into the wall, trying to dislodge him. Forsythe extricated himself from behind the bed, yelling.

"Take that man down! He's a danger to himself and others!"

Magic words in a mental health ward.

I just hoped that the needle that would finally get me wasn't the one in Aquinas's hand. I managed to get a grip around the man's wrist as the orderlies tackled us and bore me to the ground.

"He's trying to kill me!" I screamed. "Check what's in this syringe!" I managed to keep the syringe away from my neck, but it was bound to go in any second as I was overpowered.

"He's aggressive and psychotic! It's just a sedative," Aquinas yelled. I shut my eyes, breathless with pain, as the heavy orderlies wrestled with me and one of them sat on my wounded chest, but I didn't let my death grip on Aquinas's wrist go.

"Stop this immediately! This patient is in my care!" Dr. Wilson's voice, high and clear, pierced the chaos. "He trusts me, Dr. Aquinas! Let me help."

Dr. Wilson appeared above me, limned from behind with the overhead light like an angel. She caught and held back Aquinas's hand. The syringe trembled, just above my skin. "Calm down, Michael. I'm here now, and you're in my professional care."

I went instantly limp, dropping my arms to the ground, knowing that I had to play this right or I was still dead, right in front of her.

"Yes, Dr. Wilson. Thank you," I said meekly.

The orderlies sat on me an endless moment longer to make sure I was subdued.

"Get a restraint vest," Dr. Wilson barked. "I don't want him to have any more medications right now. He's having enough trouble with reality." I didn't like her words. Her expression was blandly disapproving, as if I were a naughty preschooler, and I knew she was playing to the observers. A third orderly appeared, carrying a straitjacket. The only thing between me and death right now was a petite blond woman with steely eyes. "You have to put this on, Michael. You're not safe to yourself or others right now." I heard the warning in her words. She was trying to protect me.

I allowed the men to slide the straitjacket onto my arms and bind them across my chest.

Once I was restrained, Dr. Wilson turned to Aquinas and Forsythe. "Please go. You've upset my patient. Clearly, seeing you reminded him of his ordeal."

Forsythe straightened his uniform. His face was congested with rage. "This man is psychotic. Dangerous. I'm going to recommend that he be locked up permanently."

The major strode out, chest puffed like a courting pigeon. I remembered the first day I'd met the man. I'd committed the cardinal sin of being taller than him, and he'd never forgiven me for it.

Aquinas recapped the syringe and went to slide it into his pocket, but Dr. Wilson gave a charming, collegial smile. She extended her hand, palm up. "Hey. I might need that. He could still get aggressive, and I'd like to be prepared."

Aquinas looked at me. I saw the battle in his eyes. On the one hand, I might act up and she'd inject me and end his problem for him. On the other hand, she might listen to my paranoid ravings and have the syringe tested.

"I'd like it back if you don't use it." He slapped the syringe into her palm. "I'll be in touch about the lieutenant's progress." He strode out.

Dr. Wilson turned to the orderlies. "He's safe with me."

"But, Doctor…"

"But nothing. He's meek as a lamb. Aren't you, Michael?" She patted my bound arms.

"Yes, Dr. Wilson," I said robotically, a whacked-out expression in place. It must have been pretty good, because the orderlies let go of me, moving reluctantly toward the door.

Dr. Wilson flicked her eyes again at the corners of the room, and I gave a slight nod. We still had surveillance.

"I think my chest might have opened up again." I lifted one of my strapped-down arms as high as it would go to show the spreading bloodstain I'd felt dampening the material. "Perhaps I could get some medical attention?"

"Back on the bed!" Dr. Wilson commanded, clapping her hands. "Move this man to surgical! Stat!" She was using the need for medical attention to get me moved. Damn, this woman was good.

The orderlies hopped to, opening the door and getting behind the mobile bed to push as I climbed back into it. Dr. Wilson walked briskly along beside me and undid the straps on my arms as she pretended to be checking the extent of the bleeding.

"I have to call for more help," she whispered. "And get this syringe tested. Pretend to be out of it."

I gave her that glassy stare I was getting good at. "Yes, Doctor." If the situation weren't so serious, I knew she would have laughed. Now she just touched my shoulder.

"You're going to be okay."

We got on the elevator with the orderlies and got off at the surgery floor, where Dr. Wilson raised some hell. As soon as she had an emergency surgery team working on me, she caught my eye and used her chin to point to a phone.

I gave a tiny nod, and she disappeared.

I was still vigilant as the medical team got the straitjacket and gown off me and unpacked the wound, which had opened up during the activity. I got it repacked and restrapped. Dr. Wilson appeared again, holding a clipboard.

"This man has a new room assignment," she said. "And a police guard."

Two strapping police officers had followed her in. Dr. Wilson dismissed the hospital staff and directed the officers to wheel me away. Once out of the surgery unit, Dr. Wilson took us up to the maternity ward. The officers wheeled me past rooms where babies cried and laboring women moaned, to a small room way on the end.

"No one comes in or out without my say-so." Dr. Wilson handed a paper to the officer. "He's off the hospital roster. These are the people who can see him. Check with me about anyone else. And there's a woman on her way—Sergeant Texeira. Curly brown hair, athletic build. His wife. She can come right in."

The officers nodded and took up stations outside the door.

Lei was coming. My heart pounded with anticipation, and I felt a grin pulling up my mouth. "Dr. Wilson. I owe you my life."

"We aren't out of the woods yet," Caprice Wilson said, but she smiled back. "Now, tell me what happened that caused those men to almost kill you back there."

"You were right about what happened to me. I was unconscious and head-tripping, but I didn't know that. I woke from the coma on the last day of captivity, but couldn't physically respond. I was stuck in my body just hearing stuff. Those two were talking, and they took a proof-of-life photo." I described what I'd heard and seen. "I can testify to recognizing both of them as being involved with the kidnapping. But I worry I've been discredited already."

"I think that syringe I got from Aquinas might help with that." Dr. Wilson's smile was tight. "I had a feeling you were being set up in some way. But I didn't realize how far they'd go to shut you up. I'm calling my friend Ben Waxman at the FBI. He's the Special Agent in Charge of the Honolulu branch."

She got out her phone and began pacing back and forth as she talked to the FBI. I settled back and rested, waiting for my wife. Anticipation made my stomach jumpy and my hands twitch.

Dr. Wilson looked up at me with a broad grin, the phone still to her ear. "Turns out Ben knows all about the kidnapping. Sophie

Ang was already working on it, off the books, and has a file going on Forsythe and Aquinas. We're going to get them."

I smiled back in relief. "Thank God."

The door slid open with a tiny snick. A curly brown head appeared, followed by Lei's slender form. She was wearing her usual work outfit, a black tank top and jeans, and athletic shoes that squeaked a little on the polished floor as she advanced into the room.

Lei's eyes flew open when she saw me on the bed, so wide and dark I couldn't see the pupils. Her lips, usually pink and lush, leached of color. The freckles stood out on her skin like cinnamon on milk.

"Lei!" I cried in alarm. Dr. Wilson saw Lei's knees crumpling and caught her before she hit the ground.

"For gosh sakes, who's my patient now?" Dr. Wilson exclaimed with mock impatience, her voice wobbly. She supported Lei over to me by main force, Lei's arm over her shoulder. I reached for my wife, groaning at the pain from my ribs, and hauled Lei up, lifting her onto the bed with me.

Finally she was where she belonged. In my arms, her head on my chest, her hair in my face. I pushed those springing curls out of the way as I had done a hundred times before, petting them so they lay down a little. "I'm the one who's supposed to be fainting. Are you okay?"

Lei made a little snuffling noise, and I felt her nod. She squeezed me, and damn, she was strong. "Let go a little," I wheezed. "My ribs."

She loosened her hold, but not that much. I didn't mind. God, she smelled good, the coconut oil Tiare had given her scenting her skin and Kiet's baby shampoo in her hair. She felt good, too, light and strong, but heavy in all the right places. My hands wandered a little, getting a feel of those places. She felt even better than she smelled.

"I'll leave you two to get reacquainted. I have more calls to make." Dr. Wilson sounded satisfied. She damn well should be. That woman had saved the day.

"Thanks, Doc," I called as she shut the door behind her.

I pushed Lei's hair back again, sweeping it aside with my hand and loving the texture, soft and bouncy. I tipped her face up. She was still pale, but her lips were pink again, thankfully. "Will you still love me when I'm a crazy alcoholic with a fractured skull, cognitive impairment, and a gunshot wound?"

She just kissed me. I was always the one who'd tried to tell her how beautiful she was, how she made me feel. But she just kissed me. Her mouth was like a strawberry sundae, sweet, slippery, and delicious. Those little noises she made as she turned so that she fit in her special spot alongside me—shoot me now and I'd die a happy man.

"Are you okay?" She whispered.

"Now that you're here, I will be."

"I have so much to tell you. Our ohana is getting bigger."

"Oh, yeah?" My hands were wandering again.

"I rescued some boys on my last case. I'm an aunty now, and that makes you an uncle. We have a funeral and a birthday party coming up."

"Uncle. I can do that," I mumbled, distracted, feeling myself come alive under her touch. "I have to tell you something, too. I'm different, after this. I can feel it. Something's gone that was messing with my head. I'm off the booze, permanently."

"I'm so glad." Lei pulled back a little. She undid the bone hook she'd given me when I left from her own neck. "I had a new thong put on this." She fastened the pendant on me, warm from her skin, and gave the hook a pat as it lay against my throat. "Back where it belongs."

We lay there for a long moment. I shut my eyes, feeling our hearts and breathing fall into sync as she snuggled close. Lei took my hand in hers and slid it under her shirt, placing it on the smooth, taut skin of her belly. "You better get well fast. We're having a baby," she whispered.

I thought I wasn't hearing her right. She was finally pregnant again? I felt a wave of dizziness and shut my eyes. It was too much joy after so little. My hand, fingers spread, stroked that smooth, sacred place near her waist where our child grew. "Really?" My voice was hoarse.

"Really." She took my face in her hands, looked into my eyes. "Are you happy?"

"I don't deserve this much happiness. I left you. I'll never do it again." I could hardly force the words out past the emotion clogging my throat.

"You better not." She kissed me. "Because I won't let you go."

Turn the page for a sneak peek of book twelve of the Paradise Crime Mysteries, *Bitter Feast!*

SNEAK PEEK

BITTER FEAST, PARADISE CRIME MYSTERIES BOOK 12

It always started with a body. Lieutenant Michael Stevens hooked his thumbs in the pockets of his jeans and gazed down at his newest case. "Tell me what you see."

Detective Brandon Mahoe, Stevens's young Hawaiian protégé, squatted in the narrow, chilly space of the walk-in refrigerator beside the body. Blood had spread in a pool beneath the corpse, filling the round holes of a raised rubber floor mat. The smell, more of a metallic feeling in Stevens's nostrils, was almost lost in other, competing odors: garlic, ripe fruit, mushrooms, scallions, and other produce lining the shelves.

"Male, six foot, trim build at a hundred and seventy-five pounds or so. Dark hair. Maybe thirties or younger. Cause of death appears to be stabbing." Mahoe's tone was serious. The detective wasn't being sarcastic about the handle of a large butcher knife protruding from the man's back—Mahoe didn't do sarcastic. "Probably a kitchen staff employee, to judge by the white chef's coat he's wearing."

Stevens dropped to his haunches beside Mahoe. He blew on a latex glove, inflating it to go on easy. He did the same to another, snapping it on. He pulled his notebook, equipped with a stub of pencil on a string, from his back pocket and jotted the information. "Good start."

"Can we shut the refrigerator door?" A male voice, harsh with impatience, came from the doorway. "All this food. It will spoil."

Stevens stood to his feet, a slow unfolding to his full, intimidating height. He stared down at the stocky, belligerent figure confronting him. "And you are?"

"Chef Winston Noriega. I own this place." The man, his chin outthrust, folded tattooed, muscular arms over a pristine white apron. "There are thousands of dollars of gourmet farm-fresh produce in this walk-in. I see no reason for it to go to waste just because Francois got himself stabbed."

"Back up out of here." Stevens used his voice like a lash to cut across the arrogant chef's posturing as he advanced to the doorway. "We'll close the door. But only so we can have privacy. I'm sure you wouldn't in good conscience serve food to your customers that has been part of a crime scene, even if we allowed it. Officer!" He gestured to one of the uniforms gathering the names of the kitchen staff. "Put up scene tape in this kitchen, clear this area, and put Chef Noriega in his office until I have time to interview him."

"Yes sir." The officer gestured to his partner, who shooed the lookie-loos into an adjacent area and pulled out a roll of scene tape.

"You can't do that!" Noriega said. A muscle jerked in a jaw wide and square as a bulldog's. Stevens glanced over at the officer who'd approached and now stood behind the chef. First responders had told Stevens that the chef had discovered the body.

"Cuff him if he gives you a hard time. What did you say the victim's name was?"

"It's Francois Metier, my sous-chef. Don't touch me." The chef shrugged away from the officer and stomped toward his office. Stevens stared after him thoughtfully, watching the officer accompany him to the door of the office. A woman, tall and elegant in black trousers, spoke a few words to the officer and slipped in after the chef.

Probably the wife—he'd heard that she helped manage the famous restaurant.

Stevens pulled the handle of the walk-in closed as Mahoe had begun photographing the scene. Flashes from the camera threw the tight setting into high relief again and again against his eyeballs: floor-to-ceiling shelves, packed with every sort of foodstuff; the body on the floor, one hand down alongside the body, the other curled up alongside the man's face; the blood pool.

There was a gleam of something in the palm of the hand lying along the body.

Stevens bent low to see the object. A familiar twinge in his side reminded him of a gunshot wound that had gone septic eight months ago. Healed now, that area still reminded him of his mortality whenever it had a chance. "Looks like there's a ring in his hand. Photograph this."

Mahoe approached with the department's Canon and photographed the item in question. Stevens lifted a diamond-encrusted band with a large center stone from the dead man's hand. "Looks like an engagement ring." He slipped it in an evidence bag. "Did you call Dr. Gregory?"

"Yes, sir. The medical examiner's on his way."

"Don't need to call me sir." Stevens had been Mahoe's original commanding officer, but they were working as partners now, with Stevens in a mentoring capacity.

"Yes sir." Mahoe grinned. "Sorry. Habit."

A tap came at the steel door. Mahoe, closer to the entrance, pushed the handle and the unit opened with a pneumatic whoosh. Dr. Phil Gregory entered, carrying his kit and a body bag, his cheeks pink with excitement. The portly medical examiner had been on a health kick lately, and his trademark aloha shirt, decorated with hula girls today, hung loosely from his shoulders. "A murder at Feast! This is my favorite restaurant!"

"You're looking good, Doc, so you can't have been eating here that often," Stevens said. "I've heard they're good, but after talking to the chef, I'm not wild about coming here as a customer."

"Well, he's well known for being a perfectionistic prick. That just makes for better dining, and this restaurant is all about the food. What do we have?"

The space felt crowded with three men and a body in the packed area. Mahoe sidled past Dr. Gregory. "I'll go see what's happening outside. Gather our interviewees."

"Leave the camera. I may need to get some more shots when we roll the body," Stevens told him. He turned back to Gregory. "So we got the call at 0800 hours, when Metier's body was discovered by one of the staff who'd come in early to clean." Stevens prodded the corpse with his foot. "I'm guessing this guy, identified by Chef Noriega as Francois Metier, his sous-chef, was offed last night sometime. He's in full rigor, plus the cold of this fridge, so probably after the night's rush. Must have been late in the shift or someone would have found him."

Dr. Gregory gloved up and slid booties on over his shoes as he approached the body, opening his doctor's bag to make his initial assessment. "Murder weapon appears pretty obvious."

Stevens nodded. "Gotta say, I wasn't impressed with the chef's response to all this. He seems more worried about losing his produce than his employee."

"That's consistent with what I've heard about Chef Noriega," Gregory said, squatting by the body. "So how's Lei? Has she gone out on maternity yet?"

"She's hanging in there. Got a couple more days on active duty." Stevens smiled, thinking of his very pregnant wife. She'd finally had to slow down and was often irritable. Being ungainly was tough for such a physical person. "Baby can't come soon enough for either of us."

Dr. Gregory smiled. "You think you'll be prepared, but it'll happen when you least expect it." He pointed at the knife protruding from the victim. "This stroke went in very deep—broke the skin on the other side. The murder weapon looks like one of those super sharp ceramic blades, and it went right through his kidney and appears to have penetrated all the way through his abdomen. Dropped him like a stone. Exsanguination will be cause of death, at a guess."

"No defensive wounds, either. There was a ring in one of his hands." Stevens withdrew the small plastic evidence bag and showed it to Dr. Gregory. "I'm guessing he knew and trusted his attacker."

"Maybe it's a woman," Dr. Gregory said. "He was going to pop the question in the fridge where they met, and she popped him instead."

Stevens's mouth twitched involuntarily at the gallows humor. "Very romantic. But doesn't the depth of the stab wound look challenging for a woman?"

"Easy with one of those chef knives. They go through meat like butter."

A flashback swamped Stevens's mind: his hand, fisted around a combat knife, driving up into a man's throat from below. Blood poured down his arm, only slightly warmer than the jungle air.

Not real. It never happened. He shook his head abruptly to clear it. "Early days yet for speculation. Surprised I'm telling you that."

"Of course, but this looks pretty straightforward." Dr. Gregory moved around the body, gazing at it closely. His glasses fogged slightly from the cold air. "Dr. Tanaka's been called to another scene, so can you help me? Let's remove the knife and roll the body."

"Let me pull any prints first." Stevens used gel tape to gather impressions from the handle as Dr. Gregory bagged the man's hands. "Damn. Just looks like a lot of smears, but hopefully we can retrieve something back at the station. You do the honors, removing it." He took an evidence bag from his open crime kit and snapped it open.

Dr. Gregory grasped the knife handle carefully, holding it with the tips of his fingers so as not to disturb any prints. He lifted it from the body with startling ease. "Whoever did this either knew where to stab or was damned lucky. It went right where it should go for maximum damage, and hit no bones along the way."

Stevens held the bag open and Dr. Gregory dropped the knife into it. While Stevens sealed and wrote on the bag, Dr. Gregory continued his examination.

Mahoe poked his head in. "I've got some interviews lined up, L.T. Want I should start taking statements?"

"Sounds good. I'm helping Dr. G with the body. Need a little more time. Leave the chef for me to talk to, though."

"You got it." The young detective withdrew his head.

Stevens arranged the evidence collected so far in the open area of the briefcase-like kit as Dr. Gregory performed the body-temp indignity with a rectal thermometer. He then spread the long, zip-up body bag wide in preparation of receiving its cargo. "The victim's way cold and in rigor, as you speculated, Lieutenant. Consistent with death last night. I'll know more after the full post. Let's roll and then bag him."

Stevens took the man's feet and Dr. Gregory the shoulders, and they flipped the corpse onto its back.

Blood had pooled beneath the body where the tip of the knife had penetrated through the abdomen, providing an exit wound. The vivid liquid, darkened with the hours, had spread to cover the white of the man's side-buttoned chef's coat and looked black in the fluorescents overhead. Blood trapped in the body had gathered in bruise-like, purplish lividity in visible tissues.

"I'll deal with this back at the morgue." Dr. Gregory gestured to the soaked clothing. Stevens picked up the Canon and photographed the front of the body. The man's rigor held one arm stiffly up at his side, his head turned oddly and eyes closed, just as he'd fallen.

Francois Metier had regular features and a square jaw decorated with a beard swatch. He'd been a handsome man at one time, before dusky lividity stained his face. Stevens moved in close, photographing. "Do you see scratches on the victim's cheek?" He zoomed in on the area, the flash blinding in the dim.

"I do see some sort of mark. Could be scratches," Dr. Gregory agreed. "This is looking more and more like a lover's quarrel gone wrong."

"Should be some interesting interviews ahead." Stevens set aside the camera and rifled the man's pockets. He dropped a wallet and phone into evidence bags. "Don't see anything else of interest."

"I'll do a thorough check for trace back at the morgue."

When they were both done recording and inspecting, Stevens lifted the man's heels, encased in rubber-soled work shoes, and Dr. Gregory grasped the rigid shoulders. They slid the body into the black bag.

"I brought the gurney in. It's just outside," Gregory said.

"Well, I'm not throwing my back out—getting too old for that shit." Stevens opened the fridge's door. "Mahoe! Need help here."

"What's up, L.T?" The young detective stepped up into the narrow space.

"You've got the young back we need," Stevens said. With the three of them lifting, they soon had the black-bagged corpse on the gurney and strapped down.

"I'll let you know anything interesting I find." Dr. Gregory lifted a hand in farewell. The M.E. pushed his burden out through the kitchen, accompanied by one of the uniforms, as Stevens retrieved his crime kit.

"Mahoe, can you put scene tape across the walk-in? No one goes in or out until we have a chance to have Kevin go over every inch of it." Kevin Parker, MPD's pimply-faced University of

Hawaii criminology intern, was proving a big asset at crime scenes, with an instinct for finding anything out of place and an eye for detail that had helped on several cases.

Stevens waited for Mahoe to seal the fridge with scene tape, using the time to organize his crime kit and label the evidence bags, but as he did so, a sense of dreamlike distance from his surroundings distracted him.

Stevens stripped off his gloves, flexed his hands and rolled his neck as he looked around the clean, brightly lit kitchen. Eight months after a military contractor stint which had resulted in some serious injuries, Stevens still sometimes felt a sense of unreality about his perceptions, a barrier between himself and what was happening around him that his friend, psychologist Dr. Wilson, called "de-realization."

"A symptom of your head injury," the psychologist had said when he called her not long ago to complain that the bizarre sensation was still happening. "Just weather it, along with the flashbacks. Be patient and try not to take it too seriously. Use a physical cue to ground yourself in the present moment's reality. Remind yourself that you're home, safe, and that your brain just isn't firing right."

Looking down, he rubbed the steel watch he'd taken to wearing against his wrist, eliciting a cool pinch of metal against skin as that physical cue. Lei also had a habit of rubbing something or squeezing her leg when she had similar symptoms—his wife still sometimes used the same sorts of techniques, though the source of her trauma was very different.

A loud voice, vibrating through the nearby wall, broke his reverie.

"Hell if I'm going to sit on my ass a minute longer waiting for this cop!"

Stevens heard a light feminine voice trying to calm the man. Chef Noriega was getting restless. The two voices rose and fell in a familiar cadence that sounded like marital argument.

"Let's go interview the man behind Feast," Stevens told Mahoe. "Got your recorder handy?"

"Sure do."

Stevens knocked once on the door marked OFFICE and turned the knob, pushing the door inward.

Chef Noriega had his hands around the woman's throat, pushing her up against his desk. She was clawing at his wrists, her face congested. Bulging, panicked eyes begged for help from behind the chef's shoulder.

I had to grab onto the edge of my desk to heave myself out of my office chair. "Be right there, Captain," I said into the office phone, and hung up. Once standing, I leaned back, digging my fists into the small of my back, arching to stretch. The curve of my belly brushed the edge of the desk. "We got a new case."

Pono, my long-time partner, looked up from his e-mail. "What the hell. You're supposed to be on light duty!"

"It is light duty. I hope. Another cold case. We've been summoned to hear about it."

"Yeah, and look how that last one turned out," Pono grumbled, referring to a cold one eight months before that was supposed to just be a time filler and had turned into one of the biggest cases we'd had in years.

"I don't know about the timing. I'm going on maternity in a few days." I waddled to the door of the cubicle, tugging down the dark blue smock I wore over skinny black maternity jeans. I'd had Ellen, Stevens's mom, sew up a bunch of the same garment for me, a sort of uniform that, I hoped, minimized the obviousness of my pregnancy.

Pregnant cops were awkward for everybody. The guys got all protective and mother hen, like Pono was acting. The women wanted me out of sight so I didn't embarrass anyone, and the perps didn't know how to act either. I was glad that I wasn't the size my friend Marcella had been at approaching nine months—but still, dealing with a basketball-sized belly pressing on my bladder constantly was challenging, and even light duty as a cop wasn't your typical desk job.

Pono took my elbow in the hall. I tweaked my arm away. "Quit fussing. I can walk on my own two feet. Just because I can't see them doesn't mean they aren't still there."

"Stubborn, you." Pono shook his head. "I can't wait for you to be done and out of here. I'm having a heart attack thinking you're going to drop it in our office or something."

"You must have really been a wreck when Tiare was pregnant," I panted, short of breath already with my lungs so cramped. I tried to speed up, but felt the distinctive sensation of the baby moving. These internal feelings had gone from fishlike fluttering, to kicking that felt like tiny fists, to these late-term, long, slow rolls that inevitably ended up with me feeling like I had to pee.

Which I now did.

"No one was more relieved than me when Tiare declared she was done after we had a boy and a girl." Pono spun his Oakleys by a stem as the slowed his stride to match mine.

"Quick bathroom stop." I turned toward the women's room.

Pono rolled his eyes. "Of course. I'll see you there." He went on down the hall.

In the stall, I settled myself and smoothed the sturdy navy cotton over my belly. It pushed back against my hand.

"You better be pointing downward. Not too long now, Baby," I whispered. "I can't wait to get this part over with and meet you." We'd decided not to know the sex, and I was still glad of that choice. So far the pregnancy had been healthy and problem-free, but I knew I was still trying to guard myself from the grief of something going wrong—knowing that there was no way to really do that.

If something went wrong with this baby, I'd never have the heart to try again.

I finished up, washed my hands. My face was fuller, my hair was fuller, and so were my breasts, straining the fabric of a smock sewn two months ago. "Oh well. I'm out of here in two days, and I can wear nothing but sweats from here on out, right, Baby?" There was no comment from below but another jab to the kidneys. "Ow. Maybe you're planning to play soccer for University of Hawaii."

A few minutes later I pushed open Captain Omura's office door.

"Surprise! It's your baby shower!"

Everyone was yelling. A party squeaker went off, and a popper sprayed confetti down over me as I clapped both hands over my mouth in shock. It looked like the entire department was crowded into Omura's little office, and they laughed and clapped at my surprise. Pono fired off another popper, and it rained down more confetti. I knew it was going to be a pain to get out of my hair later, but his big grin made me forgive him.

"Any excuse for cake," said Detective McGregor, a big bluff red-faced man I'd butted heads with on a few cases. Jessup Murioka, our teen tech whiz, came up to hug what he could reach of me and slip a sweet-smelling ginger lei over my head. Abe Torufu and Gerry Bunuelos hugged me as Pono handed out pink-and-blue party hats, along with pink-and-blue wrapped cigars. Guarding the huge cake on Omura's desk stood Tiare, his wife, wearing bright purple scrubs. She'd clearly come straight from the hospital, and the only thing bigger than the cake was her smile.

I made my way through the hugs and shoulder smacks from the guys to her side. "You're the monster behind this idea."

"Of course. Couldn't just let my little seestah skulk off to that fortress house without a going-away party." Tiare enfolded me in her arms. She always smelled like coconut and gardenias, and today was no exception.

One arm around my shoulder, she addressed the milling officers and support staff. "I'll cut the cake as soon as you folks throw a few bucks in for the office gift," she said, loudly, cutting across the joking and horseplay that had begun. "We're getting them one of those fancy strollers that does everything but change the baby."

She handed a gaily wrapped box with a slit in the top to Pono. My co-workers, teasing the while, dug bills out of their wallets and shoved them in.

Captain Omura, smiling and polished, came around her desk and patted my shoulder. "How are you feeling?"

"Really huge, with bruised kidneys. Thanks for asking." I glanced around. "Where's my husband? And Dr. Gregory?" The colorful M.E. was one of my favorite people.

"They pulled a fresh homicide. Out at that hipster restaurant, Feast."

"Oh, that should be interesting." I felt my heartbeat quicken with interest, and Baby kicked me in response. "Do you think he needs any help at the scene?"

"Definitely not. Part of my present to you is going home after the party—a couple of days early. I checked with human resources, and you have some comp time coming to you along with the maternity leave."

"So there's no case?" Absurdly, I was disappointed. What was I going to do for the next month until the baby came? I hadn't let myself think too much about it, but now full-time motherhood was upon me.

"You've got a case all right." Omura patted my enormous belly. "Right here, my little workaholic. Now let's have some cake."

Download *Bitter Feast* and continue reading now!

ACKNOWLEDGMENTS

Aloha dear readers!

Whew! What a suspenseful tale. This book was just amazing to write, the first novel in which I did virtually no plotting or outlining. From the moment I decided I'd be in Stevens's head for the duration, I was hooked.

Stevens had a lot going on, and resolving it and coming up with the twists at the end were some of the most fun I've ever had writing.

And then there was Lei—really growing as a woman and a mother, learning to stick to things and see them through, curbing her impulses but expanding in her ability to love and commit. Writing a series this long is such a wonderful journey!

Special thanks goes to Sergeant First Class M.L. Doyle, for being my military "expert" advisor for Red Rain. (Any remaining errors are mine.) As with many topics I tackle, I don't know much about the subject, and rely on my experts to help me get my facts within the ballpark if not perfectly correct. I first got to know Mary when she asked me to blurb one of her Master Sergeant Harper mysteries, and I was really impressed with her detailed knowledge of military criminal investigation.

More thanks go to Captain (Retired) David Spicer for his procedural read, and further to women's fiction novelist Holly Robinson, who, in spite of her own pressing deadlines, found time to do a critical edit/read of Red Rain. And for the first time ever, Noelle Pierce, my eagle-eye dangling clue finder, couldn't find anything to critique! Thanks to each of you for helping me make this the most intense story yet.

If you liked what you read, please leave a review. They're the best thanks any author can receive.

Much aloha,

FREE BOOKS

Join my mystery and romance lists and receive free, full-length, award-winning novels *Torch Ginger* & *Somewhere on St. Thomas*.

tobyneal.net/TNNews

TOBY'S BOOKSHELF

PARADISE CRIME SERIES

<u>Paradise Crime Mysteries</u>
Blood Orchids
Torch Ginger
Black Jasmine
Broken Ferns
Twisted Vine
Shattered Palms
Dark Lava
Fire Beach
Rip Tides
Bone Hook
Red Rain
Bitter Feast

<u>Paradise Crime Mystery</u>
Special Agent Marcella Scott
Stolen in Paradise

Paradies Crime Suspense Mysteries
Unsound

Paradise Crime Thrillers
Wired In
Wired Rogue
Wired Hard
Wired Dark
Wired Dawn
Wired Justice
Wired Secret
Wired Fear
Wired Courage
Wired Truth

ROMANCES

The Somewhere Series
Somewhere on St. Thomas
Somewhere in the City
Somewhere in California

Standalone
Somewhere on Maui

Co-Authored Romance Thrillers
The Scorch Series
Scorch Road
Cinder Road
Smoke Road
Burnt Road
Flame Road
Smolder Road

YOUNG ADULT

<u>Standalone</u>
Island Fire

NONFICTION

<u>Memoir</u>
Freckled

ABOUT THE AUTHOR

Kirkus Reviews calls Neal's writing, *"persistently riveting. Masterly."*

Award-winning, USA Today bestselling social worker turned author Toby Neal grew up on the island of Kaua`i in Hawaii. Neal is a mental health therapist, a career that has informed the depth and complexity of the characters in her stories. Neal's mysteries and thrillers explore the crimes and issues of Hawaii from the bottom of the ocean to the top of volcanoes. Fans call her stories, *"Immersive, addicting, and the next best thing to being there."*

Neal also pens romance, romantic thrillers, and writes memoir/nonfiction under TW Neal.

Visit tobyneal.net for more ways to stay in touch!
or
Join my Facebook readers group, *Friends Who Like Toby Neal Books,* for special giveaways and perks.